BLUE FIRE

For: Joe

A Novel by

R. J. MIKELIONIS M.D.

ISBN: 979-8-88640-436-4 (sc)
ISBN: 979-8-88640-437-1 (hc)
ISBN: 979-8-88640-438-8 (e)

Because of the dynamic nature of the Internet, any web addresses or links contained in this book may have changed since publication and may no longer be valid. The views expressed in this work are solely those of the author and do not necessarily reflect the views of the publisher, and the publisher hereby disclaims any responsibility for them.

THE EWINGS
PUBLISHING

One Galleria Blvd., Suite 1900, Metairie, LA 70001
1-888-421-2397

CONTENTS

FOREWORD

In attempting to write an introduction to this book, I found it soon became too abstract a task. I thus opted to let the story stand by itself, only adding that it is the story of a journey, a journey along the spokes of a wheel, along the numerous roads and branches leading to as many points of the compass as there are human beings, who must all somehow choose between them, without the benefit of the knowledge of any eventual destination. Or do we first determine our destination, and then the roads leading to it?

It is not the intention of this book to try to answer that, only to tell a story. It begins, aptly enough, as a journey into the unknown: In this case, the unknown world of medicine. This may sound like a paradox, for certainly there is much already known in the sphere of medicine. We are acquainted with its technical matters, its successes and failures, its flashing scalpels, transplants, and steel or gold stethoscopes. Is there anything besides?

If there is, it is seldom written; it is not taught in medical schools, nor found within medical textbooks, nor even mentioned within the confines of everyday talk in doctors' lounges. That is because it cannot be taught beforehand, it cannot be comprehended in a didactic manner, and can seldom be adequately discussed: It deals with the very core of life, and death, and whatever is in between, and the feelings of individuals watching it unfold.

I also chose not to deal with it in explanatory terms: I am not sure I have any. I have simply told a story, or rather, a collection of stories. It will be for the reader to glean from them what he/she wishes. The reader will be the judge of the realities, rules, games, absurdities, paradoxes, and dreams of this journey.

At times when this journey becomes too technical, I hope the reader remembers that the technical contents of this book are but a shadow of their true proportion in medical life. And when this story leaves medicine for other unknown journeys, I hope the reader will follow to his/her own endings.

I have been asked whether the stories in this book are real. Let me answer that it was written for the reader without any need for speculation into its origin.

Raymond J. Mikelionis, M.D.

PART I

It began long ago
Future's seed
In every changing day
Sometimes winning
Often losing
Remembering always
    to begin again

CHAPTER 1

GAMES WITHOUT RULES

Sunshine. Crackling dry gold. Steep hills of scrub brush. Sharp small shadows, running.

He ran. Downhill. As fast as he could. His eyes narrow against the dry heat. Air swept past his ribs and sweating brow.

If he spilled on rock, root or badger hole - he lost.

If he made it downhill - he won.

It was simple then. Win or lose. He made up the rules. And the rules didn't change.

Age three.

The electric motor hissed like a snake in the rocks, and the large rectangular white screen slid down from the ceiling behind the lecturer's podium. The lights went out in the amphitheater.

> "Whole and bisected nervous tissue; note particularly the position of the pituitary, its attachment to the brain proper, and the surrounding vascular Circle of Willis. Try to discern the relative positions of adenohypophysis, neurohypophysis..."

Cameron's eyes narrowed.

> "Basophils in the adenohypophysis are demonstrated particularly well. They stain purple. Acidophils and chromophobes..."

The eyelids slid down further.

> "...it is helpful to remember that the chromophobes are usually small and occur in clumps. This arrangement of cells can easily be studied..."

The eyes had closed.

> "Many small follicles are filled with PAS positive colloid. In the neurohypophysis, nuclei of pituicytes..."

Cameron's back remained straight, but his chin began its inevitable journey downward.

> "Often neurosecretory material, Herring bodies, can be observed in forms of pale, amorphous blobs..."

For a brief second, Cameron's eyes opened, focusing on the eerie lunar landscape of a nerve cell magnified 9,000 times on the electron micrograph slide. Large domed lunar rocks, craters, seas floated in a haze of black, white, and gray blots before his eyes. His chin came to rest on his wrists.

"...These predominate in the pars intermedia, and often penetrate into the pars nervosa."

The domed figures transformed themselves: A white sweater, books cradled over her crossed arms, under her chest...warmly resting in their sweater, her breasts spread softly over the edge of the books; it was amazing how they were suspended over the books like that, as if over a platter for support. And no less amazing that they spanned the entire platter.

"Thus the case can be made that Neurons are secretory cells, using micro-merocrine secretions at their synaptic vesicles!" exclaimed the lecturer triumphantly. "Proteinaceous material is produced like in any other cell in the body, then transported to cluster together at the ends of the axon!"

Cameron jerked awake. The pen slipped from his hand and clattered onto the floor. His eyes blinked open. It was still dark. The monotone resumed:

"At least six hormones, all controlled by feedback loops, are produced by cells of the pars distalis. STH, or somatotrophic hormone, 3,500 to 5,000 Angstrom range; LTH, luteotropic hormone, 6,000 Angstroms; ACTH..."

At two o'clock the lights burst alive overhead; a hundred bodies launched themselves out of the amphitheater.

"God, Cameron, I cracked up when you woke up in there!"

"Did I make a lot of noise?"

"Only like a moose. Your whole desk shook!"

"How was I supposed to know he'd break the monotone?"

"You better sit farther back next time, Cameron."

"I was in the middle of a dream, Ed. You should have seen her!"

"I bet."

"Did Dr. Multke notice I was asleep?"

"You and the twenty other guys? No, I don't think so. You better join them in the back row, though—less noticeable."

"It's just post-prandial hypoglycemia, you know."

"What?"

"I've got it figured out: Blood sugar up from lunch, causing pancreatic over stimulation with insulin release, feedback loop and all that, then blam! Low blood sugar. That, plus screen down, lights out, plus monotone—equals sleep. Elegant, don't you think?"

"What about that honey in the dream, Cameron? Also pancreatic overstimulation?"

"Hmm. Stimulation overload—of another kind."

"Know her?"

"Seen her around. In a white sweater..."

"Hold it! Let's get some coffee before we go over anatomy notes."

"She had quite..."

"No, Cameron. I need to know why the Vastus Medialis attaches at the medial upper two-thirds of the patella."

"Yeah. Here it is: Because it counterbalances the pull of the quadriceps at extension, which turns out to have a slightly lateral component from the obliquity of the femur."

"There's your component forces diagram...everything in different colors, eh? Still gunning for an A in Anatomy, Cameron?"

"Doubt it. I like deduction better, figuring things out, rather than just memorizing stuff."

"Induction, Cameron—going from the particular facts to general conclusions. Anyway, what about the inferior gluteal artery, you sure it joins the profunda femoris there?"

"Yep. Look it up in Grant's..."

Ed stared at someone that just walked in: "What about her gluteal..."
"Hey, Ed, we better head for lab."

Lights fell with dull phosphorescence from the ceiling onto the formaldehyde moistened sheets. They lay draped over outlines on silver-steel tables, lined up in rows in a room white as the sheets. Ed and Cameron slipped on their white coats from the rack, then pulled on a fresh pair of gloves.

"Blunt dissection!" shouted the Anatomy Professor, "Blunt, you understand? No sharp cutting or slicing. I don't want to see *any* scalpels or scissors in anyone's hands today! You'll damage the structures and landmarks before you even know it. If you have any questions, ask!"

Brown leathery muscles slipped under their gloved fingers. Taut cream-white tendons clung stubbornly to bone as in life. Theirs was a very thin cadaver; dissection was easier with the thin ones. Slowly they continued to separate veins from arteries, nerves from tendons, muscles from skin, bones and ligaments. Cameron kept the face covered.

The Professor paced noiselessly past, then stopped. His thick eyebrows came together for a moment as Ed asked him something; his hands paused, then began work. In minutes, structures separated under the Professor's fingers, yielded, lay peeled into explainable strands of tissues, tunnels, levers and pumps. Portions of atoms that together had walked and perceived the sun now dangled neatly like moist telephone wires.

"Did you see that, Cameron?"
"Yes."
"He's fast, ha?"
Cameron nodded.

Ed's nose twitched and watered: "I think I'm allergic to formaldehyde;" formaldehyde permeated the room and drifted along the halls of the entire second floor.

"You'd be dead by now if you were."
"What do you think she died of?"
"Our lady? Don't know. She's very thin."

Ed shook his head: "Seems strange. There doesn't seem to be anything wrong with her. Something must have just gone out..."

They patted formaldehyde into the tissues to keep them moist, then replaced the covering sheet. Cameron pulled the gloves off from his sweating hands. Anatomy Lab was over for today.

"Maybe you are allergic. Your eyes are red."

"Maybe."

"What are you going to do tonight?"

"Book. And you?"

"Book."

They crossed the Montlake bridge connecting the School of Medicine, over the lake, to the Capitol Hill of the city. It was early autumn with a foreboding of rain.

"I wonder if we'll ever be able to repair things like that?"

"What?"

"Whatever she died of."

"Maybe."

They kept walking. Underneath, the lake drifted like silver fish waiting for the evening moon.

"Just seems strange, you know."

"I know," Cameron shifted his books from one arm to the other.

"Going to play football?"

"Yeah."

Cameron dashed over the stairs of the Phi Chi house, where twenty freshman and sophomore medical students lived, and threw his books and clothes over the bed. He jumped into jock and shorts that needed laundering a week ago. "Ready, roomie?"

"Be there in a jiff. Warm up that ball for me."

"If you're as constipated as the last time, we'll be waiting for an hour!"

"Who can be constipated staring at that purple and orange sun Maximilian painted in the john?"

"Well, stare at it, Ed, or we'll start without an end."

"Is that a pun?"

Cameron clattered down the stairs with untied sneakers. "Hell, it's going to rain!" He took them off and left them in the house. It was the Phi Chi daily ritual: Whether it rained or snowed, the entire frat house played football after all day at school, before the next round of evening study.

Matsu quarterbacked. A low-arched trajectory overled Barry to the sidelines of the trees; he tipped it and almost caught it with one hand. There had been something different about his movements—fast, yet jerky and detached.

"Is he on something, Cam?"

"Dunno. I didn't know he took anything."

"Yeah. Speed sometimes."

"You sure?"

Ed nodded. "He takes something." Barry grinned from the sidelines and sauntered back, his hands not seeming to keep pace with his feet.

It began to rain. Cameron felt it cool over his skin, sliding down his back and chest. He took off his shirt. Muscles tensed in the cold, moving under his skin like smoothly lubricated layers of fingers. For an instant, a leathery brown figure superimposed itself over the field of green wet grass, a brown toe-tag under the covering sheet... Suddenly, Cameron felt an urge welling within him: To be alive; to feel. To feel all he had inside. Time stopped: Muscles tightened like poised motionless snakes. Wet grass prickled underfoot. Cool air carried a fragrance over the greyness of rain and lake. Tendons released...with a tiny vibration heard if one listened, muscles catapulted, hurtled life force into a sliding green universe. With something oval in his hands, Cameron floated a long time in the universe...it turned, reeled, finally touched his back and legs. Two hands brushed him.

"Good catch!"

Tiny pools of water filled depressions in the grass. He stood, his chest muddy. Someone patted his rump: "You slid twenty yards on that stuff! Take it easy, will you; it's slippery as hell!"

"Sure."

"Are *you* on something?" Ed grinned in the huddle.

Cameron brushed his bare toes over the ground: "Alive, Ed, that's all."

After shower and dinner, Cameron arranged his books and notes over the desk. Led Zepp cruised loudly through the adjacent walls.

Ed glanced up: "I'm sick of this shit. I'm really behind. I have to book, and I just can't do it with that noise on. How the hell does he study that way?"

"Don't know. He does well, though."

"Well, either Barry shuts off his stereo, or we go study in the library again," Ed stood up grimacing: "This time *he* shuts it off."

"How?"

"We pretend to get into a fight, crash into his room, and wreck the place. Then *he* goes to the library. Chrissake! He does this every night! He plays it full blast while booking, full blast with the chicks! He may be able to get away with it, but I can't—I've got to concentrate, damnit!"

Cameron shrugged: "All right, here goes." He hit Ed low in the body with a tackle. A chair crashed into the wall as Ed recovered, and his six- foot-five frame propelled Cameron almost instantly from their room into the corridor. Cameron's back bounced off the wall, crashed through the door into Barry's room. They landed splintering bookcase and contents.

Barry's face beamed at them benignly over a textbook of Biochemistry. His foot hadn't missed a beat of the Zepp.

Ed looked at him dumbfounded, then at Cameron, and wheeled out of the room. The library, as usual.

In ivy-covered silence, the Krebs cycle adsorbed well into the regions of Cameron's brain: Facts about oxidative pathways, carbohydrates, lipids, and proteins dove into the murky depths of his mental synapses, searching for a place in the sponge-neurons of his brain, awaiting their ultimate destiny of recall during that dreaded hour, "The Quiz."

Cameron turned, noting the beige blouse and its contents across the library table. Noted, and avoided. Beige went well with blonde hair...Hans Adolf Krebs, back in 1937, had formulated the complete tricarboxylic acid cycle for oxidation of carbohydrates and fats to produce energy...Dr. Krebs probably hadn't had to contend with a coed's bosoms resting over the table like that back then...Glucose entered the energy cycle either via the hexose monophosphate shunt, or the Embden-Meyerhof pathway; extramitochondrial process teamed with the mitochondrial to result in 38 high-energy phosphate bonds, each equivalent to 7,600 calories per mol...

She walked down the steps, her legs a smooth-marble dream curving under a white miniskirt. It was her. No white sweater this time; tonight it was light blue, fluffy. Dr. Krebs and his cycle were fluffing right out of the electrical conduits of Cameron's brain. She sat down directly opposite him.

...So... 7,600 calories captured per ATP mol, times 38, equals 288,800 calories per mol of glucose, for an efficiency ratio of...

The glistening tabletop was polished like a mirror, reflecting her firm blue contents.

...An efficiency ratio of 288,800 over total combustion capacity...

Her perfume smelled of strawberries. Combustion capacity was reached, Cameron short-circuited, and Krebs went to hell. Cameron looked at her once more, then packed his books and left. The gym would still be open. A half-hour of pushing steel and maybe the Krebs cycle would compute again.

At two a.m. Cameron tossed his shoes in the dark and slammed the books down. His roommate was snoring. The snoring continued after Cameron had tossed his clothes and gotten into bed. He threw a well- aimed pillow into the dark.

"Hmmm?"

"You're snoring again, Ed."

"Sorry..."

"Ready for The Quiz?"

"Hmm...guess so. How'd you do?" "Saw that girl again."

"The white sweater girl?"

"Blue this time."

"What's the rest of her like?"

"I'll be pole vaulting in bed all night."

"Won't get very high on *that* pole. And I don't want to hear any obscene sounds coming from under the covers."

"Shut up and stop snoring."

"Did you talk to her?"

"No."

"Why not?

"Because my pants looked funny, and I *couldn't* talk to her."

"Oh."

"Besides, what would I say to her? Can you spare ten minutes to share a hot dog and coffee between Biochem and Histology?"

"You're getting Freudian."

"I'll tell you my dreams tomorrow."

At 7 a.m. they were crossing the Montlake bridge. The windows of the University Hospital were just beginning to reflect the morning's light.

"How was it?" "What?"

"The dreams."

"Oh." Cameron was a true night person; his morning abilities extended to keeping himself on the sidewalk rather than the street, and word comprehension was limited to monosyllables until noon. The lake was choppy and green beyond the bridge. Rowing a shell, Cameron thought, a good way to wake up mornings; no talking, just rowing... a woman in a terrycloth bathrobe stood by the railing... They might even get good and row for the team...They left the woman behind.

Cameron, suddenly wide awake, shook his head and looked back. "Ed..."

"What?"

"Slow down."

"What's up?"

The somnolence had left as suddenly as the start of a race. "Don't look, just slow down."

"Why?"

"Something isn't right. The woman we just passed..."

"What about her?"

"I think she's going to jump."

"Jesus Almighty! What makes you think? I mean, what do we do now?" They stopped, pretending to look at the water. "Let's go back..." Before they were able to move, she was over the bridge.

"Jesus! What..."

"Hold it! The stairs!" They tossed off their shoes before diving in. Ed reached the woman first. She screamed.

"Let me die! Let me die! Let go of me!"

Across the short-cut hill, they walked her between them to the Hospital Emergency Room.

"Jesus," Ed repeated, "what made her do that?"

"She ran away from the voluntary Psychiatric Ward."

"But why?"

Cameron shrugged: "...Don't know...Jesus!.."

They sat for their first class, Histology, dripping wet. The Professor saw them, then continued without raising an eyebrow. The screen unwound its way from the ceiling and slid behind the lecturer's podium. The amphitheater darkened for the day's Histology class. Life magnified ten thousand times: Mitochondria, Golgi apparati, coiled saccules of enzymes lay outlined under the electron microscope gun. Dots, lakes, rivers of ions, hormones, blood serum floating behind gray shadows, playing. A game played out under beams of electron particles, a game of synaptic electricity, speeded and slowed reactions, immunologic survival: A game of the secrets of life. Slide after slide clicked on and off the screen. Shadow after shadow. Endoplasmic reticulum, plasma membrane, nuclear envelope... One more pair of alert eyes watched today: Somewhere in those shadows lay clues, rules of bioelectric movements, rules yet unknown, of life, or lack of it; clues and answers for people waiting within hospital walls; perhaps answers for those who jumped over bridges...

Cameron's pen took notes in the dark. The game had another player.

CHAPTER 2

NOT IN THIS WORLD

"A man need only be turned around once with his eyes shut in this world to be lost."

Henry David Thoreau

"What day is it today?" asked Dr. Reynolds, Chief of the County Hospital's Psychiatry Service.

"December 7," said the fifty-six year old lady. She was off by eight months. Her features were dark, with an aquiline nose and thick dark hair; a blue handkerchief kept turning silently in her hands. When the kerchief stopped moving, her hands had a fine tremor. Her head moved back and forth as though she were in a rocking chair. She'd been brought by her husband and stepdaughter for commitment proceedings.

The commitment board consisted of a judge, Dr. Reynolds, and another psychiatrist; the three sat with a nurse on one side of the oval table. The patient sat alone on the opposite side. Five third-year medical students observed from seats along the wall.

"Do you know who we are?" Dr. Reynolds asked.

The lady didn't reply.

"I'm Dr. Reynolds, Psychiatrist, and this is Dr. Klein, in Residency."

"Thank you," she said, slowly turning to everyone in the room. The rocking motion stopped momentarily, then resumed.

"Your husband tells me you get very depressed," said Dr. Reynolds.

She left the handkerchief flat on the table. "Depressed...yes... everyone get drunk and I not get drunk. I depressed."

"You don't get drunk?" inquired Dr. Reynolds.

"Thank you," she replied.

"No, I mean, do you drink much alcohol?"

"All else yes, me no."

"She gets very drunk and depressed," the husband interjected.

"Who's the president of the United States?" Dr. Reynolds asked.

"I don't know president," said the lady.

"What's one hundred minus five?"

"Ninety-two."

"Ninety-two?"

"Wait minute....no, ninety-one. No, one hundred minus five-ninety-three..."

Dr. Reynolds turned to the other psychiatrist: "You have anything to add, Dr. Klein?"

"She gets very manic at times, when she's not taking Thorazine."

The nurse nodded agreement.

Dr. Reynolds began addressing the students with a dissertation emphasizing differences between thought and mood disorders. This was clearly a case of mood disorder, with inappropriate mannerisms, anxiety, perplexity, depression, motor retardation, and alcoholism. Any questions from the students?

"Yes," John Cameron leaned back in his chair: "Mrs. Cernas appears to be of foreign origin. Could cultural differences possibly account for some differences in her mannerisms?"

"Perhaps in part," Dr. Reynolds replied, "but there is some clearly bizarre behavior not accounted in such a manner, Dr. Cameron." The title of Doctor came as a traditional courtesy for the students already on clinical services.

"Dr. Reynolds "

"Yes, Dr. Cameron "

"I also wonder how much of that could be due to chronic brain damage, as opposed to a purely psychological imbalance. In her history, for example, it was mentioned she was frequently kicked in the head during her previous marriage. May I ask her how often this happened?"

"Proceed, Dr. Cameron. Keep in mind that her answers may be unreliable, in view of her previous difficulty with dates, arithmetic, so forth."

"Mrs. Cernas, you said your previous husband kicked you in the head. How often did that happen?"

"Husband good. He no kick, no hit me."

"The other husband, Mrs. Cernas. The one before."

"The other kick me much. In head, he kick me on floor."

"How often?"

"Many weeks, much often. He do it on floor. He get worse if I cover head with my hands." They twisted with the blue handkerchief.

"Were you ever unconscious?"

"Thank you," her lips stretched into a smile.

Dr. Reynolds nudged his glasses, peering at Cameron.

"No, Mrs. Cernas," Cameron tried again, "did you ever pass out, go to sleep, after he hit you?"

"Kick hard. Go to sleep many times."

Cameron turned to Dr. Klein, who had presented the case: "Were the patient's skull series normal, Dr. Klein?"

"I don't recall that skull X-rays were taken."

"How was her neurological exam at admission?"

Dr. Klein paged through her record: "I can't verify one was done..."

Dr. Reynolds interrupted: "A neurological exam would obviously be a waste of time in this case, Dr. Cameron. What is your point?"

"Well, this patient has a history of head trauma: I wonder if her emotional disturbances could originate from an organic brain injury, rather than from a psychiatric disorder?"

"Mr. Cameron, she doesn't just have the disturbances of mania and depression: She also has evidence of deteriorating mental function, poor memory, lack of simple arithmetic, etcetera."

"I thought that poor memory and mentation were precisely indicative of an organic or structural injury, Dr. Reynolds, rather than a psychiatric illness."

"That may usually be the case, Mr. Cameron, but it cannot always be used to differentiate organic from functional causes. Anything else?"

It suddenly dawned on Cameron that for some time he'd been demoted from the honorary title of Doctor to *Mr.* Cameron. He realized he should stop now. For some reason he didn't: "The patient also gave a history of epilepsy, and may have fallen from this cause. This might also point to possible head injury. And if this indeed were the case, Dr. Reynolds, if her illness is physical and organic, wouldn't this patient benefit more from a hospital ward than a mental institution?"

"The husband denied the patient's history of epilepsy, *Mr.* Cameron. Any more questions?"

John Cameron was already in the doghouse; there was little left to lose: "Ah, well, yes...the patient is on fairly high doses of Thorazine: Aren't we taking for granted that she is abnormal *in spite* of the drugs, whereas she may actually be abnormal *because* of them? Much the same way as we, given high doses of Thorazine might do worse in an exam dealing with memory, numbers and dates?"

"We know what the effects of the drugs are," Dr. Reynolds replied, "we play the odds that the patient would be abnormal without these drugs. Is that all, Mr. Cameron?"

"Yes, Dr. Reynolds."

Dr. Reynolds had already turned to the judge. They spoke briefly, nodded, and the judge signed the white paper before him. It moved from his right hand to his left.

Another patient arrived, ushered in by an orderly. "Mr. Maugham, you're forty-four years old, and live at 227 Pine Avenue," Dr. Klein read from the resume, "Is that correct?" The patient nodded once, then reclasped his hands under his chin.

"Do you know why you're here?" Dr. Klein asked.

Silence.

"Your landlady called the police after she heard the car running in the closed garage. And you were just sitting there, isn't that right?"

He assented without emotion, barely moving his face, large black eyes staring straight ahead. His ears flapped out from the sides of the head, cauliflower ears, large as swollen fronds. He'd probably been a boxer.

"So, you were trying to commit suicide," Dr. Klein continued, "do you know why, Mr. Maugham?"

"Don't really remember that," he said, shaking his head.

"But you did try to kill yourself," Dr. Klein repeated.

The man's face and right hand moved upwards in slow motion: "Try to kill myself…" he muttered quietly, letting the words escape into the room as if watching the thought behind them, "Oh yeah…yeah…" he said, shaking his head, "I've been different, since the accidents. I guess it's been different…" His head gradually sank to its former downcast level.

Mr. Maugham's summary had included that he'd been in two car accidents requiring suturing, also suffering a mild concussion syndrome after the last one.

"What's been different, Mr. Maugham?"

"Don't know. Me. I've been different. Don't remember things…"

"What's the date today?"

"Don't know."

"Who's the president?"

"The president..." He hung his head, bewildered; the eyes focused in one place, as if afraid to move about the room.

A discussion in low voices ensued on the other end of the oval table; Dr. Reynolds turned to Dr. Klein: "Is he going to be difficult?"

"No. He's easy to care for. Feeds himself and everything. Just absent minded. Bumps into things."

"Then we'll put him in an open room."

"Sure," agreed Dr. Klein.

"I really do think he's frankly psychotic, don't you? I mean, that history of the car accidents, I don't think it has any bearing on the case—look at his affect—flat, nothing on his face, afraid to move."

The judge nodded, "We better put him in." Another white paper was signed and moved from right to left into the stack.

Dr. Reynolds looked at Mr. Maugham: "Well, you know you've been difficult lately, Mr. Maugham, and you scared that landlady a couple of times. Don't you think you ought to be in the hospital?"

"Guess so. I didn't mean to scare her at all," he shrugged, "don't want to cause any more trouble. I guess I need that."

Dr. Reynolds imparted a further elaboration on schizophrenia to his students: Deteriorating mental awareness, loss of interpersonal relations, and apathy to external stimuli, all manifested by this patient. Any questions?

Cameron thought perhaps one. But it was still early in the morning - he had no wish to get on anybody's case. Besides, if it had been that important, someone else would have thought of it also. Mr. Maugham fell into step with the orderly, and turning his head for the first time, smiled to say goodbye. He would remain at County Hospital a few more days, then be transferred to the state's institution for the insane.

Diagnosis: Schizophrenia, simple type, American Psychiatric Association number 2950.

Three more cases filed past the oval table, and the morning session was over.

Back in the anteroom with padded chairs and a coffee urn, third-year Cameron drank his coffee. Fifteen minutes later, the second half of King's County Court commitment proceedings began. The door to the room with the oval table was locked behind them.

Dr. Klein began the interview: "Do you know why you're here, Mr. Smelden?"

"I am gathering that: I really wanted a lawyer. I thought I could appeal this kind of proceeding."

"What do you wish to appeal, Mr. Smelden?"

"This entire hearing. Come now, isn't this a commitment procedure?"

"Yes, but we haven't reached any conclusions yet. I wonder why you're so obsessed about appealing beforehand. Is there anything that makes you feel this way?"

"Of course: I don't feel comfortable here. I'd like to be represented by someone."

"Why aren't you comfortable, Mr. Smelden? Have you decided we are your enemies?"

"I haven't decided anything. I'm just worried, that's all."

"Mr. Smelden, it was reported that you often fly into a rage and destroy furniture. Is that correct?"

"Often? I wouldn't say often. I slammed my fist over the table and it broke. Wrecked a lounge chair and a lamp once - I had good reason. Besides, it was *my* furniture, not anyone else's. Since when do I have to ask someone else about throwing my own furniture around?"

"You were making a lot of noise in the apartment house. And a lamp—that would be a fire hazard."

"I know it. In retrospect, throwing the lamp wasn't wise."

"What was the 'good reason' you mentioned, Mr. Smelden?"

He glanced about the table: "I'm not sure I should tell you this."

"Go ahead, Mr. Smelden. There is no reason for worry."

"Well," he began cautiously, "I was watching the news of the usual, you know—the Vietnam war and all that. They were talking of honor, patriotism, not backing down—and I saw that it was a bunch of bullshit, and only religion could cure the whole thing. Like, one has to believe in this Being that takes care of us. I became very angry that things were so senseless around us."

"And who's this Being in whom we should place our trust?" Dr. Reynolds inquired.

"I don't know if you will understand. But I know this Being, I know He exists. Few people know Him."

"Why do only a few people know him, Mr. Smelden?"

"There you go, and I realize you will probably take this wrong. But you see, I am a genius. I believe in the interchangeability of matter and spirit—like, in every bit of matter, there is spirit, and in every bit of spirit, there is matter. Nothing really ceases to exist—it just interchanges. Forms come and go, spirit remains: To where the spirit goes after changes in matter, and from where all spirit emanates, is the Great Spirit: He is Energy. He is the Universe. It took me a long time to see it, and in this context everyday matters now appear trivial and sometimes senseless—for example, your preoccupation with my destroying some material things "

"Do you have rapid mood fluctuations?" Dr. Reynolds asked.

"Well, in my metaphysical wanderings, I often feel elated. However, the depression can be great when I come down to reality."

"Then you agree, Mr. Smelden, that in your 'metaphysical wanderings' as you put it, you often leave reality?"

"You're twisting words, Dr. Reynolds. They prove nothing but your own purpose. Man as a reality-cognitive being, and also a Dream-capable being, must be able to step outside reality. In fact, he *must* do so, to be truly man. Dreams, not reality, have the power to move men's souls."

"You mentioned you are a genius, Mr. Smelden. What made you arrive at that conclusion?"

"I'm sorry some people have an innate distrust of what the word implies. However, Dr. Reynolds, since you asked, a genius is one with a greater capacity to feel and think. Who was it once said: 'Life is a comedy to those who think, and a tragedy to those who feel?' Well, I happen to do both, Dr. Reynolds. It may account for my wrecking the table. By the way, I also resent being given medications prior to this hearing. I know nothing of their effect. I would prefer to enter these proceedings with my own lucid mind, not encumbered by drugs. You understand?"

"The drug is a tranquilizer, Thorazine. The nurse gave it because you were excited and in a possibly destructive state."

"Did I destroy anything here? No. I'm not basically destructive. I even try to make friends of my enemies. I was just getting excited about a connection I had made with another facet of the Great Spirit "

"What was that?"

"I really don't believe you would understand."

"Try me."

"I'd rather not. I already feel I've said too much. Let me just add that if you comit me, I would like to appeal. I disagree with this entire procedure of you sitting in judgement of me—after all, who are you people to sit in judgement of my opinions?"

The judge raised his hand: "Do you have anything further to say?"

"Not really. Only that I resent being questioned by people I don't know, and forced to take drugs I don't understand. You've stripped me of the rights due a human being." His fists opened and closed, then clenched together. Strangely, there was no anger in his face—only a pervading hopelessness, like that of a boy in a new neighborhood playing a game with rules he didn't understand.

The judge glanced at Dr. Reynolds; Dr. Reynolds glanced at the nurse: "How much Thorazine?"

"Fifty q.i.d.; we give it intramuscular sometimes, when he gets manic."

Mr. Smelden stared at them: "Manic? What's manic for you may not be manic for me. Our minds may be on different levels of awareness. I can't help it if you are already on a dead, unexcitable level."

"He talks like that often," the nurse said, "paces the room, takes notes..."

"Have you ever looked at these notes?" Dr. Reynolds inquired.

"Not really."

"That's all right. I believe we have enough." The judge nodded and followed with his signature upon the white paper. Diagnosis: Paranoia, A.P.A. number 2970.

"In this case," Dr. Reynolds added, "we'll complete the discussion with the students after the patient leaves the room."

After Mr. Smelden was escorted out, Dr. Reynolds turned to the students: "You see, in a case such as this, any discussion in the patient's presence might serve as a reinforcement for his beliefs and delusions, which may retard any chances of improvements. Now, this patient manifested the classically aggrandized view of self, with concurrent decrease of belief in the trustworthiness of others; he also lapsed into flight of ideas, loose associations, suspiciousness, and persecutional ideations about us. You must keep in mind that Thorazine is maintaining him in check, and that he appears more rational and logical than he would without it. Do you have any questions?"

Cameron shook his head; wasn't it just possible that an individual person didn't follow a textbook presentation of a particular case or disease? Wasn't there room for flexibility, insight, for listening to an individual person rather than following every printed textbook word?

"Yes, Mr. Cameron, do you have a question?"

The one he had was only peripheral to Mr. Smelden's case: "Well, it's similar to what I'd asked before. Here we have taken for granted again that Thorazine is improving this man's condition, that without it he would be worse. How can we be certain of this in each individual case?"

"We've covered this ground before, Mr. Cameron. You aren't yet entitled to an opinion about our capacity to judge the efficacy of a drug on the actions of a patient. Anything else?"

If there was, there was also no point in bringing it up. Cameron shut his notebook and shook his head.

"I welcome your dissenting criticism, Dr. Cameron. But in the future," Dr. Reynolds peered at him calmly under his glasses, "I would hope your scalpel is sharpened with more researched facts and more thoroughly selective."

As the word Doctor preceded his name John Cameron realized he'd been reinstated, with an admonition, into the fraternity of Psychiatry 301.

The students filed out through the anteroom, another lock turned, and they were in the corridor of the Psychiatric ward. A nurse and an orderly in white pushed a medicine cart and made inspection of rooms. The corridor narrowed into the distance with doors, some thick, padded and locked, and small grated windows lined it with cubicle-like regularity. In gray flannel pajamas, most patients walked about. An indistinguishable sound, muffled, as if something scraped a padded surface, came from a locked cell. Cameron turned away, towards the bank of elevators. King's County Court for this week had ended. The Psychiatry ward's doors had slammed locked behind him.

Five floors down, he was out of the hospital. It was an early winter afternoon outside, with clouds and cool moist air condensing on the leaves of trees. He wondered: Eight cases, eight persons, eight lives in three hours; a lady beaten by her husband; a silent man awaiting death in a closed garage; a man committed because of his conceptions. Had anything gone wrong in there?

Cameron breathed the cold fresh air off Puget Sound: No, not in this world; you're imagining things, Cameron. And you still have a year and a half to go, and classes this afternoon.

CHAPTER 3

WE SURVIVED THE MADNESS

The chest X-ray looked as if a snowstorm had covered the lungs: Pneumonia or congestive heart failure were the most obvious possibilities. It was neither. Nor was it anything else they could figure.

The 48 year old merchant seaman had said he'd felt fine until last week, when he'd become suddenly short of breath. They took more X-rays: No change. They questioned him several times more: Still no clues. In the mornings, the intern and medical student listened to his lungs. He was beginning to look ashen.

"I don't know what it is," the intern shook his head, "the specialists don't have an answer either. Nothing fits. Are you sure you're not in pain?" he asked the man.

"No, not pain," the seaman answered.

The intern moved to another patient. The medical student remained. "You never had any pain before either? No pain at all?" He had asked him that question many times before. He examined the abdomen: Ascites, it contained extra fluid.

"Not a pain."

It was something about the way he said it this time. The medical student repeated the question.

No answer.

"You need to tell me if it hurts. I can't help you if you don't tell me."

"It's not a pain, Doc. I can't tell you that."

"Why can't you tell me?"

"I'm a man. A seaman. I can't tell you it hurts!"

It suddenly dawned: "It does, but you can't say it hurts. Men like you don't feel pain."

There was a small, tired nod.

When he died a few days later, they found cancer. It had spread from kidneys to abdomen to the lungs. It had taken years for it to happen.

The medical student already knew many people complained overmuch of pain. He'd just learned some didn't complain at all.

Soon he would be leaving Marine Hospital—these were the last few days on Medical Service. Then Cardiology Elective, and three months from now, it would be all over. Cameron walked to the small basement cafeteria. Several nurses stood ahead in the lunch line. Karen was there.

"Heard where you're going, Cameron?"

"L.A. County - U.S.C. Medical Center."

"That's so far."

"I know."

"Was it first choice, or did you just match up that way?"

The words sounded far away. How had it worked? A computer had mated prospective interns to hospitals: One single giant electronic brain had crossmatched the lists of thousands of hospitals for their choices of future interns, in numerical order, to the fourth-year medical students' choices of hospitals, also in order of preference. Out of this seeming chaos each student found his internship niche, and each hospital its interns. In its own way it was a fantastic feat of electronic juggling, comparable to a moon shot. Cameron wondered why he resented it. Maybe for its efficiency, but really precisely for that: For its mechanical smoothness, its mathematical precision, its infallibility. The mechanics of medicine were even now close to infallible. But the art... a seaman lay dead because of a single word he hadn't been able to say; one word had defeated an entire human and mechanical medical army.

"Cameron, *did* you match up like you wanted?"

"Yes; it was my first choice, Karen."

She shrugged. "I get off at five."

It would be good, he thought. Sure, it would be good. "Let's have dinner, then go to a movie or something."

"Tell you what—I'll fix dinner at my place, then maybe we'll go for a drive."

"All right."

Cameron sat next to Watson, his intern on General Medical service, already shoveling fork and food into his mouth at a prodigious rate.

"Coming for afternoon rounds, Cameron?"

"Sure."

"Get a move on."

Watson had been a good intern: He'd steadied Cameron's hands over the biopsy needle; he'd guided his fingers as they plunged the needle into a small pleural space between chest wall and lungs; his eyes had been silently reassuring as he'd aim for that pin-point spot in the spinal canal to reach the cerebrospinal fluid.

"Watson?"

"What?"

"I'd like to thank you for teaching me."

"You helped me, Cameron; you did your stuff, and I taught you. That was the deal." He grinned through his beard: "Ready to go?"

"Yes."

"You're still uptight about it, aren't you, Cameron?"

"What?"

"The seaman with cancer."

Cameron nodded.

"Doesn't do any good messing your mind up: He was already dead before he even got to this hospital. Come on, we've got patients to take care of."

"And you?"

"What about?"

"How do you feel?"

"Everyone deals with his insides differently, Cameron. Me, I work my ass off. Does that answer your question?"

"Guess it does."

"Good luck with your internship, Cameron. You're going to do fine." They walked upstairs to the ward."

Matsu raced past them: "Hey, Cameron!"

"Yeah!"

"What internship d'ya get?"

"L.A. County."

"I got San Francisco! I got it!"

"Congratulations."

In the evening, he left Marine Hospital. It was strange—it already felt like the last day here. The rust red brick building, twelve stories to the sky atop its hill overlooking Puget Sound, caught the last bits of sunset glow. Cameron wondered if people saw it as beautiful. Perhaps it was only in his imagination: County Hospital, Marine Hospital, they all felt like home by now; their bricks were warm, the sunset from their hills the best anywhere; those hospitals had been his stone mothers, in whose insides he'd been raised, and his mind had been fed. He'd arrived clean shaven, bright eyed, clutching papers and books; in the morning he'd walked polished corridors that by evening had seen life slip away; he'd heard the sirens scream from afar, deafen, fall silent here. It all ended here: In the night-silence. I.V.'s pumping crystal liquid. Lights. Shadows. Quiet steps. Smells. There were always smells. Bad sometimes. But always he knew where he was: Laboratory, Surgery, Peds. He was a traveler here—every sound, color, footstep, every touch meant something, good or bad.

He'd been a stranger at first. Now maps of learning and instinct crisscrossed his brain. In a way, he would always remain a stranger: People lived, hoped laughed, played, cried, became healed or died within these walls; but no one would ever know everything inside them.

He arrived at Karen's: Soft dark hair, quick glowing eyes, bouncy, always smiling. They'd met at Marine a few months ago; she had said he never smiled, and he smiled just hearing her say it, watching the glow of her eyes.

"Dinner's not ready, Cameron. I had to do some extra stuff at the hospital."

"That's all right."

"I like the way you hug me, Cameron," she rested her chin between his neck and shoulders.

"You look beautiful, Karen."

"Let's take a walk. The park's right out there—no driving, no rushing, just you and me, walking."

He held her waist under the sweater as they walked by the bridge. She stopped. Cameron hugged her again, drawing her neck close.

"You don't know how much I need that," she said.

"I guess we all need that sometimes."

"Why did you get L.A. County?"

"Because I wanted it."

"Was it really your first choice?"

"Yes."

"They work you to death out there."

They did, he knew. But it was another stone mother—large, impervious to age, a city unto itself, mazes of rooms, floors, hallways; peeling paint; interns bunched together in a few on-call rooms. It was a hospital, and he'd be a traveler again, learning. A stranger again.

"But why?" Karen asked.

He shrugged his shoulders: "I liked it."

"What about your career? I thought you wanted research. A smaller University Hospital, a teaching institution would have been better."

"It is a University hospital—U.S.C. is there."

"It's also County. They'll use you like at county hospital. Haven't you been used enough?"

Cameron shrugged again: "There's a lot of medicine there. All the medicine off the streets of Los Angeles that no one else wants. I want it."

"And a university hospital wouldn't have that?"

"They're terrific places, university hospitals: Everything works like clockwork; they sparkle like mirrors, smell like executive offices, and the best brains in the world collaborate on a single patient if need be."

"What's wrong with that?"

"Nothing. They're great academies of learning, Karen. Safe, helpful, like parents watching over our first wobbly steps. I wouldn't have had it any other way. Now I guess it's time to be weaned. I need to be where things don't always work right, where it's crowded, where everyone needs to pull together because they know it's all they've got, where medicine smells, feels and looks like medicine. That's what I need now. I'm ready for it and I need it."

"Medicine is technology, Cameron. That's where it's going, and you're not going to change it. It isn't the old times medicine of your father, and it will keep on moving. Do you think that's so bad?"

"No. Technology has done wonders, Karen: Sparkling labs, computers, transducers, monitors. It's just that "

"What, Cameron?"

"I can't explain it. I guess I want to learn the human level of medicine first, before relying on the mechanical one. I don't think we're ready to abandon the thinking and feeling to shiny electrified solid-state circuits."

"No one is asking for that."

"Not yet. And maybe eventually those things really will do everything better than we."

"What would you do then?"

"Something else, Karen. Maybe build those machines."

"Are you going to stay tonight?" she suddenly asked.

"Yes."

"You've never stayed before."

"I never had time."

"And now that you're leaving, you have time."

"What can I say, Karen?"

"Don't say anything, Cameron. Stay."

They had dinner in a one-room restaurant that grilled hamburgers and sliced prime rib right at the counter. The walls were bare, and smoke from the grill rose into the kitchen fan.

"Aren't you going to be scared of me?"

"When?"

"Tonight."

"Why?" he asked.

"We've never stayed together before. And I asked you, so you probably think I'm pushy and that I'll totally devastate you in bed. Do you think I really will?"

"I hope so."

"I can't get out of it now?"

He smiled and shook his head. "Not now."

Her two roommates were gone. Karen left the lights off.

"Hold me."

"Any tighter and I'll crush you."

"It's strange you'll be leaving so soon."

"I know."

"Let's not talk about it. That's my room."

"I can't see anything."

"Leave it like that. I'll be right back."

He felt his way onto the bed and sat down. The bed took up half the small room and he could touch the walls with outstretched arms. In the dark, his hands went over the outlines of a radio clock and a lamp. He hesitated, then turned it on. The room glowed in dim orange. It was soft and comfortable, and he felt tired. He put his head on the pillow, and sank into the bed. His own bed by comparison was like an Army cot; by the time Karen returned, he was asleep.

She sat on the edge of the bed in her nightgown, without moving. He stirred awake. She was looking at the light.

"You want it off?"

"Please."

The glow disappeared. "You look beautiful, Karen. Why did you want the light off?"

"I don't know." She lay beside him without her nightgown, carefully, formally.

He put his arm around her shoulders. She was still. "Maybe I should leave, Karen."

"No." She placed her arms around his neck, "I'm sorry. I do want you here holding me. I do." She moved over his chest, and he squeezed her gently between the wall and himself...hands under soft covers, touching her, smell of exotic flowers, moisture...he felt comfortable and far away.

"It won't...fit!" she gasped.

"What?"

"It...we don't fit together!"

"God," he mumbled, "you're a..."

"No, I'm not," she lied.

"Karen, I don't know if..."

"Isn't this how it's done? Please. It should, shouldn't it? I mean later... It does take a long time sometimes, doesn't it, Cam?" "Sure," he muttered.

Her shoulders shook. "I'm sorry I'm a virgin."

He stroked her forehead and touched under her eyes. "It's beautiful, Karen. It's just that I'm not sure you should want to be with me."

An hour later she moved her legs suddenly up and kept them there, letting out a cry. Rolling, shaking, like a tide against shore, waves over sand until there was nothing left, he went far away then returned, slowly. Different. Sad. He turned his face next to hers on the pillow.

"Now what?" she asked softly.

"Nothing," he caressed her hair. "Do you want a glass of water?"

"Sure."

He returned and the light was on her smile, bright as always, her shoulders bare on the pillow, her short dark hair furiously curled.

"You're beautiful, Karen," he wiped the moisture from her forehead curls.

"When do I see you again, Cam?"

"All of tonight."

"Then?"

"God, Karen, you know I'll be leaving."

She nodded.

He lay down next to her. "I'll miss you, Karen."

"You will?"

"Yes, damn it."

Finals, grades, ceremonies; before graduation's sendoff into the world, one last act took place—"Senior Skits." It was an act of tradition, a symbol of freedom, an act of riot, rebellion, and transition to responsibility all at once. This irreverent, turbulent happening marked the final transition from a classroom's supervision to the future's unknowns. It was an act of revenge and a celebration of thanks for four years unlike any they had ever spent before.

Students and professors participated alike. Where "Senior Skits" bordered on the profane, it was with the realization that their toils, loves, angers, times together had been fully paid for: Paid by trembling hands drawing blood from each other's veins, by eyes following the flesh-and- blood repair mechanisms of their own scalpel-scraped arms, by I.V. needles carried in place inside their own bodies testing new drugs, by heads that had fallen asleep on books, bodies that had dragged out of bed at night to observe how others might be repaired.

> "We survived the madness,
> baby, it's all done.
> So please, don't think of madness,
> it's all over, and we've won..."

Music played in the background as the curtains opened; Karen and Cameron watched the professors being lampooned or underhandedly complimented, mimicked, criticized, thanked. Conservative students who for years had worn white coats and ties gave way to a dance group attired in nothing but their jocks, briefly stunning the audience of parents, wives, girlfriends. The country's most renown and terrifying 'Professor Figure,' the Professor of Medicine, belted out a ukulele song in a grass skirt and mop wig. Skits and movies replayed the most memorable times, lines, notorious dates, loves, and near-disasters at exam time.

> "Close your eyes, feel the morning,
> go catch the rain.
> We survived the madness,
> it's all over, and we're free..."

Awards went to the most appreciated Professors and courses—a parting acknowledgement of debts and bonds that could never truly be repaid. It was their last act of Medical School. The curtain fell.

> "'Cause we survived the madness,
> baby, ain't you proud;
> There can't be any sadness,
> not here, upon our ground..."

Karen and Cameron raised glasses in a toast as Yarbrough's music faded. It was the last time he saw her.

There was no summer vacation that year. Internship began in ten days. After graduation, Cameron packed his belongings into a U-Haul trailer improbably hitched to a VW beetle, and pointed it south to L.A. In a few days he'd be in another stone building, filled to capacity with blood and flesh he'd be directly responsible for the first time in his life.

"Dr. Cameron," intoned the hoarse voice of the Chief Medical Resident during orientation.

"Yes."

"You don't know it yet, but you've already drawn lots: Your first internship service is Hematology. You are the intern on call tonight."

CHAPTER 4

THE MACHINE THAT NEVER SMILED

"Hurry," the nurse's voice said, "he's coughing blood."

The receiver hung by the wall in the night. The intern shook his head awake, scrambled up the echoing stairway.

He saw it in the stainless steel pan, under the artificial lights of night. At first, he, too, thought it was blood. Dark chunks, clots, jelly, pieces floating in thick red—the pan was full of it, air bubbles rising in sweetish smell.

He tried to clear the man's throat of the clots wedged inside. He grasped one. Soft, slippery, air hissed from it like a sponge. The intern looked at it. It fell from his hands. They weren't blood clots at all. Pieces of lung. Lung cancer. The man was blue now, covered with pieces of torn lung he'd been coughing out, and with the blood that hadn't made it into the pan.

The intern stared at the bloody tissue all around. In one day and one night, another world had passed. Things would not be the same again. Ever.

Cameron glanced at the tiny blue dots under the microscope, clustered in scores around the pink staining white cells. Staph abscess? It was rare to have a staph abscess that large.

Process: Diagnosis
1. The man had a large right lung abscess by X-ray.
2. The man's sputum contained staphylococci.

But were the staphylococci the primary invaders, the reason the abscess had originally formed? Or had they arrived later, as secondary invaders? If so, which was the real culprit within the abscess?

Process: Treatment Alternatives
1. Treat the abscess as if it were due to staph, and hope that assumption was correct.
2. Resort to open or closed biopsy of the abscess, to pinpoint the exact invader.

Either alternative was risky.

"Is this 6-B, General Medicine?"

"Yes."

"We're the medical students."

"All right. That's Dr. Underman, and I'm Dr. Cameron. You can choose whichever intern you wish. I might as well tell you with me you'll be doing CBC's, UA's, gram stains, whatever else needs to be done, just as I do. I know junior U.S.C. medical students are already above all that, but it needs to be done—we'll be doing the 'scut work' as well as the fancy stuff. You've got three months here to spend in any way you wish. But if you don't want to work, don't bother coming on rounds with me."

Three of the students left to see Dr. Underman.

"You sound tough," said the one remaining.

"I'd rather work alone than with someone I can't depend on."

"Thanks. What do you have against U.S.C. students? You from Harvard or something?"

"U.S.C. students are bright and lazy. And no, I'm not from Harvard."

"You're overworked and uptight."

"Right."

"I'm Mel," said the medical student.

"I'm John Cameron."

"Anybody ever say you should smile more often?"

"As a matter of fact, yes."

"Where do we start?"

"The Resident shows up in a half hour for patient rounds. Before he arrives, we review lab results and fit together the pieces of the puzzles."

"What can I do?"

"Relax, Mel. Today's an easy day: We go on rounds, talk to patients, check that meds have been given, run down X-rays and lab results, do a liver biopsy, maybe one lung. You can look over the charts, and in the evening we'll finish up with rounds again—to make sure our patients are better off than when we started this morning."

"And if they aren't?"

"One Resident, one intern, and one medical student are going to think and sweat some more."

"Maybe smile more, too."

"You've got a deal. Let's review Mr. Navarro first—here's the chart, let's go talk to him."

The man with the lung abscess spoke a mixture of mostly Spanish with little English: No, he wasn't short of breath; yes, the chest pain was still there; so was his cough.

"He trusts you," said Mel, "he's calm as a church and knows you're going to cure him."

"No—he knows I'm going to *try* damn hard. Now you know the story, Mel: What do you think?"

"Can I see the X-rays?"

"Listen to his chest first, Mel; Clinical before Lab, remember?" He turned to Navarro: *"Quiere escuchar a su pecho, bueno?"*

Mel passed the stethoscope over Navarro's chest, then shook his head: "Can't hear much of anything unusual. Only some decreased breath sounds anteriorly."

"Where anteriorly?"

"To the right of the sternum."

"That's right. You found it. It doesn't sound like much to you now, but you'll get used to listening. Pretty soon that'll sound like the whistle of a locomotive to you. Here are his X-rays."

"The abscess, right? And you said the sputum gram stain showed staph—so, staph abscess, probably *staphylococcus aureus.*"

"Good, Mel, but a little fast. You didn't go through the entire process: Is the abscess sac broken in any places?"

"Doesn't appear to be."

"So whatever organism is causing the infection, it's still inside the sac, right?"

"Right."

"But since the sac isn't broken, the staph we found in the sputum came from *outside* the abscess sac."

"You have a point there."

"Then how do we know that the staph we retrieved from *outside* the sac is responsible for the infection *inside*?"

"We don't."

"Right. We're guessing, because staph could be either the primary or secondary pathogen. Hold it! I just missed something myself!"

"You have, Harvard?"

He nodded: "There's the possibility of an abscess presenting itself on a bronchial tube cancer, predisposing it to infection. Always think of something hiding behind the obvious."

"So, what do we do now?"

"What do you think, Mel?"

"I don't know."

"Exactly. At this point we ask for help: The pulmonary specialists. They'll see Mr. Navarro this afternoon." Cameron wrote a request for consultation on the chart.

"How many more do we have?"

"Eleven."

By evening rounds, preliminary lab cultures had returned on Navarro: *staphylococcus aureus*, resistant to all antibiotics except

Methicillin. The pulmonary specialists had already recorded their recommendations: Agreed it was probably an abscess caused by staph, best treated by a trial of antibiotics rather than biopsy. Cameron tried to remember if Navarro had good veins—Methicillin could only be given I.V., it was painful, and it would take a long time.

"That's it for today, Mel."

"And tomorrow?"

"Tomorrow we're on call for the wards; the day after for admitting new patients."

"See you at breakfast, Cameron."

"Sure."

He thought of telling him sleep might be better than breakfast for tomorrow, but he didn't.

"Hey, you're smiling, Cameron!"

"Right. See you."

The next day two patients were well enough to go home; Navarro was still feverish; and the other fourteen were gradually improving. The day went by uneventfully.

"So what happens tonight, Cameron?"

"We eat dinner fast and wait 'til they call us."

"Call us for what?"

"Any problems in the General Medical wards tonight, while the off- call interns sleep."

"*All* the General Med wards?"

Cameron heard his name paged. "Let's go."

"You weren't kidding about eating fast."

"Mel, you might as well learn how to brush your teeth with one hand, and piss with the other."

They took the elevators to 7A. The patient lay cool and sweating, soaking the linens; sixtyish, eyes closed, forehead glistening. Cameron squeezed hard over his shoulder muscle: No response to pain; in coma.

"How long has he been like that?" Cameron asked the nurse.

"About six hours. But his pressure was good until just now, when he bottomed out at sixty over zero."

Cameron glanced at the I.V. bottle.

"What was wrong with him before that?"

"We don't know. He was admitted yesterday"

"To McLaren's service?"

"Yes, McLaren was the intern"

Cameron winced. "Show me the patient's chart."

"What's going on?" asked Mel.

"If it's one of McLaren's patients we better take it from the top." Cameron glanced swiftly through the chart: No history listed other than shortness of breath, and a few crackling lung rales found on physical. Diagnosis: Congestive heart failure. Treatment: Water expulsion with Lasix. Cameron paged over the lab results, vital signs, medications, then turned to the progress notes. That section was empty.

"Did McLaren see this patient today?"

"I don't think so."

Cameron flung the chart into the wastebasket; "Tell McLaren to keep his charts where they belong."

"What's this all about?"

"Never mind, Mel. Let's see the patient." He touched his forehead: After the initial coolness of sweat, he felt the furnace underneath. "Temp?"

"One-hundred-four two," the nurse answered.

Cameron got into gear:

H.E.E.N.T. (Head, eyes, ears, nose, throat) - No significant findings.

Neck - No increased veins.

Chest - Inspiratory rales, the sound of rustling silk when the patient breathed in. McLaren was right about that; there was also a dull sound in the right lower lung.

Heart - Grade 2/6 systolic ejection murmur, loudest at the aortic area. Maybe also a faint Grade 1/6 diastolic murmur.

Abdomen - Soft, no changes of organs.

Genito-Urinary - No significant findings.

Extremities - Pale, pulses faint. A red, moist sore on the right heel.

Skin - drenched in sweat.

Neurological - Patient comatose; reflexes still normal.

Cameron stood back and thought a minute. "Get me a cut down set and CVP line. Mel, you know how to do a cut down?"

"No."

"Watch. You'll be doing the next one." Cameron cleansed the skin with iodine and alcohol, fastened towels around it, and opened a straight red line one inch inside and above the elbow crease. A blue tube popped out. "Basilic vein, Mel—our highway to the heart. Next to it is the antecubital. What's this?"

"Looks white, like a nerve. The median nerve?"

"Get some gloves on. Feel it."

"It's pulsating."

"Right. The brachial artery—a highway we need to avoid." He placed a tiny slit into the vein, and blood flooded into the oval wound. The bleeding stopped after the vein was lifted onto a bridge of silk threads, and a plastic catheter slipped its way to the heart's right upper chamber. The manometer pressure registered between 7 and 9 centimeters of water inside the heart's chamber. Cameron tied catheter to vein and back to the skin, then closed the wound.

"Let's get a portable X-ray to confirm cath position."

"Why did we put a CVP cath in?"

"Watch," Cameron poured 300 cc's of intravenous fluid through the catheter. The manometer reading remained unchanged: "What does that tell you, Mel?"

"A relative lack of fluids, I guess."

"Right. This patient is in shock, not from excessive fluid due to congestive heart failure - since in that case the pressure would have gone up with the additional load of 300 cc's - but due to the opposite, fluid depletion. Nurse, two blood culture tubes, please. Mel, can you draw them?"

"Sure."

Cameron wrote the rest of the patient's orders:

1. I.V.'s - Ringer's lactate 1 liter over 4 hours; add 10 meqs of KC1.
    Then 1 liter D5/W water over 4 hours with 15 meqs of KC1.

2. Antibiotics - Keflin 2.0 grams I.V.; Kanamycin 0.5 grams I.M. stat.
3. Oxygen, 4 liters/minute by mask. Maintain oral airway and suction as needed.
4. Arterial blood gases stat.
5. Sputum gram stain, culture and sensitivity.
6. Gram stain, culture and sensitivity of leg sore.
7. Hydrocortisone 1 gram I.V. stat, and q 6 hours for 24 hours.
8. Portable chest film and previous films for comparison
9. E.K.G.
10. CBC, UA, creatinine, sugar, electrolytes, stat.
11. Foley catheter.

Cameron scratched one out: "Better yet, we'll do the gram stain ourselves. Give my regards to McLaren."

"What was all that about McLaren?" asked Mel.

"Most interns are pretty good about leaving their patients well cared for before they split for their night off. McLaren leaves his work for the intern on call instead. I'll have a heart-to-heart with him tomorrow."

"Will he make it?"

"The patient? We'll have to wait and see."

Mel scratched his chin: "Cameron, I realize what you did. I'm just not sure *how* you did it."

"All right, how do you think I did it?"

"You probably thought the patient was in septic, infectious shock, and ordered antibiotics and fluids to counter it."

"What would you have done?"

"The same, I hope. It was a pretty good diagnosis to make."

He shook his head. "No, Mel. We don't make diagnosis: We feel, we see, we listen, think and we're *led* to a diagnosis. We keep the circle wide, then draw the net in. Example: This patient's in coma, shock. He has a temperature, a heart murmur, strange lung sounds, and a sore on the foot. Process:

1. Neurologic shock from a stroke is a possibility, but not enough evidence to support this view, so discard.
2. Hypovolemic or fluid depletion shock, caused by infection, medication, or a metabolic disease; retain this possibility.
3. Cardiogenic shock from a heart attack, myocarditis, defective heart valves, or aberrant blood chemicals such as a low potassium caused by Lasix; retain this possibility, but remember that this type of shock would more likely be present with congestive heart failure and fluid overload, which we don't have in this case.

Finally, 4: Septic, infectious shock due to bacterial toxins; the increased temperature, lung sounds suggestive of pneumonia, and pattern of this shock go along with this more than any of the other choices. The pneumonia could provide the original source of bacteria for the sepsis, so could the heart murmur, where bacteria could be growing on the valves; and so also could the sore on the leg. Probably all three are connected. And of course Lasix would aggravate this type of shock. So, the pattern fits.

Now we need to confirm: Do a complete blood count, culture the blood, lungs, and leg sore, repeat the X-rays of the chest, finish chemical blood analysis, and do an EKG. Since in this case there isn't time to wait for laboratory results, we begin treatment: Oxygen for the lungs, antibiotics for the probable infection, and increased fluids for the shock. Then we watch and wait."

"You're a machine, Cameron."

"Right. And machines don't smile."

"What if we're wrong?"

"We may not have a second chance."

"What if"

"Yeah, there are many what ifs. There are no absolutes in medicine, even if you think you're one hundred percent correct. Remember it, Mel. Always rethink, reevaluate, and look at the patient again."

"Dr. Cameron," crackled the page, "Dr. Cameron, you're wanted on 7-B."

Mel placed his breakfast tray next to Cameron's and his eyes blinked open.

"Coffee?"

"Sure."

"Tired?"

"Hmm. Aren't we admitting today?"

"Yep."

"Well, I'm not going to miss it, Cameron."

"Turning into a real go-getter, aren't you, Mel?"

"Can I work up any of the new patients?"

"Let me do it first for now; then you can write your own report and compare."

"Compare myself to a machine?"

They finished breakfast and went on rounds. "Navarro doesn't seem any better from the methicillin, and his vein hurts," Mel commented.

"The antibiotic will diffuse only slowly into the abscess sac. It may take a week, or it could take a month. If it works at all."

"If it doesn't?"

"The machine tries something else," Cameron smiled.

They didn't finish rounds on their previous patients. Their first new admit was a young girl, curly chestnut hair, cheeks smudged by mascara, breathing shallowly. The emergency red-blanket was over her feet.

"Red-blanket," muttered Cameron, "looks like an overdose."

"Do we know what she took?"

"No idea. Usually we never find out. The stuff on the streets has so much mixed in, not even the labs find out in time." Her pupils were small and reactive. Reflexes slow. Heart and lungs normal. Cameron squeezed hard over her shoulder muscles; nothing. Stage 2 to 3 coma.

"Hypnotic or sedative, Mel; or a combination. Strychnine, LSD, PCP usually show more agitation…Nurse! Gastric lavage set with three liters of Mag sulfate. Wait, give me a 7.5 ET tube and straight blade first."

"You're going to intubate?"

"Going to try. If she's in deep coma, without a gag reflex, she could vomit and aspirate into the lungs. As many die from that as from the

O.D. itself. The 'Playmate of the Year' died of it." Cameron held the lighted intubation blade in his left hand, drawing the tongue out of the way; vocal cords shone white under the light. He eased the plastic airway in. The girl coughed spasmodically, and bit firmly down on the tube. Cameron pried it loose.

He shook his head: "She's not awake to protect herself from vomiting and having that aspirated into the lungs, yet she's not asleep enough to allow the tube into her trachea to protect the lungs."

"What now?"

Cameron shrugged. "We still need to wash her out." Cameron placed the tip of a lubricated nasogastric tube into her left nostril. It slid two inches, then stopped. He twirled it, until a cartilaginous softness gave way.

Droplets of blood oozed from her nose. Her eyes opened, then tightened, mascara running down the cheeks.

"You're hurting her."

Cameron said nothing. The tube continued its journey down until a bilious yellow fluid began to return. "Stomach contents, set up lavage. Start an I.V. D5/W Send blood to lab for a drug screen." Twenty minutes later the fluid returning from the stomach was clear. Cameron removed his gloves and turned to Mel: "Look at her teeth."

"They're clenched shut."

"That's why we didn't put the stomach tube through the mouth; it would have caused less pain, but she would have clamped it shut just like the airway tube."

"Oh."

"Smile, Mel, Smile. She's only our first O.D. of the day."

Before it was over, two congestive heart failures, one pulmonary edema, one red-blanket in D.T.'s biting the stretcher rails, a woman with a blood clot inside her lungs, a young man with the crayon-like yellowness of hepatitis, and two more O.D.'s had arrived at their admissions ward. At 3 a.m. they took a break and visited the man in D.T.'s. He was calm now, wide-eyed and sitting up in bed within the padded room.

"How are you doing?" Cameron asked.

"Fine," replied the man. "There are rats in my bed."

Cameron pointed to thin air: "That one there?"

Mel took a step back.

"Yeah, it's a big one," said the man.

Cameron looked intently and waved his hand back and forth in the air: "It's a nice one, isn't it? It won't hurt you, see? It's a nice one, and you can pet it just like this."

Mel looked at them both as if they were lunatics.

Cameron walked out and closed the padded door. Mel stared at him: "I think you ought to get some sleep."

"Oh, that. They're D.T. hallucinations, Mel. You won't convince him otherwise, so you might as well agree with him and talk him down slowly."

"Whew!"

"Had you worried, ha, Mel?"

"Yeah, Harvard."

An hour later, the Resident's voice crackled into the receiver and somewhere inside Cameron's sleeping brain vault: "You awake, Cameron? We've got a kidney failure. That's all I know about it. An old lady. Can you take care of it? I'll go over the case later."

Cameron swung his legs over the edge of the bed. He was already dressed in wrinkled blues; by the time he hit the lights of the corridors, his steps were already straight.

The lady was 79 years old, too short of breath to talk or even moan. No matter what Cameron examined, there was something wrong with it. He called the Resident. "She's ready."

"What's the story, Cam?"

"Chronic renal failure. Uremia. She had a heart attack tonight, and went into pulmonary edema. She's also got pneumonia."

"Is that all?"

"I called her private doctor and asked why he sent her here. He said he didn't want her to die at home."

The Resident shook his head. "What have you done so far?"

"Nothing."

He looked at Cameron. "Get going—Central Venous Pressure line, Lasix, antibiotics; hell, I don't need to tell you what to do. The works."

"She's dying, Roger."

"She's not dead yet."

"She's been dying for years. Nobody's going to put her on a kidney machine."

"Start the CVP, Cam."

"No veins."

"Cut her down, then."

"You want me to cut her in the last few minutes of her life?"

"What's wrong with you, Cameron?"

"Nothing."

"That's an order, Cameron."

"Roger. Will do."

"Do I have to stay up to watch you, or will you do it?"

"I'll do it. I'll do the whole bit."

"All right, then."

The nurse quietly opened the cut down tray, then cleansed the arm in preparation for the search for veins. Just as quietly, she left. Cameron draped the arm, leaving a square open above the elbow. He remembered promising the next CVP for Mel. He looked at the woman: Eyes closed, breathing through puffed cheeks, skin like wrinkled paper. No one needed this cut down. Not Mel. Not anyone.

A thin red line flowed under the scalpel. Red beads burst from the skin's edges and oozed out over the parchment-white fibers of connective tissue covering the muscle. No veins. He pierced it like paper, and began the hunt below. It was a bloody hunt. Not even the anesthetic could numb all the prying dissection. Cameron glanced at the woman: Her eyes were open, staring at him. A few beads of sweat squeezed out over her forehead. Then she died.

Cameron closed the cut down tray methodically. Methodically he closed her eyes and methodically he drew the sheet over her. Methodically he walked the corridor, then climbed the stairs to the twenty-fourth floor. There were always unused sleeping rooms there. He lifted the receiver.

"Yes?" came the night operator's voice.

"I'll be at 2633."

"Who is this?"

"Dr. Cameron."

In the quiet darkness, behind the locked door, he could still get an hour's sleep. Instead, he stared at the ceiling. It was all right, he thought. After all, machines didn't smile, and machines didn't need any sleep.

CHAPTER 5

INDIAN SUMMER

He had red hair and was twenty-five years old. With the thick moustache, blue eyes, large shoulders, he could have been a movie star. The intern saw him on morning rounds, stopped by his bed, opened his chart. But he seldom wrote on the chart or talked to him. He didn't know how.

Afterwards, in the afternoons, the intern would see him sometimes wandering about the hospital in flannel pajamas and robe. At times he felt like stopping to talk to him. But each time he didn't.

The lumps underneath the robe grew all the time. They were noticeable only under the pajamas at first. Now they bulged under the bathrobe as well—over the chest, back, stomach, arms. Malignant melanoma: Two words told the young man's story.

He continued to pace like that, silently in his pajamas and robe, along the corridors, sometimes by the patients' cafeteria. There was a lump over his neck now. Initially the lumps had been removed, of course. But one couldn't cut out a hundred of them, growing like that. Growing inside. One couldn't do anything. It was strange, though, how strong he still looked, red hair still shining, eyes bright and unblinking. The intern wasn't certain about the eyes, though. He didn't look at them.

Outside it was an Indian summer. The sun fell on hospital walls and windows from a clear blue sky. There was no wind. It was a magnificent summer. On a court not a hundred yards away from the hospital, the intern sometimes played basketball. It was one of the few times he felt happy, covered with sweat.

The redhead still walked with his strange energy, clean-shaved and hair combed. But he was growing pale. The lumps had their own energy:

The energy of cancer. Taken from him. The way cancers always took their energy. The redhead that looked like Robert Redford was the same age as the intern. But he would never get out of those corridors alive.

The redhead knew it, walked alone, and didn't ask for anything else. Others avoided him, not knowing what to give. Aside from rounds, the intern avoided him also.

One morning the two met downstairs. The intern finally looked at his eyes.

"Here," he extended a basketball, "there's a hoop and sunshine out there."

There was nothing else the intern could do or say. The life of someone dying didn't fit into any charts, words, or understanding.

Mel collected the blue-coded charts for rounds. Each intern had his own color code—Cameron's was blue.

"What do we do with this one?" said Mel, glancing at the "Expired" label.

"Take the name off our list."

"And the chart?"

Cameron looked away. "Send it to Medical Records."

"Did you finish the final summary?"

"Yes."

"Any lab or X-rays you want me to pick up on the way?"

"No."

"We're missing some."

"Get them then."

Cameron lined up the remaining charts. He reviewed all the indexed sections: Orders, Vital Signs, Nurses Notes, Lab, X-ray, EKG, History and Physical Progress Notes. Today it seemed somehow odd. Progress? Guarantees didn't exist, and all the indexed and color-coded charts in the world couldn't put them there.

Mel returned panting from the stairs.

"Ready for rounds?"

"Yes."

The diabetics foot wasn't covered by the bedsheets. It twitched a little. There were several ulcers, but no smell yet.

"What's bothering you the most?" Cameron asked.

The man stared at Cameron. "The leg."

"What about the leg?"

"It hurts."

Cameron knew it hurt. But he needed to ask. He couldn't put words in a patient's mouth.

"Where?"

The patient pointed.

"For how long?"

"Three days like this, bad."

Cameron glanced at the next bed. There were no partitions between the six beds in the room. No one talked. The boy in the next one was nineteen. He had diabetes also; and something else that had kept him in hospitals for much of his life.

"It hurts about here?" Cameron already knew what it was, but he was trying to be precise.

"The whole leg hurts."

"Any fever or chills?"

"Yes. Every day for three days."

"How long have the ulcers been there?"

"Long time." The man with diabetes was used to the ulcers—diabetic neuropathy. But he wasn't used to the pain.

"Let me look at it."

"Hurry up. It hurts bad."

The second toe was already black. Several ulcers on the foot were still dry, with a translucent thin layer of crust. Cameron pressed one; the crust broke with pus.

"Did that hurt?"

"No."

There was no feeling over the foot. All the feeling and pain was above, where the rest of the leg was infected. It twitched again under Cameron's hands.

"Christ, that hurts!" The man had a chill. "When am I going to get the pain medicine?"

His temperature was 103 degrees; with the infection, his right leg was four centimeters larger than the other.

"Finished, Doc?"

"Yes."

"When do I get the pain shots?"

"I'd rather stay away from pain shots, Ron."

"Pain medicine," the man repeated hoarsely, "aren't you going to give me any?"

"You've been taking a half grain of codeine already, Ron. It should keep you for a while."

"Hasn't helped."

"You've got an infection in the leg. When we start antibiotics it should hurt less. It's the best way of knowing that it's getting better."

The patient didn't know yet that it was gangrene, or that he might lose his right leg.

"I hope so. I can't bear this."

Cameron glanced at the boy in the next bed. He stared straight ahead, past the walls. Cameron finished writing on the chart and left.

The Resident leaned over Cameron's desk. "Who'd you write up?"

"Ronald Reed, 48 years old, next room, first bed as you go in."

"That's the eleventh admission today," the Resident muttered.

"I know. I'm still two behind."

"What's this one got?"

"Septicemia, gangrene of the right foot going up the leg. Diabetes like all the rest."

"So start him on Kana and Methi, and call an ortho consult. How's the Ketoacidotic doing?"

"Out of coma now. By the way, this one has already been taking Methicillin—no good so far."

"So try K and K."

"He's in pain, too."

"Give him pain meds, Cameron."

"Yeah."

The Resident left.

"Is something wrong?" Mel asked.

Cameron nodded. "We'll wait, Mel."

Most of the patients slept during morning rounds. Only the boy and the man with gangrene were awake. The boy looked like someone who'd been in a hospital on his back a long time. The man complained of pain almost as soon as they walked in.

"I've been in pain all night long! Can't you do something? I told you I had pain!"

The Resident leafed through the chart, then scribbled on the Doctor's Orders sheet. "Temp down any, Cameron?"

"No." Cameron turned to the man: "Any chills since last night, Ron?" He shook his head. "Just the pain."

"The fever will drop," Cameron assured him, "so will the pain."

"I don't give a damn about the fever! Only the pain, Doc!"

Cameron had seen the Orders where the Resident had written for Demerol. When they went outside, Cameron looked at him: "Don't give him Demerol, Roger. I've seen his old chart."

"And?"

"Drug addict. I.V. drugs."

"O.K. Then keep him on codeine."

"He does have a lot of pain, Roger. But I think the codeine should hold him and tell us how his leg is doing."

"Sure. Keep him on it."

Cameron canceled the order for Demerol and increased the codeine to a full grain.

Mel called him from the ward during lunch. "Cameron, Reed's acting up."

"I'll be there."

Cameron walked in with the chart. Mr. Reed's tray was untouched. He shook his leg: "Doc, this here medicine's not doing any good." "Is it any better at all?"

Cameron measured the leg again. Less swollen. But another toe was black.

"Well, Doc?"

"The fever is down, and your leg is not as hot."

"So?"

"I think we're beating the infection."

"You haven't beat the pain! It's worse than ever! I can't go on like this!"

"Look, Ron. I can't give you pain shots."

"Why not?"

"You know why not."

"Why?"

"You've been an addict, Ron. It's on your old chart. Maybe that's how this all started. Maybe you injected something and got an infection."

"That's it, ah?? I've been an addict, sure. But I'm in pain now. P A I N he spelled it. "For Chrissakes, give me something!"

"Codeine is strong medicine, and I would rather give you medications by mouth rather than shots, Ron. Your infection is getting better, and with it the pain will stop also. Hang on a while longer, Ron."

"What do you think I've been trying to do? I can't make it, Doc! I know I've been an addict. That was two years ago " His leg twitched and he stopped to catch his breath. "I haven't touched the stuff. Honest. I've proved I can stop. I've been on the streets right where it's at and everything, and I can control it!"

The intern stared at him. "I can't give you the shots now, Ron. You know I can't." Cameron turned around and walked out of the room.

"Chrissakes, I might as well be suffering outside this hospital then! Let me go home!"

Near midnight a nurse called to say Reed wanted to see him again. Cameron pulled up a chair by the bed.

"Look, Doc. I haven't had any sleep. Not the night before, not the night before that. How long you gonna keep me like this?"

"I can change your sleep medicine."

"That won't do any good. It's the pain medicine I need."

Cameron looked at him. The fever was almost completely gone, the leg was cooler. But the area of black continued to spread. Less infection, but more gangrene. He was winning, yet they were both losing.

"You're going to have to give me the pain medicines!"

"You are getting them, Ron. Every six hours. Four, if you want." "Those pills don't do any damn good! They don't do anything! I can suffer at home too!" His mouth quivered as he tried to sit up, his eyes burned from pupils small and dark.

"If you go home you might lose the leg. The whole leg. You might even die."

"I don't care. Let me die! I want to go home! I can suffer there!"

"You mean you want to sign out against medical advice?"

"Yes, damn you! Can't you hear me? I'm going home! Tell the nurse to get my clothes!"

Cameron walked into the corridor. He touched the nurse's shoulder. "Seventy-five of Demerol and twenty-five of Phenergan, every four hours if he asks for it." He wrote it on the chart and returned to the room. "You'll get the Demerol, Ron. Be careful with it."

"I'll be careful, Doc. You know I will. I can control it, you'll see."

Cameron replaced the blue-tagged chart within the rack. The nurse unlocked the narcotics cabinet. "You know he's an addict, don't you?"

"He was," Cameron said

"You mean you believe his story?"

"It doesn't matter."

In the morning Mr. Reed was sitting up in his bed, his legs lifted so they curved up higher than the rest of the body.

"Good morning, Ron."

"Good morning, Doc."

"Feeling better?"

He nodded. "Feel good. That lifting of the leg helped too."

"Good." Cameron looked over the chart. Mr. Reed had asked for the Demerol every four hours.

"You know, I didn't mean to be sore at you yesterday, Doc. It's just that "

"It's all right. Forget it." He looked at the foot: Still dying. Cameron glanced back at him. "I'm glad you're doing better. Be careful with the stuff. You know there'll be more danger now Oh, what the hell, what am I telling you this for?"

"I can do it," Reed smiled, "sure, I can control it."

Morning rounds finished fast, the rest of the day was slow. Cameron rewrote the orders for Mr. Reeds narcotics. Narcotic orders had to be reaffirmed every day. As he got into his car to leave, Cameron turned the radio on. He didn't like thinking about people that were going to have their legs cut off. Tomorrow, if Mr. Reed wasn't any better, he would give him some more Demerol. And he would have to call the surgeons.

Cameron put the car in gear and left rubber tracks behind.

CHAPTER 6

NEW YEAR'S

Rowing on a moon-plated lake, the water quietly drifting past, a sweater wrapped around her shoulders...

Buzzing; shrill-splitting a dream in half; sound bouncing off four dark walls. The intern's hand groped for the button on the wall above the bed. The buzzing stopped. The other hand reached for the phone.

"Yeah?" He was on back-up call for overflows on the medical wards.

"Cameron? Sorry again, Warren here. Got a burn patient going sour, and a seizure downstairs." "O.K."

"How fast can you come?"

"Two minutes."

"Thanks. You want the burn or the seizure?"

Words didn't register in the dark. He swung his legs over the edge of the bed. Two minutes, burn patient, Warren...He'd been rowing at night...a quiet lake with someone...wind blew her hair, sparkling in a reflection of water-stars...

Cameron stopped: Wind rushed along the dark street separating the General Hospital from the Staff quarters. He was awake now. He glanced down. On his wrist, 4:30 a.m. Below, jockey shorts. He'd forgotten interns on call should always wear their scrub suits to sleep.

He would be off on New Year's evening. Other than that it would be a New Year's like any other. That is, it would be a regular day, then at the stroke of midnight, it would turn into a new year. Very simply and just like that. The difference was he wouldn't celebrate it. He'd decided on that all week. It wasn't really a momentous decision: he'd simply thought it too contrived, with the funny hats, horns, bells chiming, cars tooting and everyone getting jolly drunk and striking up in song. Not that any of it was bad—just done so routinely, artificially—these were the things to be done, at a certain time with a certain merry look, whether one felt like it or not, much in the manner of an excuse finally provided to fondle a secretary's, nurse's or a stranger's ass, when all the rest of the time it was not exactly fashionable.

Not that he minded the latter. Like any warm-blooded intern, after days and nights of trying to pull patients' bodies together, drained of what little was left, after all computer fuses had blown within his cranium, and time off had finally arrived, his eyes and hands wished to go wild on anything that reminded him of beauty. That is, he could easily become an animal—which could scare her when the leash broke—like the time he'd pulled her sweater off by the bridge under the lights, people passing by, and he hadn't realized she had nothing on underneath.

But for some reason now, he rebelled against the idea of a New Year's revelry-on-call, the massive exuberance at the stroke of midnight. For after all and what the shit, it was just another day. There was nothing in the stars ordering January first to be New Year's—it could have been May or July just as well. Besides, he was against the whole mechanical, assembly line, served up at-the-stroke-of-midnight routine, and the drug-like hypnotic effect—like mob psychology or war—that this day had upon people.

For a while, Cameron actually considered he might be crazy, viewing New Year's that way. He realized he wasn't, though, since he still normally appreciated all the hugging, kissing, and the rest—that he would sincerely miss.

"What are you thinking, Cameron?"

"Not much, Mel."

"Got anything cooking for New Year's?"

"No."

"There's all kinds of parties going on."

"I know."

"One of the guys is having one at his apartment - B.Y.O.B."

"Thanks, Mel."

"You're not on call, are you?"

"No."

Mel shrugged: "Want the address anyway? I won't be seeing you again; Medicine rotation is over for us tomorrow."

"Hey, that's right, Mel."

"Thanks, Harvard; I learned a lot. Going to miss your computer style."

Cameron smiled: "I'm going to miss you telling me to smile. Good luck, Mel."

The rest of the week was filled with talk of parties, advance reservations at so-and-so's tavern, shows, or music places, and B.Y.O.B. or not? Now reservations at a bar Cameron just couldn't handle—it was about as spontaneous as waiting three months for a camping spot in Yosemite. Besides, he had no girl now—he hadn't called her since the incident by the bridge—and revelry on such occasions without a girl left something to be desired. Furthermore, another girl he did like was already going to a party. And it was too late to get another decent, or even indecent chick.

The last few days and invitations passed by—an ordinary choice of ordinary parties. What the hell, had it been an orgy or something, an experience, in his rebellious mood he might have tried it. But he'd decided to cut out the regular, assembly line type stuff. He'd decided to say fuck it. He'd do something different this time. Go out alone someplace. Wander. Read a book. Go to bed early. Maybe get drunk someplace. Anything he felt like at the time, and not at the beck and call of a machine-stamped twelve. Maybe he'd even meet a truly wild, rebellious honey in his wanderings who felt the same way, and instead of quaffing beers, swapping hats, and tooting horns at midnight, they'd just destroy a bed. Dreamer.

At any rate, he could always go to bed early. He could use it after a hundred-hour work week. Still, he could admit to himself he was a real asshole for being against New Year's—like motherhood, apple pie, and all that.

The night before New Year's rolled in uneventfully: A usual load of comatose diabetics needing blood sugars monitored every half to one hour; burn cases that hemolyzed blood; stab wounds, bleeders, and chop-cases in general. He got a few hours' sleep.

Morning brought two more comatose overdoses, a victim of assault, and one victim of just plain bad luck. The old year was dying in the new year's light and victims were being served up the world's disasters and the smell of death's night like shuffled cards being spread across a table by fate. Nothing calendar-set or assembly line about that—just a deck of cards falling at random, any time, any place, for anyone.

Cameron was off early, had a late lunch, and went to play basketball. Afterwards he took a walk. He missed his old city, far away. This time of year, the high-rises would be glowing in darkness; from the hill, upright like small matchboxes, one could almost touch them. The old stone-domed church would lean like a steel beam upon the slanted streets overlooking the Smith Tower. And beyond everything was Puget Sound: The Sound, silver clad in reflections of a waning sun, calm, shimmering, stretching lazily over shore and islands to where one saw no more; sailboats leaned small as white commas; heavy ferries left their smooth, regular wakes, musical notes written on water, read by the drifting clouds. A ferry, still far away, would be churning in from Bremerton, with red and yellow glows in the twilight.

Another time, another place. The street was quiet and the wind cool and mild, like a bird swooping treetops. There were few people about on early New Year's eve: Even the hospital, on the side away from the Emergency entrance, appeared calm. Cameron remained outside and lay on the grass where they sometimes played football. The buildings became shrouded in darkness.

He'd almost forgotten it was New Year's eve. He brushed the grass from his clothes and walked to the basement cafeteria for dinner.

Jim and Warren were still there; the other interns had gone. Jim talked smoothly to a student nurse, and Warren told of a party he was giving. Two girls from the fifth floor, dietetic interns, were also going to a party. The girl Cameron liked, with curly shoulder length hair, quick blue eyes and sharp Swedish face with naturally red lips, was already spoken for.

Cameron ate his dinner and tried to shut out talk of parties and festivities. He wouldn't be needing that. He'd already decided on the freedom of whatever he felt like doing tonight.

After dinner, Cameron stopped at the library/lounge on west wing of Staff quarters. The room was small, paneled in wood of fifty years ago; an old dusty sofa, three armchairs, a pile of old TV guides, hospital directories and a profusion of scattered medical journals completed the room. Cameron coaxed the ancient TV into proper vertical hold with a few slaps and other quaint adjustments. Black and white images flashed across the screen. Curtained and dim, the lights barely cast shadows: In fact, probably no one had ever seen the entire room by light of day or night. Yet generations of interns had found this a haven, cozy as a fireplace, and the history of medicine sat in decades of medical journals and books, harboring spiders.

After the news on TV, Cameron pulled on gloves and played handball in a converted basement room of Staff quarters. He took a shower and returned the key to the telephone receptionist.

"How come you're still around?"

"Dunno."

"On call?"

"No."

She shook her head. At the hospital entrance, an old man in a frayed grey overcoat sat at the end of a long wooden bench, waiting for an elevator. His hands shook; his ruddy face was veined under the unkept white beard. He'd been in the hospital many times before, as a patient. Now he was a visitor—a bottle made a bulge under his coat—one old man bringing New Year's eve to another.

Cameron crossed the street and returned to Staff quarters. Punctuated every twelve feet with closed doors, the bright corridor was empty. The upstairs lounge was empty. He sank into an old cushion chair, and perfunctorily paged through an old Playboy. He returned to his room. A Cardiology textbook lay open on his desk. He got into it.

The radiator creaked and sputtered with bursts of steam; it couldn't be turned off and he opened a window. Moon shadows stirred through the flapping curtains and came to lie on the wall above his bed. Cameron closed the Cardiology text and lay down. With the radio at hand's reach, he watched the shadows. Somewhere on the desk, between the books, was a bottle of whiskey. Without moving from the bed, he found it, used it.

Cameron was keeping his promise of freedom from a mechanistic New Year's. Half dozing, he thought of taking another walk. To see what souls were about—maybe even some free ones. Then they would sit at the edge of nowhere in the dark, and watch the lights of buildings go out at dawn while dew fell through New Year's night. He decided to take the walk, put the bottle away, and pulled on a T-shirt. Still in the dark, he groped for a sweater.

There was a knock on the door.

He knew the place should be empty. The interns on call would be at the hospital, the others gone.

The knock returned.

Maybe Karen...hell, no. He hadn't seen her since she'd returned from the Peace Corps...

He opened the door.

A woman in her late twenties, with an electric blue scarf about her neck and tight dark blouse stood shivering without a coat, her makeup as heavy as her smell of liquor. She wasn't pretty the way she was now.

"Where's McGuire?" she asked quickly.

"Dr. McGuire?"

"Yes, him."

"I don't know."

"He lives here. I know it. Tell me where he is."

"I don't know. No one's around tonight."

Her voice grew shrill and tremulous: "I have to find him!" Cameron wondered what had gone on between them. He knew McGuire was out with the long-legged, dark-haired nurse that was probably the prettiest of the lot. McGuire wouldn't be back tonight. But he didn't want to explain that to this woman just now.

"Where is he? What's his number?"

"I don't have it."

She grasped his shoulders and pushed herself into the room. Her purse slipped from her shoulders and a small derringer clattered to the floor. "I have to find him, don't you see?" she wrung her hands.

He did see, and wondered if she planned to shoot McGuire. He wanted her out of here quickly. Cameron led her down the corridor into a phone booth, and dialed the hospital operator. The booth was very small for the two of them, and the operator took a long time to answer.

"Dr. McGuire's extension, please."

The receptionist didn't recognize his voice: "I'm sorry, I can't give out that number."

"Pete's sake, Anita, this is Cameron. I need his number."

"Oh, Cam; all right."

"Three twenty-six," Cameron told the woman in the booth. He opened the door and took her out: "three twenty-six, and now you have to leave. Women aren't allowed on this floor." He placed her by the elevator, returned to his room and slammed the door. The elevator creaked to a stop, then resumed its journey.

On its desk in the dark, the radio glowed with orange dials and played on. A bottle of whiskey glistened opaquely next to Chapter 11 of Cardiology. Cameron placed the derringer over the desk. He didn't like the way he'd dealt with that woman. He remembered he should take a walk.

From a distance suddenly came the sounds of sirens, tooting horns, shouts and singing from the apartments nearby. It was too late. New Year's had arrived. Cameron took off his clothes, and went to bed.

Maybe noise, singing, and cheerful people were what the woman had needed tonight—even if it was artificial. Perhaps artificial was better than nothing. And right then, she'd had nothing.

What the shit. She was drunk. She'd calm down in a few days. It was only New Year's, and people acted like that on New Year's.

Cameron watched the shadows from the curtains, playing across the open window onto the ceiling.

As he wished, it had been an unusual New Year's. He half-smiled in the dark. Be careful of what you wish.

CHAPTER 7

SATURDAY, SUNDAY, AND MONDAY

A drunk had fallen down a flight of steps.

The intern pointed to a thin dark line across the skull X-rays. "It's a fracture," agreed the Neurosurgeon.

"When will you take him?" the intern asked.

The Neurosurgeon shook his head: "We won't. He's too unstable. His blood pressure and pulse are all over the place."

"But he's got lateralizing signs."

"Stabilize him first. Then we'll take him."

Christ, thought the intern, there was nothing more he could do for a large bleed in the brain. Neurosurgery had to take him and operate.

But somehow the man stabilized: The intern measured out medicines, steroids, and prepared and changed the I.V. bottles himself. By thirty-six hours, the man was still in coma, but his vital signs were normal.

The Neurosurgeon didn't come for another twelve hours.

"He's stable," the intern said.

"It's been three days—it's too late."

"Two days."

"He's probably got irreversible brain damage by now anyway. We'll have to wait and see if he shows any signs of improvement."

"Isn't it enough he's alive and stable?"

"No. We have to see if there's anything improving inside worth operating."

"If he does improve, he won't need surgery."

"Right."

"And if he doesn't, you won't operate."

"That's right, Intern."

"You son of a bitch."

"What did you say?"

"Nothing."

"What's your name, intern?"

"I'm John, John Cameron," he crouched to look at her ski bindings.

"I'm Julie Ann." Their heads touched; her hair tumbled straight down without a ripple, almost to her skis.

She looked at him: "It may take a wrench to move that binding." He touched her hair. She was beautiful. He didn't know what to say.

"You seem happy," she told him.

If he was, it had just happened now. "I'm afraid I'm not helping much with the bindings," he said.

"You have a nice smile."

"I do?"

"Yes." She stood up and the curves of her body uncoiled slim and beautiful. Her skin was pale like a wheatfield in the sun; she would get an awful sunburn today. "I'm skiing with some friends. Do you want to ski with us?"

"Sure."

"You're very calm," she said.

"You should put on some sun lotion."

"See what I mean?"

"It's just that you'll burn."

"I already have some on."

Her friends were not at the lodge or on the sundeck. "A bunch of us came up," she explained, "Carey twisted her ankle and we stopped awhile. I don't see them around. Shall we ski? Or do you have to meet someone?"

"No."

"Which runs have you been skiing?"

"I don't know this mountain very well."

"Never been to Mammoth before?"

"No. I just had two days off, and came up."

She nodded: "We're up two days also. Usually we all come up; my boyfriend's a ski fiend, but he couldn't make it this weekend. I came up with his friends." They took the chair up, soon cruising above the trees. A blanket of radiant white snow slipped beneath them; a bird's nest perched over a pine branch. She looked at him: "How come you are alone?"

"Not much time to think of it, I guess."

"You can ski with us; if you don't mind, I'll show you the mountain." They were off the chair. With a twist of her hips, long legs touching at the knees, she was down the slope. His own form felt like a billy goat's by comparison.

He churned to a stop at the edge of the trees, Julie Ann turning in beside him. "You're not a careful skier," she said.

"I don't have to be careful out here."

"Not a bad skier, though. Where'd you ski before?"

"Washington—I'm sure your boyfriend skis better."

"He's a natural athlete—football, baseball, basketball, and just crazy on skis."

"What about you?"

"I like to swim and ski. I guess I'm a good swimmer."

He thought of her pale skin in the sun. "Maybe we should see if your friends are back."

"Let's go."

They still weren't back at the lodge. "We must be just missing them on their runs."

"Do you want to wait?"

She shrugged. "We can just ski. Unless you're getting bored with my pace and want to ski on your own."

"I like skiing with you."

"Then we'll take the top run. You feel like going there?"

"Sure."

They skied together the rest of the afternoon. On the lifts, they talked of books, weather, Washington and California, and disagreed completely about politics.

"Why did you meet me today?" She glanced at him.

"You had trouble with your bindings."

She laughed: "And you had a nice smile, Cameron. You really don't mind skiing with me?"

"I like being with you, Julie Ann."

"It's strange," she mused, "I feel comfortable with you."

There was a silence.

"I have a boyfriend, you know."

"You told me."

"I'm living with him."

"Let's ski," he said.

At the end of day they caught up with the rest of the party on deck. Carey was nursing a hot rum and had her bad ankle propped up and wrapped in a woolen sock.

"This is John Cameron," Julie introduced him.

"How's your day been, Julie?"

"Snow's good, and Cameron lost his wallet in a fall. Where've you guys been? We've been looking for you."

"We cut out early for Carey's ankle and been lodge-skiing ever since. Maybe tomorrow we can help find your wallet." Cameron found a beer thrust into his hand.

"Doesn't matter about the wallet. Probably covered in snow." Carey giggled as he pulled off the sock to look at her ankle.

"Well, what do you think?" she asked.

"It's just a sprain of the lateral ankle ligament. Keep it propped up, put ice on it, and maybe you'll get into your boots tomorrow. That should provide enough support to ski, if you're up to it. I don't think anything's broken, but it will take the ligament about six weeks to heal."

"You sound official, like a doc."

"I am a doc."

She laughed: "I didn't know. I thought you were just looking, you know...you don't look like a doctor."

Cameron remembered something. "I guess for two days I'm not."

"Thanks for looking at it."

Cameron finished his beer. "It's been nice meeting you," he said without looking at anyone. "I better get going. Bye."

Julie Ann walked with him to the steps. "Is there anything wrong?"

"No. Just time for me to leave. I've got some reading to do."

"What are you doing about dinner?"

"I guess I'll eat someplace."

"Without your wallet?"

"I've got some money in my pocket."

"We're cooking chicken tonight. You're welcome to dinner."

"They're your friends, you know—a group. I wouldn't feel right crashing in like that."

"What's wrong? You wouldn't be crashing anything."

"They're nice people, Julie Ann, thanks. But I'm not sure I would feel right, and I have some reading left to do." He touched her hair, the same way as when he'd first met her. "You're very nice."

She hesitated. "Skiing tomorrow?"

"Sure."

"Meet you here, Cameron. Now go get your reading done."

Sunday they took the chair to the top. "Do you like what you do?" she suddenly asked.

"I like medicine. I don't like some of what I have to do."

"Like what?"

"I don't know. Hard to explain, I guess."

"Anything bothering you?"

"Yeah." He paused. "I left a man back in the hospital, with a skull fracture, and all his medicines and I.V.'s lined up on his bedside table to give while I'm gone."

"How is he?"

"In coma now for two weeks."

"What will happen to him?"

"No one thinks he's really alive; no one wants to operate. He'll stay that way until he dies."

"Can't you do anything for him?"

"I can give him medicines to just barely keep him alive. I don't know how long it will last. I had two days off and left him to someone else's care."

"You don't think they can do it while you're gone?"

"You don't understand. It's not the same: Things can be done by the book, but I've watched that face and closed eyes for two weeks; I know how he responds to every drop by IV drop."

"I'm sorry."

"Skip it. What do you do, Julie Ann?"

"I teach retarded children."

"Swell. Don't we have anything happy to talk about?"

"It *is* happy, most of the time. Every little bit helps, and you'd be surprised how fast they learn sometimes. Mostly they're just happy in their own way of looking at things."

He glanced at her face as if for the very first time: "You're quite a lady," he said quietly.

"Did you get all your reading done last night?"

"Some."

"Why wouldn't you have dinner with us?"

"I wouldn't have been any fun."

"Why?"

"I felt strange remembering I'd left that man in the hospital."

"Cameron, these are your days off."

"I also felt strange because they were your boyfriend's friends."

"You minded that they were his friends?"

"No. They were a good bunch of people. But they might have minded me."

"Why?"

"Because I like you."

"You do?"

"Isn't it obvious?"

"I don't know. You're so calm about everything. I can't tell what you're thinking."

"Look, Julie Ann—you're living with him, he sounds like a great guy, and I just met you here for two days while he's gone. You're happy, and why should I change that?"

"I guess I'm mixed up. I feel comfortable around you."

"And I like being with you."

"Can we leave it at that, Cameron?"

He didn't reply.

"I couldn't see you again without telling Jeff."

He nodded: "I know. I would like to see you anyway."

"It wouldn't do any good."

"All right."

They had lunch with the whole group. Carey tried to pry the boot off her sprained ankle.

"You want to ski more later?" Cameron asked her.

"Sure. I'm just going to release some of the pressure."

"Then leave your boot on and have a beer. Your ankle will swell as soon as you take the boot off, and you'll never get it back on again. Were you4 comfortable skiing?"

"Not too bad."

"Good." He looked at all of them: A world of laughter, strength, health, playing like children. In the world of children, diseases when they came ran into energy's wall of life; a body still growing, digging in to fight back. He liked the fighters. The drunk with the broken head that should have died two weeks ago—he was a fighter. No one could see it, but something inside him kept on, kept the heart beating, the skin perspiring, the lungs transporting oxygen into the cauldron of life. Something inside hadn't been broken. Something hung on. Except Cameron. Cameron had left. He'd be back soon, he thought. But still he had left.

"Let's go, John," someone patted him on the back, "let's hit the slopes."

Julie Ann smiled: "Don't make it any harder than it is, Cameron," she told him softly. It was strange how she had read his mind.

"Is that how you do it with your kids?" he asked her.

She nodded and took his hand: "I guess I don't expect as much. I'm happy over the little improvements they make. It keeps me going."

"Yes," he said. "It's strange what keeps one going."

On their last run together they swung over a knoll and stopped. He removed his gloves and looked at the mountains. Bordered in red sunset, white mountain crests dimmed in a thickening blue darkness above. Far off a few brilliant specks glistened.

"What are you thinking?" she asked.

Cameron shook his head. He looked at her face, then slowly pulled on his gloves. He slipped his hands around the grips of the ski poles.

How could he tell her? How could anything like that be told? It was kept in. He'd learned that by now.

"I'm taking one more run," he told her.

"The chairs are closing. There isn't time."

"A fast run. I need it, Julie." He shook the snow off the skis.

"I'll be waiting below."

Her words drifted in the air above. Why had she said that? She didn't need to say that. She wouldn't be there, of course, and that's how it would end: A Saturday and Sunday, nice days, nice weekend. Nice, to be remembered nicely sometimes. But the beauty of that evening almost broke his insides with what there was no room to say.

He skied the last run without stopping. Thoughts he wanted to shut out crowded like splinters of light. A restlessness coursed within him that needed to end. His skis downed the hill like quivering arrows, heart racing out into scattered space—skis, snow, blood rushing—into a place of no remembrance. There was nothing now. Nothing but space. Time. The need to control two laughing arrows. And only laughter to respond with. He didn't know who he was. He didn't know what he'd left behind. Or whatever would lie ahead.

She waited by the ski chalet. He hadn't believed she would.

"Julie," she said smiling, "Julie Ann Hartley, remember?"

He took off his gloves and touched her face. "You're here," he said.

"I said so, didn't I?"

"Why?"

"I wanted to."

"I'm glad."

"It feels strange to say goodbye, Cameron."

"Then we won't say it." He smiled at her and waved. Afterwards, he didn't look back.

On Monday morning he found the table he'd lined up with I.V. bottles and medicines empty. The man with the skull fracture was gone.

Cameron lay in his bed at night wide awake. The radio played. He glanced at the clock - 3 a.m. What was he waiting for? Someone to tell him it was all right? He wanted to call her now, talk to her. Talk to someone. That was it, he thought—it was only that he needed to talk to someone. He turned on his side and listened to the radio.

The next Monday and week and Monday after were the same. Then he called her.

"Cameron, is that you?"

"Yes."

"How did you know I would answer?"

"I didn't."

"What if Jeff would have answered?"

"I don't know. I would have asked for you, I guess."

"Just like that?"

"I don't know any other way. I'm sorry I put you on the spot."

"I'm glad you called."

"You are?"

"Yes. I already told him about you. It's the first time something like this has happened, and I don't believe he's very worried. He knows I love him."

There was a silence on the other end of the line.

"How was the man?" Julie asked.

"He died."

"When?"

"When I was gone."

"Jesus," she paused.

"The autopsy showed a new bleed on top of the old one."

"You're not responsible, Cameron. Those were your days off."

"Sure. Those were my days off."

"Don't say it like that."

"Let's drop it. I just wanted to call you, Julie Ann, to hear your voice."

"I sent you a card today, Cameron. Did you get it?"

"No. Where did you send it?"

"To the hospital. Isn't it funny you called the same day I sent the card? I wanted to send it for a long time, but I finally sent it today." "It took a long time, but I called you."

"I want to see you, Cameron."

75

"Sure."

"Just like at the ski slopes," she laughed and imitated his voice, "sure."

"When, Julie Ann?"

"Tonight. Is that all right, Cameron?"

"Are you kidding?"

"I'm coming over. It's an old Volkswagen—on its last legs and falling apart, so it'll take me a while."

She had curled her long hair and looked very fragile in her thin red coat. She sat down. "I feel strange coming here."

"Can I take your coat?" he mumbled.

"Yes. How about a beer?"

"I should have one around someplace," he searched the refrigerator.

"I'll need to tell Jeff about this," she said. "I love him, do you know?

I do, and I don't know why I'm sitting here. I've never done this before." She fidgeted with the belt of her coat.

He touched her, and took her in his arms.

"Do you know why I finally sent that card?"

"No."

"Because you touched me like that the day we first met."

CHAPTER 8

RED BLANKET

Emergency Service. The place of red blankets.

"Can you take an ambulance run, Cameron?"

"Sure."

"Bethlehem Steel, someone fell from a scaffolding."

They carried the man into the ambulance. He had fallen three stories onto a stack of metal. There was a red crescent line under his ribcage, by the spleen. Cameron stuck an I.V. into his arm. The ambulance lurched as the sirens started. Cameron began to get car sick.

At Emergency three stretchers nearly collided in the corridor. Cameron shoved the stretcher past a girl with curly red hair, turned up nose and blue eyes, and white coat over blouse and corduroys. "Skip the paper work, Nellie. It's a red blanket."

As they wheeled past the waiting room stretchers collided again, and a ruddy faced woman, geniality exuding from all her being and perhaps from the bottle she carried, patted the man on the stretcher. "You poor dear! Whatever happened to you?" She felt his forehead, and the man stopped moaning for a bewildered moment.

"Well, I got to go now," said the ruddy faced woman, "I have to take a piss."

Stretchers unscrambled again, and they rushed to the operating room. The man's T-shirt opened under the scissors, and Cameron felt car-sick again.

A campers' convention of about seventy thousand surged onto the outskirts of town for boating, swimming, sun basking, and beer.

They brought the boy over on a stretcher, wet red trunks and sand pebbles still on his feet. He shivered under the ambulance blankets. Both hands were folded over his chest. He was nineteen years old. He'd come from Oregon to volunteer for lifeguard duty at the reservoir.

Cameron felt the boy's forehead, hands, and watched his breathing. A strange feeling that he couldn't shake crawled under his skin. He watched the boy. "What's the matter?" he finally asked him slowly.

"I'm cold."

"I see that. I'll get you another blanket." Cameron pulled a red one and placed it over the boy's abdomen and chest.

"I can't move," said the boy.

Again the strangeness crawled under Cameron's skin. He felt cold himself. "You can't move anything?"

"I can move my head, I can shake my neck."

Cameron moved instantly and held his head still. "No. Don't move your head." Cameron tightened the cervical collar. He looked at the boy's face upside down from the head of the stretcher—freckles, sunburnt apple cheeks, sand in his hair—all American lifeguard kid with upper teeth like a beaver's grin. His eyes and face were calm as he continued to shiver.

"What happened?"

"I dove into the water."

"From a board or something?"

"No. I just ran in. About a dozen steps."

"You just jumped in?"

"Yes. It was shallow, I guess. A sand bar."

"Relax. You'll be all right. You're shaky and scared. Just take it easy and let me look at you. Cameron examined the boy's reflexes. They were absent.

"How far below the water was it?" Cameron asked him.

"About one or two feet."

"How did you hit?"

"I don't know. Didn't see it... I woke up under water. Couldn't move, I remember that. Nothing moved... I held my breath and felt water all around me. I shook my head so someone would maybe see and come get me."

"Someone pulled you out?"

"Another lifeguard. They pulled me out over the beach."

"Were you able to move at all?"

The boy tried to shake his head again. Cameron stopped him. "Just my head," the boy said, "and my neck..."

"No. Don't do that now. What's your name?"

"Chuck."

"I'm Dr. Cameron. I'll be taking care of you. I want you to remember not to move your head."

"I'm cold."

"I know." Cameron listened to his heart and lungs—normal, like any freckle faced nineteen year old lifeguard's should be. Now for the neurological exam.

"Move your toes."

"I don't think they're working," the boy said.

"Try again, Chuck."

He turned his eyes up: "Anything happening?"

Cameron felt a shiver. "Try your knees."

The boy clenched his teeth. Nothing happened.

Cameron took the boy's hands in a grip: "Crush my hands, Chuck." They felt soft and rubbery.

"I can't feel your hands."

"Crush them anyway."

The rubber-like feeling remained unchanged. The boy was quiet.

"Relax," Cameron said, touching his arm. "Now move your elbow."

It slipped lightly on the sheets.

"Good! Now move the left one."

It rose an inch and a half from the stretcher.

"Great! Now shrug your shoulders, Chuck."

The shoulders moved well. The elbows moved a little; the wrists, like the legs, not at all. Cameron checked and rechecked the wrists, hands, and fingers. They just drooped. He tested skin sensation with a needle—nothing below the collarbones and upper arms.

"How about here, Chuck?"

"No."

"Can you feel that?"

"No."

"Here?"

"Something. I can feel you touching."

"Is it sharp?"

"No."

"But can you feel it?"

"I think so."

It was dull on places of the chest, but completely numb below the navel. Still, there were fibers left intact, Cameron thought: Something was still left, and it didn't just stop at the neck. And they were going to try damn hard, because it wasn't going to end like this. It just wasn't.

"You can move your elbow, Chuck, and you can feel here. Those are good signs. Now we're going to take X-rays, then we'll talk."

The boy said nothing.

A moist film of white, grey and black shades rolled from the developer into Cameron's hands. He positioned it over the X-ray viewer and opened his eyes. Bones, soft tissues, lines like ghosts skipped within his head; then a black line: A thin black line that crossed the upper part of the 6th cervical vertebra. The neck was fractured clear through.

The Radiology technician looked at Cameron: "Good cross-table lateral?"

"No."

"You want me to take another one?"

"I didn't mean technically." Cameron went out into the room with the stretcher.

The boy didn't ask anything.

"I'm going to keep you in the hospital," Cameron told him.

"All right, Doc."

There was a silence.

"How is it, Doc?"

"I'm having the X-rays checked over," he said slowly, "right now it looks like a break. But it doesn't look like it moved much and everything around it is in place. That's good. Do you understand that, Chuck?"

"Yes."

"It will depend on how far the neck moved. Your exam looks good and there are fibers still intact. For the rest, it's too early to tell: There could be a blood clot choking up your movement in the spinal canal, or just pressure from the swelling after the injury. Both of these could clear up."

Cameron knew that the boy understood they also might not.

"How long could this last?"

"Hard to say, Chuck."

"The neck is broken, right?"

"We'll have it checked again. It looks that way right now. But even if the bone is broken, that doesn't mean the spinal cord is damaged."

"Can you tell?"

Cameron shook his head. It was easier than saying it.

"I would like to call my dad."

"Sure. We need to brace your neck first. It won't take long. Then you can talk to him."

Cameron left the neck carefully padded with sandbags around the cervical collar, and called the Neurosurgeon. He arrived at the X-ray room. "It's clear through," he said, "the neck is broken. How is he?"

"Breathing on his own; moves his shoulders and elbows a little, nothing below that. There's some feeling down to the navel. You think he's got a chance it's not severed?"

"Dermatomes can skip three down, Cameron; we see that every once in a while: They still have feeling below the level of the break only because there is cross-innervation between the segments. Let's go see him."

Results were the same as before: Reflexes absent; muscle groups at 6th vertebral level weak; below that, gone. Cameron's eyes followed the needle's tracks testing the skin. Small red beads sprouted where it had touched. Chuck didn't blink. The surgeon's eyes also remained unblinking, unchanged in their sockets as he halted the examination.

"We'll put in Crutchfield tongs," the surgeon said. It was a statement to no one in particular. A statement, terse and brief, to hold the line. Defeat did not exist. No one spoke of it. Medicine was a succession of lines, a series of trenches, fought over quietly with unblinking eyes. Cameron watched and wondered why the eyes did not blink. If an Army was in retreat behind those lines, no one would ever know. Perhaps it was why they didn't blink.

"The tongs will hold your neck straight in traction," the surgeon explained, "then we'll operate. It won't hurt you. Is there anything else you would like to know?"

"I want to talk to my Dad."

"Where is he?"

"Salem, Oregon."

"Let's put the traction on first, then you can call him while we prepare the operating room. All right?"

"Yes."

The skin over the temples was shaved and a pale circular welt rose as the anesthetic seeped from the needle under the skin.

"Did it hurt, Chuck?"

"No."

"That's the worst of it. You won't feel anything else."

"I'll still be able to talk to my Dad?"

"Yes. This is only a local anesthetic. We'll put you to sleep only after you talk to him." A half-inch line turned red over the temple, then revealed white as the scalpel struck bone. A drill burrowed into the skull.

"You okay?" the surgeon's voice asked muffled through his mask.

"Yes."

"See?" the muffled voice continued, "the bone has no nerves. You won't feel any of this." A sweet smell rose from the living bone dust. After three millimeters of burrowing, the arms of an hourglass tong tightened into the shallow wells at the sides of the head. Weights dangled from Chuck's head over a pulley.

"How are you doing?" the surgeon asked.

"All right."

"Now for the call to your dad. Anything else I can do for you?"

"Just the call."

The surgeon put a hand on his shoulder: "The operation will take a few hours. We'll put you to sleep, and see what we can do to decrease the swelling back there, in the spinal canal. Did Dr. Cameron already talk to you about that?"

"Yes."

"Later we'll put the neck bone back together again, then see how the spinal cord reacts."

"Thank you."

The surgeon's eyebrows didn't move as he pulled off his gloves and went into the doctors' lounge.

Cameron spoke into a telephone from a corner of the room. "Is this Mr. Conrad?"

"Can you speak up?"

Cameron repeated it.

"Yes, who is this?"

"I'm Dr. Cameron, from the County Medical Center. Your son was brought here from the campers' convention."

"Is he alright?"

"He dove into shallow water. His neck might be broken." It was easier to say it fast and all at once.

There was silence on the line. Then, "How...what do you mean?"

"There is a line across the sixth cervical vertebra," it was also easier to use the technical terms; it made it more abstract that way. "A fracture line; he's breathing all right and all his vital signs are normal. He wants to talk to you. Do you understand, Mr. Conrad?" There was no need for him to speak so softly; the boy was in another room.

"This is all sudden."

"I know, Mr. Conrad. I'm sorry."

"How is he? What does this mean?"

"He wants to talk to you. I don't want you to worry, or to worry him, you understand?"

"Can I see him?"

"You're hours away. We'll have to operate before that. Let me explain it to you." Cameron told him the best first, then the worst. The last part took longer.

"It's...a very sudden thing," the father repeated.

"Yes, Mr. Conrad."

"How long will he be there?"

"A week, two weeks."

"Before you know?"

"About the same."

"What if...it's like you said, the spinal cord. How long will it stay that way?"

"That would be permanent."

There was a long pause. "So sudden...So you don't know which way it is yet?"

"Not for sure. We're going to try to relieve some pressure on the cord; then wait, and hope for the best."

"Does he know?"

Cameron shook his head. "He's a very brave boy. I'm not sure."

"Dr. Cameron, let me talk to my son."

Cameron wheeled in the stretcher dangling with weights, positioning it beside the telephone. Watching the boy's calmness, he almost forgot: He tried to give him the telephone. The motion stopped in mid-air, above the boy's motionlessly folded hands. Cameron stood frozen for a moment, before bringing the receiver to the boy's ear.

"Dad," the voice was high pitched initially, then returned to normal. "Dad, I'm all right. No, I'm all right. I'm in the hospital. Don't worry, Dad."

The boy was still shivering as his red blanket was removed to drape surgical sheets over him. Above the masks, none of the eyes around the operating table blinked. Cameron understood now why they didn't blink.

CHAPTER 9

END OF SERVICE

After the workout his limbs tingled, tightly warm, pleasantly tired. He stopped outside the *dojo* to look at the photographs: People in white *gis* broke boards with bare hands, flying side-kicks, double front kicks.

A young boy of about six pressed his nose against the window. His eyes drifted over the samurai helmet, photographs, karate handbooks and gear. A poster showed two men on a snow-bordered lake in Japan: One stood with bare feet planted in the snow, legs apart in a fighting stance; the other was suspended in mid-air above his shoulders, legs tilted to the sky in a karate kick, floating. Sunshine reflected from the snow and white *gis*. They played by a blue lake and sky under the snow covered trees.

The intern looked at the window-gazing boy. He had seen others like him. It was nothing new. But something inside him now shook: He was just a man on the sidewalk now, watching a boy looking at a window full of dreams.

He'd been talking to a pretty girl after karate class, but couldn't finish the sentence. He put on his sunglasses and left without explanation.

What's wrong? he asked himself in the car. You've seen them before in a wheelchair like that. And this one maneuvered it well, thin legs dangling over the edge, seeming quite happy watching the photographs.

Yes, you've seen them like that before, the intern repeated. Even small ones with dark curly hair. He put on his sunglasses and drove slowly into the street.

It was one of those days, continuing the same way into the night. At eleven o'clock, Cameron was very tired. After midnight, it no longer mattered. At two twenty-five a.m., an ambulance arrived with a red blanket over an old man's legs, convalescent hospital and ambulance checklist forms pinned to his stretcher. By a process of random rotation, an old man in his red emergency blanket, and John Cameron, intern, met on the admissions ward of General Medicine, sixth floor.

The sight of the red blanket brought Cameron's reflexes as alive, as what it contained appeared lifeless. Cameron placed his fingers over the radial pulse and a stethoscope over the old man's chest. The heart was still beating—feebly, but still going. What had happened to this man?

A metal chart lay over the red blanket. Cameron glanced at the forms: Hugo Petrovic, 86 years old. He placed the chart down and stared at the contents under the blanket: Eyes shut within sunken shadows, shallow breathing, lips pulled back over dry purple gums. Where to start?

Cameron examined the ambulance checklist:

Name - Hugo Petrovic
Sex - Male
Blood Pressure - 92/70 @ 2:10 a.m.
Pulse - 84 @ 2:05 a.m.
       115 and weak @ 2:10 a.m.
Respirations - 24 and labored @ 2:05 a.m.
Color - Pale
Alert - No
Short of Breath - Yes
Medications en-route - None
Aid en-route - 5 liters p/m O2
Remarks - Coma state

Medical Referral from Convalescent Hospital:

	Social Security Number	Birthdate
Name	Medicare Number	
Male	Single	No religion

Economic status - Medicare

Name of friend to notify - none

Reason for referral - "Patient is usually aggressive and noisy; today he developed rapid respirations, low blood pressure, pallor, labored breathing, and coma state. Patient is usually confused most of the time, cannot walk, cannot talk, cannot hear, cannot see, cannot feed self, and is incontinent."

Medications - Thorazine 50 mg t.i.d.

Quaalude 150 mg h.s.

Empirin #3 with codeine q4 hrs. as needed

M.O.M. 30 cc's as needed

Valium 5 mg t.i.d.

Cameron stared at the stretcher: It was another of those cases after all. An 86 year old man with everything going wrong, and if he could somehow pull any of it together again, it would only be for a short while, resembling the proverbial dictum of vegetable more than human being. Cameron stood and stared at the stubble on the old man's face.

As a matter of routine habit, Cameron began to talk to the old man, to obtain a history. His fingers were already poised to write on the chart: "History and Chief Complaint unavailable, patient unresponsive." Cameron lifted the patient's eyelids with his fingers—blank gaze. He talked into his ear—same gaze. He shouted into his ear...the old man's eyes moved. Cameron sprang back, looking at the old man's face.

The eyes were small, lids narrow at the edges; wrinkled cheeks, a glistening film appeared at the inside corners of the eyes. Cameron placed the chart down. The old man was crying. He should have been too dehydrated to have any tears.

Cameron slowly ascertained that Hugo Petrovic really could hear, if one shouted in his ear; that he could really see, if he thought there was anything around him worth seeing; that he could even try to talk, with dry palate and toothless gums, if he believed anyone would be there to listen. Cameron finished the physical. Shaking lightly, he glanced at his written diagnosis:

1. Dehydration
2. Urinary tract infection
3. Probable pneumonia
4. Possible pre-renal azotemia
5. Incontinence, secondary to B.P.H. or cancer
6. Overmedication with sedatives and narcotics.

Cameron continued to shake. It was because of something not recorded on the chart at all. Hugo had been like this for weeks, maybe months, at the convalescent hospital. They had thought he couldn't hear, couldn't respond or feed himself, and was just an agitated broken-down body producing shit. Perhaps they hadn't even stopped to consider he might be agitated precisely because he did produce it, and no one bothered to clean it up for hours. Instead, he got sedatives and narcotics. So he responded less and less, and became less agitated. And everyone was happier, so long as he was quiet. Very quiet, finally: Like this. Snowed, so snowed he hadn't swallowed food or water for days.

And even that wasn't exactly why Cameron shook: Because at two thirty a.m., staring at the foot of this old man's bed, he had almost done the same thing.

At four a.m., I.V. bottle dangling half empty above his bed, Hugo sat eating shakily with a spoon. He was telling Cameron he'd left Yugoslavia at age fourteen, had been a steelworker among many other jobs since, and now at the age of eighty-six had nothing left to return to. He would talk better if his plates were repaired, he told Cameron. Where had he been before the convalescent home? At an apartment. Had anyone looked after him there? No. What did he do by himself? Nothing. There was nothing to do. The Social Security payments were too small to do anything with anyway. Then Hugo asked how he would pay for the hospital. Cameron told him not to worry, it would be taken care of. "Oh no," nodded Hugo, "Of course I'll have to pay for part of it."

Later that morning, the laboratory results returned: A sodium of 155, BUN of 77, and acid phosphatase so high it had gone off the scale. Diagnosis: Confirmed, unfortunately so for diagnosis number five.

Cameron returned to see him that evening. Hugo inquired whether his dental plates had been found and repaired—he wanted to be able to talk better. Cameron promised to look for them; he left him sitting up and eating, and himself went to bed. He had forgotten today was his last day on the General Medicine service. Tomorrow he would transfer to another ward.

Early in the morning, before rounds on the new service, Cameron returned to General Medicine to complete his off-service chart summaries. Each intern did them for his incoming counterpart, to provide necessary information without having to page through a patient's entire chart. He was nearly finished when he heard a low, muffled scream. He followed the commotion.

Hugo Petrovic was being held to keep his arms still; leather restraints were being wrapped around his ankles and wrists.

"What's going on?"

"We're trying to draw the blood tests you ordered, Dr. Cameron. He's been kicking up ever since he saw the needle."

Cameron walked to the foot of the bed. Hugo's eyes were wide open. "Have you told him what you wanted to do with the needle?"

"What difference would that make?"

Cameron took and needle and syringe. "Let go of him."

"Restraints too?" the nurse asked.

"Let go of him."

"Yes, but"

"Did you see any orders for restraints?"

"No"

"Then get them off."

Cameron sat by the old man, leaned close to his ear. A cracked smile opened on the parched face. Hugo extended his arm, veins up, towards him.

"What did you tell him?" asked the nurse afterwards.

"Just that we needed blood drawn." Cameron walked out of the ward.

Weeks later, at a noon teaching conference, another intern approached Cameron. "You took care of Hugo Petrovic a while back, didn't you?"

"Yes."

"He's back again—Convalescent hospital sent him back in worse than before."

"I'm on tonight; I'll drop by."

"Thanks."

Hospitals changed at night: Rows of I.V.'s, stark white beds, peeling paint were all swallowed up in darkness. Lines on faces smoothed, loud chatter was replaced by whispers, rapid steps became mellow; beads of light glistened over transparent I.V. lines like candles in dimmed caverns. Cameron usually liked hospitals better at night.

Hooked up to one of the thin clear lines reaching from arm to I.V. bottle against the wall, Hugo lay on his back. Leather straps protruded from the metal edges of the bed where they fastened onto his ankles and wrists.

Cameron pulled a chair up to the bed. The old man smelled horribly. He was lying in his own shit. Cameron didn't look at him for a while. Finally, he peeled back the sheets and covered the feces. Hugo opened his eyes. The intern heard his name spoken.

"Yes," he answered.

The old man said nothing else. Cameron undid the leather restraints. Hugo's hands went up slowly, to Cameron's face and hair. Since he'd been lying in it, they were not clean.

After a while, Cameron walked out to the nurses' station, and took Hugo's chart. Technically, he wasn't supposed to write on it since his General Medicine service had ended. Technically, he didn't give a damn. He took out his pen:

> "No doubt this patient's treatment at the convalescent home prior to admission was unacceptable not only on medical grounds, but in failing to meet even humane criteria.
>
> It is sad to consider that this human being will be subjected to the same cycle of neglect, oversedation,

dehydration, and admission to a hospital until he dies. Perhaps it is time to place the dictum 'To do no harm, heal sometimes, comfort always,' back into practice, so that this person and others like him might die with dignity rather than with bound hands and feet."

Cameron closed the metal chart, and left the night corridors of the Medical wards. Usually, he liked the nighttime better. Usually. His footsteps clung to the walls like shadows.

At Thanksgiving, he remembered he had promised Hugo to visit him that day at the nursing home. Cameron went the day after. The old man had already died.

PART II

Glorious is the way,
Glorious and true.
God is on our side,
And we'll do the rest.

CHAPTER 10

DEPARTURE

BUPERS ORDER
119605

LT. JOHN CAMERON, MC., USNR

VIA COMELEVEN

WITHIN SEVEN DAYS AFTER RECEIPT THESE ORDERS PROCEED AND REPORT MEDICAL OFFICER DESIGNATED IN FIRST ENDORSEMENT FOR PHYSICAL EXAMINATION, INCLUDING FLIGHT PHYSICAL IF BEING ORDERED TO DIFOT. IF FOUND PHYSICALLY QUALIFIED IMMEDIATELY RETURN ABOVE ADDRESS, UNTIL SUCH TIME AS NECESSARY TO COMMENCE TRAVEL ON OR AFTER 1 DEC AND PROCEED AND REPORT CO, NAVAL AMPHIBIOUS SCHOOL, CORONADO, SAN DIEGO, CALIF. ON 5 DEC, TEMPORARY ACTIVE DUTY UNDER INSTRUCTION ABOUT THREE WEEKS. COMPTEMDIRDET PROCEED PORT IN WHICH COMDESRON NINE MAY BE, ARRIVAL REPORT DUTY STAFF.

ACCOUNTING DATA 1721453.2250. T 22 N2G2 2G CIC 1/ N2G2/1L/ 02634

D.H. GUINN
VICE ADMIRAL, USN
CHIEF OF NAVY PERSONNEL

"When are you going?" she asked

"Saturday."

"Everything is happening so fast."

"Yes," he answered.

"Jeff knows we've been seeing each other." She still had on her red coat, like the first time she'd come to see him.

"What did he say?"

"Nothing. He's a very confident person. He doesn't believe I could leave him. Neither do I; I really don't think I could. Do you understand, Cameron?"

"I think so. There's nothing I can do about it."

"See? You're always so very calm about everything."

"I'm not really. I just look that way."

"We're having a party the weekend you're leaving, for his friends. I won't be able to see you off."

"That's all right."

"That's shit."

He didn't reply.

"What happens afterwards?"

"I suppose I'll be going with the destroyer squadron to Vietnam."

"For how long?"

"I don't know."

"Why did this have to happen, Cameron?"

"Because they call up the youngest ones first, even doctors."

"Don't be so literal, Cameron."

"Have you had dinner?"

"No."

"Then let's go, Julie Ann."

They went to a small Italian restaurant along the main avenue. It was cool and quiet and dark inside, with red checkered tablecloths, and her eyes looked very blue in the candlelight.

"You look beautiful, Julie Ann."

"Sit closer to me, Cam."

He took her hand.

"You look so straight, Cameron; like a little boy."

"You look pretty straight yourself."

"I'm not: I am living with a guy I can't leave, and here I am with you. I drink and I have even seen pornographic movies in Tijuana. Have you?"

"No, not in Tijuana," he smiled.

"See? You're so straight compared to me. Look at those people in the corner, they're probably thinking, 'What's he doing with that Jean Harlow blonde?'"

"They're probably staring at us because we look good together."

"You think so?"

He wrapped his arm around her shoulder, "Come here, Julie."

"Oh, God!"

"What is it?"

"That guy sitting there—he's a good friend of Jeff's!"

"Here?"

"Yes, here. Miles away, in the middle of nowhere, and we run into him!"

"Has he noticed you?"

"I don't know."

"We can leave."

She held his hand: "No. It just happened this way, and we'll stay."

"Will you feel all right here?"

"I feel fine, Cam."

"Sure?"

She nodded. "Did you know my hair was bleached?"

"I didn't think about it."

"But only a little," she added. "It's really quite blonde anyway."

"You look beautiful."

Afterwards they walked on the beach. "What am I going to do while you're gone?" she asked.

"Same that you've been doing before."

"I guess in a way it will be good. It will give me time to sort things out, see if I should stay with Jeff."

He didn't say anything.

"How's the hospital been?"

He dug his toes into the moist sand. "Worlds passing, Julie Ann; worlds passing by so fast...you see them one day, and they're gone the same night."

"Are you sad, Cameron?"

"Yes."

"Because you're leaving?"

"No. I think it's because it doesn't really make any difference what I do."

"Yes, it does, Cam."

"Maybe. It just doesn't seem like it now."

"I will miss you, Cam. Look, maybe you can still apply for a C.O. or something; And there's always Canada."

He shook his head. "I can't do it, in my own mind. That's just it: Because it wouldn't matter whether I was there or not, they'd still be killing each other. But it will be strange now working on people who are killing each other on purpose, when before it only happened by accidents of fate."

"It seems so stupid."

"It is."

"Then why are you letting them do this to you? Why are you going, Cameron?"

"To see if I can make any difference, I suppose."

"You just said it wouldn't make any difference."

"Then to see what people are like when they don't make a difference." She sighed. "Let's go now, Cam. We don't have much time together." "I'm glad you're here, Julie. I'm happy being with you." He lifted her in the air and kissed her. They ran back, over the sand.

She looked at the packed boxes and empty drawers in his room. "You're already packed."

"It's not important now," he placed his hand under her coat, drawing her waist closer. Her light hair clashed with her bright red coat, and felt like soft fresh snow against his face.

"Can we lie on your bed?"

He carried her there. He was surprised how light she was; she was almost his height.

She sat on the edge of the bed and removed her blouse: "I'd like to be with you."

He sat beside her and touched her.

"I'd like us to be together, you know, Cam? We don't have to do anything, just be together. Can we do that?"

He nodded.

They were before the dresser mirror. She stood and removed her jeans. Her chin was over his shoulder and her hand on her hip. "You know, we do look good together, Cam."

"Yes." They really did.

"They say if you put a pencil under your breast, and it falls, they're firm enough so you don't need a bra," she said cupping her hands.

"Have you tried it?"

"Yes."

"What happened?"

"I guess I don't need a bra," she blushed. "I'm cold, Cam."

They drew the sheets and blankets over them.

"Are you happy?" she asked him.

"Yes."

"I can't, Cam. You know that, not now."

"I understand."

"Are you still happy?"

He nuzzled her chin. "Yes."

"Maybe it's strange, Cam, just being together like this. But it's comfortable and good. I've never felt bad with you. I don't ever want us to do anything we'd feel bad about or need to lie about later."

"It's all right, Julie. Really, it's all right..." They fell asleep holding each other, his arms under her breasts.

He spent a month in Coronado in the Navy's Medical indoctrination program, and returned to place the rest of his belongings in storage before sailing. The room was empty. A clock radio on the dresser, uniform, dog tags and duffel bag were all that remained for departure. Cameron turned the radio on and waited. Two hours later she still hadn't come. He turned the radio off, left the door ajar, and went to dinner.

The door was open the same as he had left it. Eleven o'clock. He walked outside, expecting somehow to see her. He returned alone. The radio played something from a movie he didn't remember. Late at night, he walked outside again. There was a time he could almost foretell when she would be there. The street was quiet and empty now; the trees moved dark in the wind. She would come, he knew. He simply knew it.

He went to bed with the door unlocked and the radio on; two hours later, the radio was still playing. The door was still unlocked. And she hadn't come.

She wouldn't come now. There was probably some party with Jeff's friends. Of course, she had already told him of it; he had forgotten. Cameron tossed over on his side and listened to a song on the radio. It was 4 a.m., New Year's first day. In five more hours, they would be sailing.

The phone rang.

"Cameron?"

"Yes," he answered in a morning-hoarse voice.

"It's me."

"I know."

"I'm going to meet you in Hawaii."

"You are?"

"I couldn't get away tonight. When does your squadron arrive in Hawaii?"

"I don't know exactly."

"You are stopping there, aren't you?"

"Yes, I think so."

"I'll be there. I've got to go now, Cam. I'll see you there, I promise."

"You're crazy."

"I want to see you. I love you."

He didn't sleep anymore. He took a shower, dressed and drove to the pier. He'd already sold the old MGB and the new owner would pick it up at the pier afterwards. Cameron left the keys under the seat, and watched the fog. Two hundred yards away, an occasional flicker of lights showed over the squadron's invisible gray hulls in the fog. They had said the weather would be good for the day they sailed. But there was fog. Not a thick pea- soup fog, but it was fog, all right.

"Dinner is served for First Class Petty Officers " Cameron glanced at his watch - 1715 hours; the wardroom would soon be open for Officers' dinner. He turned off the cassette playing Kris Kristofferson and hopped down from the upper of two bunks.

"General Quarters! General Quarters! Man your battle stations! Condition Zebra! Close all water mains and hatches! Lights out! Condition Zebra!

Cameron grasped his emergency chest and darted up the gangway to the bridge. Metal hatches had already been shut tight, secured for "Zebra"—the ship was compartmentalized in case of a hit. Rotating the ratchet wheel over the hatch, Cameron got through the circular porthole and secured it behind him. He ran up the two decks to the Combat Information Center and bridge. Except for the radars and markers on maps, everything was dark in the C.I.C. Radars shone a pale, luminous green as they swept past dots, squares, and circles in faint grays or whites. In dull red, dials marked course and distance from targets.

Cameron didn't know what had happened: Their 5 inch/54 gun mounts hadn't fired, nor had the 3 inchers above his bunk. There had been another sound, a strange sound, like thunder rolling in a wind, that he'd never heard before. All of Staff was in the C.I.C. Something had to be happening. The radio came in scrambled:

> "Volo Song, Volo Song—come in. This is Alpha Whiskey; repeat, Alpha Whiskey. Come in, Volo Song."

Their codename had changed. Cameron watched the radar screen: Three scales of topography zoomed in and out like a telephoto lens; all of North Vietnam and Laos on one scale, a smaller part of North Vietnam on another; and on further closeup, details of a few miles of Vietnamese coast. The radar scanner continued its luminous green sweep. Ships of the fleet, carriers and planes shone in friendly dots and circles; red X's marked the enemy.

"Like an X-ray, eh, Doc? You get used to it. See," Jim pointed, "here are the mountains and coast. They never change on radar. It's the other blips we're after."

"Yeah. Just like an X-ray," replied Cameron.

"Volo Song, come in! This is Alpha Whiskey. Repeat, Alpha Whiskey! What's going on?"

X-rays were slightly different, though. Not targets, Cameron thought. Targets? What kind of targets? Gun emplacements? Sure. People? Sure.

Anyone that shouldn't be there, like a dog, cat, or a child? Probably. So not quite like an X-ray....

"Repeat, come in Volo Song! What is going on?"

Noise level rose in the C.I.C. Talking. Radios. Whispering. A few terse commands. Radios crackled again. Alpha Whiskey called again. More whispers. A few questions in the tide of noise. But efficient. Despite the urgency, no words wasted.

Whoosh, whooosh...The entire ship shook, chips of paint showered down. The ship's guns were firing now.

The X.O. whispered to the Commodore: "There go another two, Commodore."

"Did we hit anything with the first?"

"Lookouts say there was a bright flash, others saw it hit. The blip went off the scope. Commodore, I think we hit a MIG."

"Are you sure? A MIG?"

He nodded. "It went off the screen, just a few miles away."

"We hit it, ah? With the first two salvos of Terriers?"

"Yes, sir. Probably the second."

"This is Blue Bolt calling. Repeat, Blue Bolt. Over. Volo Song, we are on fire. MIG bomb. The aft gun-mount is blown off. Deck has separated. Trying to flood the magazine and projectile room "

"Alpha Whiskey, come in, this is Volo Song. Alpha Whiskey, do you read me? Over. Alpha Whiskey, Blue Bolt is on fire. Extent of damage unknown. Repeat, extent of damage unknown. Over."

"Doc, get your emergency bag."

Blue Bolt, Cameron thought, that was the codename for his old destroyer, a World War II tin can he was scheduled to be riding now before last-minute orders had transferred him here, to the DLG, Leading Guided Missile Destroyer.

"Are they flooding the magazine?" asked the Commodore. "They have to flood it or they'll blow sky high! Get them on radio!"

"Volo Song, this is Blue Bolt. We haven't flooded magazine yet. No water pressure aboard"

"They haven't flooded," muttered Jim, the First Lieutenant. For an instant, his eyes left the radar screen. Two more noises shook the ship. Probably outgoing Terrier missiles. Perhaps incoming Russian Styx. It was difficult to be certain of anything now.

The Commodore paced. "Did you hear that? They haven't flooded yet! Jesus! Their whole stern is on fire, and they haven't flooded the damn ammo!"

"Volo Song, this is Blue Bolt. Flooding magazine and projectile room. Manually. Repeat, manual flooding. Over."

"Ready Doc?" asked the Commodore.

Cameron nodded.

"Need anything else, Doc?"

"The Corpsman is bringing our large emergency chest. Do we know how many people are hurt?"

"Maybe they'll know at the bridge."

Cameron went to the bridge. Past the window panels, it was still light outside. The Captain stood over the plotting chart. "Captain, do we know anything about their injuries?"

"No. They just requested medical assistance. We told them we had you on board. There are two more doctors on Alpha Whiskey. Maybe we'll send one of them instead."

"It was my old ship, Captain. I was to be on it before my orders changed. I'd just as soon go."

"You'll be taking the helo. Big Mother Six-0 is coming in to take you."

"I'll be on flight deck."

The Captain looked at him: "Someone get the Doc a helmet!" he shouted.

"No more helmets, Captain."

"C'mon! Look around!"

A communications helmet, wide at the sides where the earphones fit in, was passed on. It had no chin strap. "May I go now, Captain?"

"Yeah. Hey!...Give the Doc a decent helmet! That's a talker's helmet!"

A new one came from somewhere; Cameron tightened the chin strap and walked out on deck. The only others above deck were the sailors manning the port and starboard 3 inch guns. The 3 inchers were not computer guided and had to be worked manually. It was cold and windy; one of the sailors greeted him with a nervous sweep of the hand.

Smoke poured like a cloud trailing out of Blue Bolt against the horizon in the shadows of dusk. How many, Cameron wondered, how many might be...He reached the helo flight pad. The helicopter still hadn't arrived.

"Have you heard, Doc?"

"Yes."

"You know anything else?"

"No. Is the Corpsman here with the emergency chest?"

"Right here, sir. Can I go with you?"

"Depends on how many are hurt. I don't know. They haven't said. There's a good Corpsman already on board, if he's still all right." "I would like to go with you, Doc."

"What if something happens here? I don't think I should take you."

The computerized 5 inch/54's began firing. "PT boats," said the Flight Controller. "Saw a few of them out here. Saw the MIG, too. Strafed Blue Bolt on a straight dive, rolling up…Then bang! We got it! Blew it sky high! Just disintegrated "

Two more blasts quivered the end of Flight Controller's sentence and the ship's hull. Streaks of smoke hung in the air.

"We're not protected here," someone said. They were in the helo's open hangar. "Stay away from the metal beams above. Heavy if they fall."

Cameron wondered what was taking the helicopter so long. Probably skimming the waves, dodging the MIG's. It would be difficult for the MIG's to chase after them that way and then roll up in time. "Still want to go?" he asked the Corpsman.

"Yes, sir."

It was a time for waiting, hearing sounds, feeling the wind, and the evening light dim. Maybe there was also fear. But anything that would happen, would happen wherever one was. Cameron was glad he was outside, the wind drifting over his face and hands.

Flight Controller listened to the radio. "Magazine's flooded now. And they're sending a Doc from Alpha Whiskey instead, leaving you here in case something happens, Doc."

"Is he there already?"

"Wait a minute," he cupped his ear close to the earphone: "Yes. Situation in hand. They won't be needing additional help." "Doc," the young Corpsman muttered, "I wanted to go."

"Phone the bridge. Tell them we'll remain on deck in case anything changes."

It darkened slowly on the ship's deck. Their guns fired occasionally. The targets were out of view. They remained between Blue Bolt and the

North Vietnamese coast until it was out of range. A smoldering trail of smoke still hovered in a streak darker than a moonless night over the limping destroyer. Phantoms dipped their wings overhead, returning to their carriers. The helicopter came into view shortly; it landed quickly, without the usual hovering over the bullseye that marked the deck's center.

"Secured from Condition Zebra. Secured from General Quarters," blurted the loudspeakers. "Set material condition Yoke. Make damage reports to Damage Control Center."

The hatches and passageways were once again open as Cameron returned to the bowels of the ship.

CHAPTER 11

ADRIFT

"Attention all hands. This is the Captain speaking. This afternoon we were honored by Admiral Bergen's visit. He was proud indeed of our battle performance. I want to thank every one of you, and extend my personal congratulations for a job well done. As you know, this was the first MIG kill ever by missiles from a surface vessel. Congratulations, and let's go back to get another one! Let's do it for Admiral Bergen!"

And for motherhood, and apple pie, and football, and....

"Did you hear the rest of the story, Doc?"

"What story, Jim?"

"About the MIG's. It was a setup, or rather, was supposed to be. There was a new airstrip nest of MIG's at Dong Hoi, so we were to shell it and stir them up, so the MIG's would take to the air. Then Navy Phantoms from the carriers were supposed to knock them out."

"That's not exactly the way it happened."

"No. Several blips on the radar screen took off westward over the mountains at about the same time. Our Phantoms chased them instead. They turned out to be Air Force fighters."

"Our own?"

"Yep. In the meantime, the stirred up MIG's came flying over us. Actually, I don't think you're supposed to know all this, Doc. Classified, you know."

"Probably not."

"Did you see Admiral Bergen today?"

"I was at Sick Call."

"Anything bad?"

The usual—a few colds, VD's, and less accidents; the sailors were getting used to ducking by now and not hitting their heads. A Chief Petty Officer had come in with a hugely swollen glans penis. It was like a water filled sac, soft, not painful, and nothing else wrong. It would have been somewhat explainable from overvigorous activity—but there were no women on board. No diagnosis seemed to fit.

Cameron tried to think: "Have you been under any stress lately? Sometimes a psychological stress can cause a physical reaction." "No, not stress," the C.P.O. answered.

"Anything else you can remember?"

"Well, I just killed two MIG's yesterday."

"How's that?"

"I pulled the missile triggers on them, Doc. I killed them. Did you see the hits? They say it was a beautiful blast of colors with that fucken' MIG blowing up!"

It was an interesting physiologic reaction: War as a substitute for sex. Cameron had heard about it before, but never quite believed it until now.

"Well, did anything interesting happen during Sick Call, Doc?" Jim repeated.

"No, not really, Jim."

"They're putting up decals of red MIG's all over the place. Everyone is claiming the kill."

"I know."

"They've even got them over their bunks."

Cameron shrugged. "I hope they don't run out of decals."

"Looks like we'll get a citation for it, too, Doc."

"What citation?"

"For the first MIG kill by a Terrier missile. And Combat Action medals—you'll get one too, Doc."

"I'm not here for medals."

"You'll get one anyway. It was really lucky, you know—two more seconds and that MIG would have been all over us. Or the other MIG—there were two, you know. It's amazing they hit Blue Bolt and not us, we were really closer. That PT boat and Styx missile could have also got us."

"What PT boat?"

"We're not sure if we knocked out the PT or the missile itself. We're still analyzing the radar tapes. But it sure looks like there was a Styx missile coming straight at us."

"It's clear God must be on our side, isn't it, Jim?"

Jim glanced at him. "Going to the movie tonight, Doc?"

"Maybe."

"You might as well. We've all been extended here for another two months."

"Where did you hear that from?"

"Admiral Bergen passed that on today, along with the congratulations."

In a way, Cameron felt an irrepressible urge to laugh. "See you later, Jim."

The night's movie was another John Wayne flick and Cameron didn't wait to see the ending. He walked back to his stateroom, found the upper bunk in the dark, pulled off his shoes and stripped to the waist. Beads of sweat rolled over his forehead and chest. He wiped them with the edge of the sheets. At least it was less than a hundred degrees tonight. Less than a hundred, and in one more hour, their fifty-fourth consecutive day at sea would be over.

"Taps, taps, lights out. Silence above and below decks. Taps, taps..." The waterline at the level of his bunk brushed like an ocean's embrace against the skin of the ship.

Before morning Sick Call, Cameron visited the C.I.C.

"What's happening, Jim?"

"We're entering P I R A Z."

P I R A Z - Positive Identification Radar Advisory Zone - meant that their ship would be providing closeup shore radar monitoring and guidance inland for carrier-based fighters and bombers. The war was full of such pseudonyms.

"I don't suppose we know what the targets are."

"Don't suppose so, Doc," Jim smiled back. "By the way, I heard you were being transferred to another ship."

"News to me. I better confirm and start packing—where am I going?"

"The 'Gunline' I think. They've got missions going on over there and no doctors. You better check it with Mike."

Cameron checked with the X.O., then packed his toothbrush, razor, two extra uniforms and his black bag into his duffel. Big Mother Six-O lifted off the deck a few hours later. Cameron watched the waves recede in the distance, like small crests in a wind flurry. The helicopter fluttered between the blue sea and sky.

His new destination enlarged gray-hulled in the horizon. "You're going to have to push me out, Bob. I'll never get used to jumping out of one of these."

"Don't worry, Doc. We'll be smooth."

Bob placed the hoist under Cameron's arms and opened the sliding door. A gust of air blew into the helicopter as it hovered over the destroyer below.

"Ready, Doc?"

"Sure."

A boot pried him loose from the edge of the helicopter where his feet had been dangling. Cameron was in the air, over a bouncing sea. He straddled the gun mount before his line shifted back to the ship's stern.

He touched down on the wet deck of DD 937 with a mild electric shock from the static induced by the rotor blades.

"Doctor John Cameron reporting, sir."

"Welcome, Lieutenant Cameron. Welcome to 'Freedom Train'."

"Freedom Train" began at night. A convoy of destroyers—codenamed Truck, Argentina, and Walter, made steam to approach the North Vietnamese 'Gunline' coast to hit the areas between the D.M.Z. and Dong Hoi. Walter went in first, lining up three miles off shore.

"Ready?"

"Ready, Captain."

"Mount 51, guns free."

"Aye, aye, sir. Mount 51, guns free!"

Fifty times the guns roared with a red and blue tail of fire. The ship trembled like cardboard from hull to superstructure.

"Flat faces, sir."

"How many?"

"Two, sir. Also four cross slots on us, sir."

"Mount 52 ready?"

"Ready, sir."

"Mount 52, guns free."

"Aye, aye sir. Mount 52, guns free!"

"Sir, we hit the village. We can't see it very well, but we hit about a half dozen buildings. Truck confirms it. The explosions might have been petroleum or ammo nearby."

"Good. Enemy radar still on us?"

"Yes, Captain. Same as before—two fire directing radars and four scanners."

Explosions cracked at some distance away.

"Counterbattery fire, sir."

"How far?"

"A thousand yards, sir."

"We have another target: Mount 51 ready?"

"Ready, Captain."

"Guns free."

The fifty rounds hurtled out to their destination in less than a minute and a half.

"Flat faces tracking, sir. Counterbattery fire eight hundred yards."

The thudding sounds approached like drums on a chessboard, to both port and starboard now.

"Five hundred, sir."

"Prepare to come about. Full speed ahead."

"Aye, aye sir."

Truck and Argentina went in next. Both gun mounts soon jammed on Argentina, and Walter returned to provide suppression fire; Argentina sailed out of range, a black shadow, guns silent. The muzzles on Walter turned a dull red in the night.

They went in five more times at different parts of the coast. Their official mission was dubbed "H and I," Harassment and Interdiction. Their official targets, unknown but to top brass. Their results, same. With dawn at 0527 hours, they were secured from General Quarters.

"What do you think, Doc?"

"I wonder what we hit."

"Why?"

"Don't you?"

"No. The targets are chosen by someone, maybe Special Intelligence. I just plot the coordinates."

"What if S. I. makes a mistake?"

"Like what?"

"What do you think would be a mistake?"

"Doc"

"Yes."

"The Captain wants to see you."

"Sure."

The Captain sent him to the Information Control room where a sailor with a knife had barricaded himself behind the machines. The sailor sat with his glasses dangling over his nose, crying.

"What's the matter, Tom?"

"Christ, Doc!"

"What's going on?"

"I can't take this anymore!"

"So tell me about it."

"I'm in real trouble, Doc."

"What happened?"

The sailor adjusted his cap. "An officer called me a bastard. I pulled a knife on him."

"Did you cut him?"

"I don't think so."

"Well, let's figure out what we can do."

In a while, the sailor was more calm and returned the knife to its sheath. They both walked to Sick Bay. The sailor began to shake.

"Hey, Tom, take it easy."

"I'm in real trouble, Doc, aren't I?"

"It's going to be all right, Tom, take it easy."

"Freedom Train" next night was uneventful under a moonless night. A few scanning cross slots found them, and an occasional flat face tracked them. They encountered counterbattery fire on only one run. A lone enemy plane contact turned out to be a star. In a total of six coastal raids, over five hundred rounds had gone off somewhere into the night. They were secured from General Quarters at dawn, then cruised out of range. "Freedom Train" was over until next midnight.

Cameron woke up sweating - 2030 hours. He'd slept past dinner. He brushed off the sweat with a rumpled sheet and dangled his legs over the bunk. Slowly he opened his eyes and gazed at quarters. Cast in shadows, without portholes, four gray bulkheads nine feet apart flanked a bunk bed, clothes locker, and foldout desk. Everything was metal, warm in the heat. Cameron hopped to the floor. He tried to dry his sweat by standing under the blow vents that rushed in warm to hot air, depending on how the ship's boilers were running. Today they were running hot. He stuck his face under the cold tap. It was warm also. The uniform on the chair had partially dried.

Along the passageway, small red lights at knee level guided his steps; only shielded red lights were used within the ship after sundown. The lights disappeared a few steps away from their source. Outside it was pitch black, or however dark the clouds, moon and stars decided. Cameron took the gangway past the main deck and onto the command bridge. A gust of air hit his face as he reached the bridge's open wings to the sea. Except for the metallic clang of the rudder and the commands of the Officer on Deck to the helmsman, everything was silent. A phosphorescent blue night surrounded them without shadows, throwing incomplete outlines, slow moving forms like ghosts against the windows of the bridge. At a cruising speed of twenty-two knots the humid air glanced off the tropical waters like a stormy hot night breathing. Cameron held his breath a moment, then walked outside onto the wings. The stormy air swirled.

"Hiya, Doc. Watcha doing here?"

Cameron glanced at the place where the words had issued. He couldn't tell who it was.

"We'll be getting started pretty soon," the voice said.

"I suppose so."

"Wasn't the movie any good?"

"Didn't stay for the movie." Cameron looked closer as the cigarette dot described a red arc around the edge of a face: "You shouldn't smoke, Justin."

"Why? Because of the light, Doc? It won't carry far."

"Because of your lungs."

Midnight appeared as if a bright moon had suddenly come out. The sky became light, edges of clouds turning white, pink, and red. For a moment, Cameron didn't recognize what it was. They had arrived noiselessly, the B 52's from Thailand and Guam, like lightning without thunder over the land. Planes oddly too high and away to be heard, but their bombs splintering the night like miniature suns. Cameron now remembered officers talking, hoping the President would allow return to "Alpha Condition," the opening again of unrestricted air strikes over the North. This, then, was "Alpha": From the ship, the vision of a silent thunderstorm in the night. Elsewhere... Cameron was glad he didn't know what it felt like elsewhere.

The edges of land continued to dance like sudden flashes under a strobe. Then "Freedom Train" went into action to shell the coastline and Highway 1. It was odd enemy vehicles still moved with their lights on, despite the shelling. It had to be a very bad road. The 308th North Vietnamese Division kept moving south.

"Counterbattery fire, Captain."

"Where?"

"Seven hundred yards starboard, Captain. Two cross slots and a flat face tracking us, sir."

"Mount 52 ready?"

"Mount 52 ready, sir."

"Guns free, Mount 52."

"Aye, aye sir. Mount 52, guns free!"

The last of the rounds went off rhythmically. "Counterbattery fire bracketing us, sir. The snipes can hear them exploding by the hull. Sonar places them at less than a hundred, Captain, sir."

The order wasn't formal: "Haul ass!"

The destroyer quivered as its four boilers squeezed out their maximum RPM's.

"Zigzag out!"

"Aye, aye, sir!"

Flares popped into the sky overhead. The ship's edges became clear as a knife. Two more flares from the shore parachuted overhead.

"No smoke from those boilers! Let's not leave a trail a mile long!"

"Aye, aye, Captain!"

Cameron watched the flares, wondering how they remained drifting slowly above, like bright stars tacked to the sky.

A hoarse thudding jackhammered on both port and starboard.

"Where's our suppression fire?"

"Argentina is jammed again, Captain!"

"Damn Argentina! Open up our 52! Open it up!"

"Unidentified aircraft, sir. Two of them, three miles away."

"Continue evasive action. What's our range?"

"Seven miles from shore, Captain. Aircraft turning away."

They were silent.

"Twelve miles and opening, sir."

"Aircraft?"

"Due west."

Another silence.

"Fifteen miles, sir." "Flank speed."

"Aye, aye, Captain. Flank speed."

At 0220 the sky became dark again over land and sea. The bombers had stopped. "Freedom Train" reformed; they had three more night-raids to go.

The next day was calm. Sailors sunned themselves on deck and slept, a portable radio played below the gun mount. Cameron glanced up: Clouds slow-drifted overhead. Then it seemed as if the clouds went still, and their deck became a rotating spaceship, moving in the sun-filled firmament of a universe's worlds gliding by. Cameron watched the blue green sea and felt the sun. A small whirlwind crossed his chest and circled the deck like a miniature warm tornado.

Two more weeks were left of "Gunline."

CHAPTER 12

GOD IS ON OUR SIDE

PAGLOT2CDS02265   KLJ741
ZNY CCCCL ZOC—RUMFULD RUMGORA

FM CTF SEVEN SEVEN
TO TF SEVEN SEVEN

CONFIDENTIAL
1. PERFORMANCE OF ALL HANDS IN TODAYS OPERATION WAS
SIMPLY GREAT. YOU HIT THE NORTH VIETNAMESE WITH
EVERYTHING BUT THE KITCHEN SINK. THE SHELLS AND
BOMBS THAT RAINED IN THE NORTH LEFT NO DOUBT THAT
THE U.S. MEANS BUSINESS. YOU DID YOUR COUNTRY PROUD.
WELL DONE.
COOPER
20 72

"You're going back to the D.L.G., Doc."

"When?"

"Today."

"'Gunline's' over?"

"For you it is."

Cameron shrugged. There would be something going on at the guided missile destroyer as well—they wouldn't be transferring him here for nothing.

The next day he was aboard DLG 32 via helo. In broad daylight, DLG 32 and four advance ships sailed into a harbor, laying down a barrage onto Coastal Defense sites, army barracks, anti-aircraft mounts, petroleum stores, and whatever else lay on targeted coordinates. It was a total surprise: The sporadic enemy counterbattery fire ripped off only a first aid kit from the port bulkhead of DLG 32.

At 1000 hours, the planes came in. They swooped low, dark objects parachuting into the water. Two MIG "bandits" scrambled overhead meeting them in dogfights visible above the ships. Other ships had joined now, dotting the horizon with smoke and gunfire, forming a ring around the harbor. More planes and parachutes drifted across the sky. Helo Big Mother Six-O dashed low over the water to retrieve the crew of a downed F-4.

"How are they, Doc?"

"Fine. Backs a little sore from the ejection seats."

"That's all?"

"That's it. What's going on out here, anyway?"

"Confidential, Doc."

By the time Cameron returned on deck, it was over. They were steaming away.

In the afternoon they had a barbecue and cokes on the fantail. It was a hot, hazy day, with the water very still and the ship not rolling at all.

"Guess that went off pretty well," Jim remarked.

"I wouldn't know."

"You're not the only one that didn't know—nobody knew. We just mined Haiphong harbor, Doc."

"Did you know?"

"Yes."

"How many others knew?"

"Only a few."

"Why? Most of us have Secret clearances."

"Does it bother you, Doc?..Here, put some chili on that.."

"I guess it does bother me."

"Why? A matter of conscience?"

"Maybe. How in hell do I know what we're doing out there, where those shells are exploding?"

"Orders, Doc. We get them, we do them."

"*You* do them. This isn't Germany and I'm not an S. S. trooper."

Jim looked at him. "You think I am?"

"Maybe we all are."

Two officers from the C.I.C. joined them: "Good going," one of them shook Jim's shoulder, "What do we have left to prove now? We've got PT boats, a MIG, and a harbor all under our belts."

"Ask the Doc here."

"How are you, Doc? How were the pilots?"

"Fine."

"I'll tell you what we've got left, Jim," said the officer. "We've got to get us a submarine. That's it, a submarine!" It sounded like a toy for Christmas. "Wouldn't that be a jerk off? Pass me the ketchup."

Two sampans with bamboo sails cut through the haze. One of the officers looked up from his hamburger: "Blockade runners; gonna have to intercept them!"

"We don't have an official blockade," Jim told him.

"No," winked the other. "Not official. Lt. Hallinan will take care of them."

"Sure I will."

"Any more points for the kids?" someone asked.

"Of course. They make a smaller target."

It was a joke. Jim looked at Cameron: Of course it was a joke. But jokes had a way of changing the longer you were out here at sea, away from home.

Lt. Hallinan got one of the sampans, then returned to finish the barbecue. After the meal, the fantail was cleared for scheduled machine gun practice.

"Hey, Doc, want to try it?"

"I don't think so, Charlie."

"Say, Doc," Jim said slowly.

"What?"

"Not everyone's like them, you know, Doc."

"Right, Jim. And God is on our side, isn't he?"

In the evening, while the movies played in the sailors' mess and officer's wardroom, Cameron returned to his stateroom. He left the lights off, and felt his way to the desk. The skin of the ship was hot even at night. He turned on a dim desk lamp and gazed at a drawerful of medical magazines several months old. The med journals were the only magazines still consistently arriving by mail from the States. *Time* and *Newsweek* were often "lost" on the carriers along the way, and *Playboy* subscribers had no chance whatsoever—waiting hands on the fleet carefully guided them away before they reached helicopter mail.

Cameron slumped in his chair and carefully arranged the magazines before him: *New England Journal of Medicine, Postgraduate Medicine, Prism, Lancet, Hospital Practice, J.A.M.A.* The October issue of the N.E.J.M. had an article on "Enzyme Replacements Therapy for Adenosine Deaminase Deficiency;" articles on "Increased Levels of Transcobalmin II," "Decreased Bioavailability of Digoxin," and "Platelet Survival and Morphology in Homocystinuria" floated before his eyes. Cameron couldn't bring himself to read them. Those things didn't really matter out here, ten thousand miles away from home. He put them together again and dropped them back into the drawer.

Here death and survival were measured at the end of 3 inch, 5 inch and 8 inch guns. They splintered the night a hot-red, then steamed away, never knowing what they had hit. A-7 Corsairs, F-105's, Phantoms rode ship's radar inland and watched their targets on TV. "Black Crow" B 52's, sky-silent and unseen, unloaded 20 exploding tons on plotted crosshairs, coordinates, and coded numbers, then headed for home. AC-130 specters, Cobras unleashed thousands of rounds per minute as "death was their business, and business was good." Guerrillas planted booby traps, mines and fecal-covered stakes. "Freedom Train" strafed for liberty, "Protective Reaction Strikes" carved craters into the land, "Pacification" uprooted families, and "Defoliation" sterilized the earth. And all the while "Body Counts" kept the score. Aseptic, clean, and efficient—with a codename for everything. Except murder. The other side did the same. The words of reality were never used.

And somewhere, someone studied piles of "Confidential" and "Secret" papers, pondered clicking computer numbers, and thought he had won. His opposite, in another part of the world, standing with arms folded before a map with different colors, thought the same. In between, most just killed or were killed. They killed from a ship's console without seeing, sighted a plane's crosshairs without caring. Or they died in some mid- reflection of life, bits of flesh raining down on some dusty field, or limbs left in odd positions on a muddy earth's road. Cameron remembered the words of a reporter in something called "Nothing, And So Be It:

> "...how hypocritical it is for the world to rejoice when a surgeon substitutes one heart for another, but accepts the fact that thousands of people with healthy hearts are slaughtered like cattle..."

He understood that now. There was nothing more to be said. The rules were simple again. Only he no longer wanted part of the game. So what was he doing out here? Why was he staying? Probably because he couldn't swim away. And because he'd never really believed anything like this could happen on mankind's earth. "Man," he thought out loud, and "kind"—was any of that still left? Now, like in a dream, he had to see the ending. Perhaps, also as in a dream, when he finally awoke, mercifully it wouldn't have changed him.

Kicking off his shoes, Cameron rolled into his bunk. In the dim light of the desk, quiet shadows played on the bulkhead like desert rocks hibernating under a cold moon. Outlines of a calendar and the muted colors of a few pinups gazed back in the dark: A pouting blonde with a tiny bikini on the verge of suddenly thrusting her firm breasts free over the edge; a brunette with a bosom even more strikingly overcrowded, beneath an incongruously fetching, homegrown smile; a glossy *Playboy* redhead with tiny freckles across the bridge of her nose, azure eyes, and pink, firm nipples blazing atop high-set breasts. It suddenly occurred to Cameron that he had already changed: He looked at them differently now, and preferred the dark haired one with unkept hair and deep sad brown eyes.

Cameron's gaze went out of focus and settled onto the ceiling. He tried to imagine where his feet would be, how his body would fall, if the ship were listing or sinking. The power and lights would be out, it would be dark. It was strange to think it could happen—a lone MIG, a PT boat's missile...It was even more strange to realize he didn't really care.

He lay on his bunk but didn't sleep. Finally, he slipped from his room out to the main deck. The moon lay fore and to starboard; wind brushed warm against his face and the night appeared clean, almost light. A moon-streak fell like fire across the dark ocean. The moon-fire touched the ship. Cameron rested on the railing, watching the ship's prow hide between the shadows of night and dark deep water. The moonbeam glided evenly, serenely dispassionate over the ocean. Its light pursued an unchanging diagonal, falling like a light-well from the talons of an eagle- sky, down through dark shrouded horizons of air and water, continuing like a geometric God towards the ship. The moonbeam's cocoon of light enveloped its metal in soft gold. It followed them like that over the sea, as if the ship were some point of reference in a celestial game, a cosmic Pythagorean triangle—the sky, a moon-streak ethereal, and a small toy ship in the ocean.

The ship's hull reflected the light, as if burnished in the night. Cameron was surprised how clear it was, how easy it would be to see for anyone looking for them. Silver fingers of foam rose along the ship's sides like phosphorescent white wings, sparkling in the night. Waves played like apparitions, shadowing, throwing diamonds over each other under the moon. Cameron looked away. There was something strange about this light. Something that kept one from looking too intently, as if into the sun. He shook his head. DLG 32: Leading Guided Missile Destroyer, 4,500 tons of displaced blue water, half steel, half aluminum, four boilers, two propellers the size of tractors; commissioned four years ago, it was named after a Navy Lieutenant who had exploded along with his patrol boat in the Mekong Delta. Sleek, efficient, silent, beautiful. It was strange its efficiency was guided by men with a purpose of less beauty than the ship itself.

The wind blew hard across Cameron's face. They were turning about. The ship crossed portside, then lost its luminous moon casing. The triangle was gone. Dark once again.

"Morning, Doc."

"Morning, Jim."

"You look tired."

He shrugged. "It was a strange night outside. I didn't sleep."

Jim looked at him: "Yes. Two ships got hit. Three dead, seven wounded. No news of the others yet."

CHAPTER 13

HOMECOMING

Casualties On Human Beings And Homes:

Dead: 73,884 (Survey taken in 1954. Increasing yearly).
Injured: 74,909
Victims: All citizens (about 300,000).
Houses affected: 18,409
Completely burnt houses: 11,574
Half destroyed houses: 5,509

Area Burnt:

6,712,455 square meters

Nagasaki, 1945

"Change of Command Ceremony is at 1430 hours; are you going, Doc?"

"Don't know, Jim. Should I?"

"You probably should, since you're part of Staff. We're getting a new Commodore. Besides, all officers are to attend."

"Guess I'll be going. How well do you know the new Com?"

"Not too well. I have a feeling he won't be as good as the old one."

"What makes you say that?"

"Don't know, Doc. Just seems that way. I'll miss the old man; he wasn't that bad after all. What about you?"

"I don't know much about the new one."

"Well, you gave him a physical."

Cameron shrugged: "High blood pressure, anxious, eyes that jump around a lot."

"Did you pass him?"

"What else? The Navy didn't send him ten thousand miles here to get turned down by a Lieutenant who thinks the new Commodore's eyes seem odd."

"What do you do about the physicals, really?"

"What do you mean? I just do them, that's all."

"What about the Nuclear Clearance physicals? Aren't they different? Aren't you supposed to look for, well… something else?"

"Sanity? Make sure they aren't crazy? Yeah. I suppose I try to make sure they're more sane than the rest."

"How can you be certain?"

"Hell if I know, Jim: Doesn't seem like you can be sure of anything out here. None of you really seem sane. I'm not even certain I am anymore."

Jim chuckled. "I know what you mean. Kinda scary, isn't it? What time out here will do to you."

"Yeah."

"It's all right, Doc. We're getting close. Two more weeks and we'll be in Japan for R and R."

"How many days do we get there?"

"Five. What are you going to do, Doc?"

"Leave the ship; get a room with a sunken Japanese bathtub, put my shoes out at the door, and look out over green terraced land until the sun goes down."

"I'm taking the bullet-train to Kyoto. I hear it only takes four hours. Aren't you going to visit anywhere?"

"What's close?"

"Nagasaki is close. I don't think there's much there, though. Kyoto's the old Imperial capital—gardens, palaces, classy, old and relaxed. Some of the guys are even bringing their wives or girlfriends to Japan."

"That's nice."

"You're going to stay alone, Doc?"

"Guess so."

"What about that girl I saw in the picture?"

"She's back in the States."

"You could let her know by radio. There is still enough time."

With the Stars and Stripes in the background, the new Commodore gave his command speech, and the old one left the same afternoon. Two weeks later they were anchored in Sasebo, Japan. Green islands rose like pearls from the ocean. The war seemed over.

Cameron walked a straight line from the ship through the naval base, past the "O" Club, into town and a street gently sloping to the green hills. When he was tired, he simply stopped and left his shoes in a hotel's lobby. The room had silk Japanese embroidered curtains, polished marble walls and a sunken bathroom.

Orders came for him the next day to detach from the squadron and fly back to the war. One of the ships was without a doctor. That left a half day: Back in uniform, Cameron took the train to Nagasaki.

He was in a city again for the first time since the States. Railways, diesel buses, cars darted to and fro, factory stacks rose in the air. Cameron stood in a small park, in front of a black obelisk fifteen feet high. The realization—first slow, then speeding, cold, hard like a steel train on tracks of infinity, ran over him—less than thirty years ago, this city had ceased to exist. A plaque on the black obelisk read:

"This is the epicenter of the atomic bomb. At 11:02 a.m. August 9, 1945, the atomic bomb dropped from the B-29 exploded about 1,000 feet in the air above this black stone pillar. By blast and thermal rays exceeding 300,000 centigrade and radioactivity, the entire area in this neighborhood was transformed into ashes and debris."

Time had stopped at 11:02 at the Atomic Bomb Museum. Clock hinges were torn, pocket watch hands bent, faces warped and melted. After that time, a variety of double, triple-headed, and grotesquely shaped onions, potatoes, and other vegetables had grown from radiation. Left were the death masks of those burned to death or buried alive; children whose faces were half-gone. There was a picture of the plane that had carried the grisly gift: "Boxcar," it read on its fuselage decal with a caricature of a winged train boxcar issuing flames and smoke; "Nagasaki, Salt Lake City," said the bottom of the decal. It was strange to be here in American uniform, staring at the deeds of quarter century before. Cameron walked out into the sunshine of the park.

Groups of Japanese children in different uniforms had arrived by bus and milled through the park. Girls wore sailor blue outfits with white fringes, or blue skirts and white blouses with blue kerchiefs; boys were in stiff-necked collars, dark jackets and caps. They had come on field trips to visit the Peace Memorial. They ran, giggled, laughed, and romped. They smiled on seeing his white Lieutenant's uniform, and occasionally came close before shyly turning away. A seven year old in a white-shirted uniform finally approached and extended a small square blank book at arm's length. It looked like an address book.

Cameron stared at it.

The boy gave him his pencil and indicated he wanted an autograph.

Apparently that started something: Others came for autographs, one for pictures, and finally they all took turns posing together at the foot of the Peace Memorial. They were of another generation. They didn't remember. They laughed and patted the uniform of a strange foreign visitor, curiosity in their eyes, who was also of another time, and had no part of that past. Above them loomed the figure of the Peace Memorial: A man with arm extended palms down to the horizon, signifying peace, and the other pointing upward to the danger from the sky.

In less than twenty-four hours, Cameron remembered, he would be thousands of miles away from this park. His uniform would change from dress white to battle khakis. And the Vietnamese had slant eyes too.

After a week on another ship, Cameron rejoined his old destroyer squadron, now returned from R and R. His first duty was to respond to the new Commodore's call: He was in the usual after R and R state, status post hangover.

"Dr. Cameron reporting, sir."

"Hi, Doc. Sit down."

"Yes, sir."

"I'm depressed, Doc. I don't know what's wrong with me. If the crew sees me like this " Devoid of his gold blazoned cap, with violaceous bags under heavily lidded eyes and a sad dropping at the corners of his mouth, he suddenly was pathetically vulnerable. "Do you have anything for this, Doc? I'm down, really down. I'm nervous. I haven't been drinking on the ship," he shook his head, "you know that."

"Yes, sir. I know."

"I haven't, Doc, really. I drank on shore. The officers saw me drunk. They've lost their respect for me, seeing me like that."

"You have a right to drink on shore. It has nothing to do with that. I don't think anyone minded that."

"Really?"

"Yes, sir."

"Has the Staff said anything about me?"

"No, sir."

"They haven't mentioned anything about me being drunk?"

"No, sir."

"You're the only one that's seen me like this, Doc. I haven't been out of the cabin for two days. Don't you have anything to cheer me up?"

"You need some sleep, sir."

"I haven't been able to sleep. I'm depressed. And you tell me I have high blood pressure, and I haven't seen my old lady in months "

"It's understandable the way you feel sir. All of us have been away a long time." It was strange to be talking like this to his commodore, the one responsible for them being here. Yet, seeing him like this, Cameron realized something: The Commodore wasn't really responsible. He was just another cog, another gear in the machinery, more aggressive perhaps, more anxious and ruthless than most for promotion, but still only a link, a part of a dynamo that reached a long way from somewhere, ultimately transforming, pressuring, penetrating his defenses, breaking him down, as it did slowly to everyone here, in time. It was a self-perpetuating machine, that ended nowhere, started everywhere, with no simple part or button to press that said—"Stop this."

"So there's nothing you can give me, eh, Doc, to make me feel better?"

Cameron took his blood pressure. "It's a little up now, but we'll take it down to normal. You probably haven't taken your medicine in a while."

"I forgot for a couple of days, Doc."

"It's all right. Take one and go to bed."

"You're the only one that's seen me like this, Doc. I need help. Please don't tell anyone. It's between you and me. Don't you see? If the others knew, it would destroy me."

"They won't know. I'm your doctor."

"All right. Don't tell them, Doc. Thanks."

The old man had asked Cameron as a doctor, and as one human being to another. As such, he never told anyone. But at other times, as a different human being, John Cameron wondered if he should have.

The Commodore recovered quickly. Two weeks later, he called Cameron again.

"Come in."

Cameron saluted.

"At ease, Doc. Did you see S.N. Tomlinson today?"

"Yes, sir."

"Guess you did," the Commodore said coming around his desk, waving a folder. "I saw your report. Did you really believe he's a conscientious objector?"

"Yes, Commodore. As far as I can tell."

"He didn't express himself very well in your report. I'm wondering if there is enough there to classify him as a C.O."

Cameron remembered the pale, nervous Tomlinson: He'd said that he didn't believe in violence, "because violence didn't accomplish anything for the betterment of people."

"His statement was brief, sir. But there was no inconsistency in his beliefs. I have no reason to think he is lying," Cameron replied.

"I can't let this catch on, Lieutenant Cameron, you understand? I won't allow everyone in this squadron to do this. As Medical Officer you prepare the reports. But remember you're just that—a Squadron Medical Officer and Lieutenant first—doctor second."

"I wasn't aware, Commodore, that people could be changed that easily."

"Lieutenant Cameron, do you still think S.N. Tomlinson is a legitimate C.O.?"

"Yes, Commodore, I do."

"You may go now, Lieutenant."

Cameron left the room. One sailor out of two thousand, Cameron pondered, one out of two thousand - what about the rest? What about himself? He could have missed this ship's duty himself, a week ago back in Japan. All it would have taken was to miss one train, one plane connection. Instead, he had caught each just in time to make it back to the ships of war.

They sailed on a bright and sunlit morning with three ships of the squadron into a strip of sea between the curved fingers of the North Vietnamese mainland and two islands. Cameron leaned over the wing's railing and adjusted his cap against the wind. Slashes of white foam gushed upward in geysers as shells entered the enemy's water almost silently. In fractions of a second, ten to twenty foot bursts of foam rose in the same places from the sea, exploding in showers. Except for the cones of foam and dull thuds afterwards, the incoming shells surrounding them were soundless and invisible. It was difficult to believe the ships were right between the concrete gun blockhouses of the islands and those on the mainland.

"Doc! Hey, what are you doing up here?" a sailor asked on the bridge-wing.

"It's sunny."

"Where's your helmet?"

"We're short on helmets."

"Christ, Doc! What about a flak jacket?"

The sea was calm and the sun out like a day on the beach. The shell foam showers rose like fireworks drifting against a clean blue sky.

"Depth, thirty feet, Captain. Twenty-eight, twenty-five...twenty-two, Captain!...Captain!"

They were running aground in this bay. It reminded him of a cannery, where freshly caught salmon were boned, pressed, and preserved. Cameron felt the cool railing in his hands, and looked at the day. The wind felt good on his face. The air was warm like spring. He smiled. If that's what it was, it was best to die as he had been born, feeling the elements of the earth on his skin.

"Commodore, request permission to turn about," the Captain's voice asked evenly from the bridge.

There was no reply.

"Twenty feet, Captain!"

"Commodore, we're running aground," the Captain said calmly.

"Out here, Captain, when it comes to glory, it's every man for himself. And I to grab my share of it, Captain!" answered the Commodore.

There was a brief pause.

"Come about!" came the Captain's order.

The warship steamed churning mud. Though the Commodore had overall direction over the squadron, each Captain was still master of his own ship. The showers of explosive foam continued around them, then slowly widened of their mark as they sailed out of the bay. The other ships followed suit. They had left the cannery. Away from land, the ship's red-hot barrels began to cool.

Removing his helmet and binoculars, the sailor on the wing wiped his brow: "What were you doing out here, Doc?"

Cameron shrugged: "As good a place to be as any."

In a few weeks, ships from the Atlantic Fleet arrived to relieve them. They had been a long time coming since the Suez was closed and they'd had to round the African Cape. After a period of training, they would take over and parts of the Pacific Fleet could head home.

"Well, Doc, we're going home!"

"I'll believe it when I can see California, Jim."

"We're leaving for Guam tomorrow."

"Are you kidding?"

"No, we really are."

So they were going home: It was difficult to believe it was over, whatever "over" now meant. They stopped at Subic Bay in the Philippines, and Cameron went swimming for the last time at Cubi Point. In the pool near the beach, a five or six year old boy swam and talked to himself. Perhaps he was talking to someone who wasn't there. Or perhaps one of the officers there was his father. Maybe his father wasn't even alive. It was a windy day and the boy's towel blew into the pool. He continued to play in the water, laughing and talking loudly to get attention. But there was no one there for that. Not even Doc Cameron.

On their last night at sea, before arrival at their home port of Long Beach, the sky was a limpid dark gem, full of clusters of brightly winking stars. Cameron stood on deck and felt small under all that brightness. A lot had happened under those stars: And for the first time he wondered whether above them God wasn't after all.

Morning time they sliced in slow formation past the breakwater. A band played at the pier. People cheered and waved flowers and many colors of handkerchiefs. Cameron searched briefly for faces, then went below deck. It was a return for heroes. He didn't feel like a hero. There was so much brightness and so many beautifully colored shirts, and children laughing and smiling and jumping on tiptoes. He didn't want to take the chance she wasn't there. He didn't want to know. It was better to remember it as it had been. That is how he kept his loves—by losing them.

John Cameron waited until the band had stopped playing, and the last clatter of high-heeled shoes and shuffle of small feet was gone. He shouldered his duffel bag over the dress white uniform, at the gangplank saluted, and left.

CHAPTER 14

WITHOUT HARBOR

A shadow fell across the white wall: The head, neck, and shoulders etched black against a flower covered tavern wall with a roof of vines in the open air. A black cat crossed his shadow, merged with it. People laughed and music played.

He watched, not a part of it all. A shadow. One with the cat. Prowling the outskirts of the crowd. Searching for the things of life he still remembered. And for those he had yet to know.

And what will you do with the answers once you find them?

I don't know.

You will sit in some other corner of the world, and watch your shadow again.

Cameron stirred in his sleeping bag and adjusted the jeans he used as a pillow. His hand touched something hard and cold. The muzzle of a rifle. His eyes blinked open, completely awake. Black boots, green uniforms, topped with two crooked hats stared from above.

"*Passaporte.*"

He searched it out of his jeans. The rifles remained stuck in the sand next to the boots as they examined his passport. "Ah, Americano," they returned it with a wave, "*pero no se queda. Hay contrabandistas.*" They walked away, their boots seesawing in the sand.

Cameron dove into the sleeping bag again. It was getting light. There was something about the light, an orange blue light over the water. He propped himself on his elbows, and looked out over the rim of his sleeping bag. A red orb dripped like a slow candle into the waves rolling to shore: Perhaps this was why it was called the Costa del Sol. Cameron zipped the bag up and watched. When the orb rose completely above the ocean, he propelled himself from the warmth and felt the sand squeeze cold between his toes. Searching out a stick with a fork at the end, he waded out to the sea. He rested a mirror between the fork, and waist high in water proceeded to shave. Salt water made a poor medium for lather. He washed and toweled off. It was time to move on. It didn't matter where.

The high Sierras Nevadas of Spain were hot and dry and gypsies lived in caves dug out of the mountainside. Ramshackle doors and windows made of cloth opened onto a cloudless heat. There could have been palaces built into the mountain behind those doors, for all he knew. Cameron stopped along the road and brushed canteen water over his lips; through the haze of eyelashes caked with dust, he watched the window-cloths motionless in the hot air. There weren't palaces there, he knew, although it was nice to think so. They were only small huts dug into the dirt.

After weeks in the mountains he saw the sea again—the Costa Brava. It was easier to let his legs follow the asphalt road down, winding seaward. Perhaps that was why he had gone to the mountains—to experience the ease of going down to the sea. Or perhaps it had something to do with a past. Cameron shook his head: It didn't matter.

He traveled because he had to move on, because there were roads and forks and crossings ahead, and he never knew which he would take until he got there. And there was never any need to remember which was the way back, because there was nothing ever left behind.

It began to rain near the sea. The high, clear mountains had been dry, and here over the white sand of shore the sky melted into ocean in a uniform, quiet shade of gray. The dust over his boots and from his hair washed out over puddles of rain. He realized he was near a harbor: Mast lines and sheets fluttered about the boats moored all around; a seagull swooped with a cry of gieck, gieck, gieck, parting the drops of rain. In the evening, gold danced over his shoulder against the hills he'd left behind as the sun washed over the mountains. Grass buds sprouted like green diamonds at the edges of pools. The rain had stopped.

Soaked, Cameron walked into a laundromat of Barcelona. As his clothes tumbled in the dryer, Cameron noticed an old man and his white dog. The old man's hat was gray like his overcoat, surrounding the white bristles of his face. His worn boots paced the floor softly, shiftlessly, followed by the dog at a distance. The dog's fur hung loosely over its bones. Whence they came, where or when they ate, where they slept, or sheltered in which doorway when cold, was anybody's guess. The old man shuffled to a stop. The dog followed, scabs over its joints and tufts of hair missing from its face. Quite naturally, the old man pressed his face against the warmth of the dryer and smiled.

At night, in one of Barcelona's cafes, a thin guitar player strummed so quietly one could hear his labored breathing. He would pause a long time, with his wild mustache almost the thickest part of him poised above quivering lips. He would wait, search, then play again. He didn't sing. His whole body was one sad melody. After a while, the guitarist stepped down, collected the coins from his cap, and went to the waitress for his drink and dinner at the far corner table.

A girl took his place: Thick woolen white sweater, hair tucked in under a cap, and cradling a guitar case over her arms. In one continuous motion she removed her cap and pulled the white sweater over her head. Long dark hair tumbled out, and she tossed it from side to side over the cream colored blouse, heavy at the bosom. Her lips were plump red, her waist small, her hair thick and shiny in the light. Cameron knew it was time to move on. It was better that way: Without reasons or seasons or memories to stop his movement.

Because somewhere between the emergency red-blankets and the dying old men tied up to their beds, somewhere between a redheaded ghost pacing the hallways and a woman that cried when a spot on her lung turned out to be cancer, Cameron had stopped believing. The rigid logic of the processes he'd learned had failed; hope's warmth had ceased. He had watched wide eyed children staring, wondering why they were in white rooms with white beds and white-dressed men and women all around them; and under the light, inside their large dark eyes, Cameron had seen the red stains of leukemia pouring from the broken clots in their eyes; and no one ever told the children, but somehow they knew, without having anyone tell them. Sometimes afterwards they still smiled, a different kind of smile. And Cameron had wondered why. Somewhere between their smiles, and the young men that met their accidents on some hidden sand bar of life, or those that met their more deliberate fate from brief orders of war issued by those who would remain safe, sanctioned by others who dared not stop it—Cameron had wondered why. Words had unleashed muzzles red in the night, orders had obliterated targets on maps—and finally, when the scores were seen on news pictures and TV, they were slant-eyed and dying too far away and in too many numbers for anyone to care or ask why.

Now Cameron didn't either. And he would never again stop to remember and never again ask why. He'd known it on that night standing under the stars coming home. Cameron paid for his drink and walked out of the cafe, to keep moving.

He rose at three a.m. in the Alps with all his clothes and shivered in the dark. The sleeping bag was too cold. He got up to walk. With the morning light he stopped by a boulder with a sign pointing to nowhere. Next to him, on a smooth edge of the slab, a squirrel quivered alone, its furry tail blowing in the wind. It was a cold wind, and the squirrel didn't move. Its lids looked heavy and it must have been sick.

Cameron stopped at a guest house for breakfast. The coffee with milk was warm in his hands and a creamy froth on top kept the heat from escaping. He took a long time drinking it. The mixed fruit marmalade was smooth and the bread fresh with assorted bakery smells still on it. Cameron raised his cup in a silent toast: His eyes flashed like those of a wolf, tracking places, days, hunting a future that didn't resemble a past. And wolves recognized traps and avoided them all; perpetual movement, roaming, was the cure: Snows under padded feet, or sands of a shore. On reaching the horizon, after a brief stare from restless, through-seeing, indifferent eyes, the roaming began again. Traps were only for those who remained in one place for too long.

Across the Rhine, castles of thick walls stood along damp banks for longer than anyone could remember. Rivers flowed at their feet. Cameron rowed a boat upstream the Neckar—he liked to row. Even wolves fell into some traps of the past. Sweat dripped from his forehead and blisters shot up on his hands. A girl with light brown hair and pretty eyes leaned against a bridge; she walked close as he shipped his oars and put away the boat. Her smile was nice and her eyes coal-dark.

She didn't ask his name: "Do you have any friends?"

He shook his head.

"Do you travel alone?"

Perhaps it was already on his face—he traveled alone because others weren't going there, or had different reasons for going. He had no reasons anymore: When he got tired of rowing and listening to the radio on some river, he would leave.

On Heidelberg's beer row, in a bar's crowd and walls jammed with noise and shadows of lights, Cameron gulped his beer and wondered what others did, how their eyes saw. He glanced through the amber of his beer mug: Another world unraveled; fireflies zigzagged in the night; burning tiger eyes lurked behind black forest shadows surrounding a campfire; people huddled while far off thunder crackled on distant dark mountains. Cameron shook his head: Like before, cigarettes moved jerkily about in many hands, small orange lamps hung from darkened walls, drums of a band beat out the music. Momentarily, he had glimpsed another world—how many more worlds were there? Perhaps as many as there were eyes observing. Yet Cameron didn't feel he belonged to any.

He returned to his amber-filled glass: White owls with large round eyes flittered from tree to tree, with their stately white chests in motion. In another world, they were the waitresses in white blouses serving drinks.

After closing time, Cameron waited at the Bismarkplatz for a bus.

He was still observing, but the world unraveling was now real: A boy, alone with all of his fourteen years, circled spastically on crutches, jerking eerily forwards at the hips; he circled and circled, breathing fast, a look of unknown terror in his eyes. The circles continued to twirl, ten or twelve feet wide, as fast as the crutches would allow. The faster the circles, the more spastic his gait became; the crutches pounded the pavement threatening to fly out from under the deformed elbows in this mad carousel on Saturday night at the Bismarkplatz. Other people watched; a couple sat on a bench and kissed. Their eyes moved once towards the spastic, but didn't understand. Neither did Cameron.

Cameron just wished to be back at that bar with the white-chested owls. He didn't wait for the bus any longer and walked away. He stopped on a bridge that night, watching the stars over the calm flowing river, for a darkness that seemed like years.

PART III

Run out of beliefs
Out of causes and self
In the end
It is a very simple thing
    that moves us.

CHAPTER 15

FREE FALL

The voice was so clear, soft as white clouds settling over a mountain. It didn't matter in what language she sang.

The eagle in his brain listened, hovering over the abyss. The sounds were too distant, the eagle shook its head. Then plummeted to oblivion. Air rushed past in void-dive. Cold. Black. Silent. The eagle screamed into time - blind now - the dive of an arrow.

Slowly sounds returned, touching softly. Coal-black cliffs broke onto a glistening pale blue, oceans gliding over pebbles and sand. The eagle's wings spread slowly, shaking against space. Shore pebbles continued to grow, spiraling below like bright galaxy crystals. The sands' warmth rose, hitting the eagle's chest.

The next instant, its dive pulled out, into the sun. The eagle soared.

He tilted his head: A large oak hovered in the windless evening above grapevines of the open-air *taverna*. The *taverna* was on a narrow dead-end street; the street had no signs. Tables were set for twos and fours, with red checkered tablecloths and napkins. In the early evening it was still hot, and most of the tables were empty. He went to the juke box and played that song again. He'd come here for the song.

It was some time before he realized there were two voices: The other was soft, quietly following the tune. When Cameron turned, the song had ended. The girl had auburn hair, slim, with light blue eyes. She looked at him, then turned away.

It was quiet now in the *taverna*, Between the vines and dark oak leaves, the stars were already gathering in the night of Athens. He looked at her again, her profile motionless. Wavy hair fell to the shoulders, her hands were clasped under her chin. Her breathing had a strange quality, as if she'd just been running. He felt something strange inside. He felt himself stop.

What is it, Cameron?

I don't know.

You've just seen her. You've just heard her.

I know.

You're imagining things, Cameron.

Her cheekbones brought light out from shadows, her eyes made their own. Her eyes found his. As if that same strange breathing moved it, her pale neck shook slightly. Then he realized the breathing was his own. And the pounding in his neck the rushing of each beat's heart-blood: At that moment, she wasn't the most beautiful woman he'd ever seen. She was the only one.

It isn't possible, Cameron.

Of course not. I don't care if it's possible.

Their eyes remained like that: Locked. Time passed, both of them in it, traveling to a place where it began and stopped. Finally, he stood up. He didn't know what was happening. He didn't need to know. He stood without thinking. Moving between the tables, he gathered her hand in his, and watched their fingers fold together.

She smiled. Her smile was a warmth from long ago - of another time, another place - a smile that had never left him, and yet he'd never found before today. Their hands remained touching like that, over the table. He felt calm now. He was surprised he had done all that. It was as if after many roads of cold snows and ice under snow laden trees, he'd finally reached a place light and warm, and walking inside, found that place was home.

"I'm glad you're here," he said finally, touching her hand. He had forgotten she might not understand him: They were at the edge of an ancient world, and the language of the tune she'd been following was Greek.

"Yes," she said simply. Her eyes looked into his without need for explanations.

"I suppose I should have a more formal and proper introduction for the occasion," he said. "I don't."

"Yes," she pressed his hand, "you do. You came and took my hand." Her voice was a soft melody, washing ashore.

"I don't know what else to say."

"Don't say anything."

"It feels good being here with you."

"How long have you been wandering?"

He was surprised at the ease of her question. "How did you know that?"

She shrugged: "How is it you're here?"

"I just happened to come here, I guess."

"It is very beautiful," she said quietly, tilting her head. "But that's not why you're here."

"I came to listen to the song."

"You liked it?"

He nodded without trying to explain. One couldn't explain magic.

"I know," she said reading him clearly. "The song goes on forever, doesn't it? The melody never stops, like the sea and the wind and the sun: Even if we'd lose everything else, we'd still have that. Did you understand the words?"

He shook his head: "You were following the tune pretty well. What did it say?"

She laughed: "Whatever you want it to say."

"Good."

"So what did it say to you, then?" she smiled.

"If I told you, you wouldn't believe me."

"Why not?"

"I'm not sure I believe it myself."

"Is it good?"

"Yes."

"Then believe it."

He didn't say anything.

"It's so strange. Strange but beautiful. Why did you come and take my hand?" she asked him.

"Because the way I felt inside, it would have been more strange not to do it."

She studied him, her eyes half crystal-question, half oracle's knowledge: "I feel as if I've known you before, that I know you now. It's so strange..."

"I know," he touched her face and her hair where it curled over her cheeks, "what are you thinking now?"

"I'm not thinking anything really, just feeling."

"Good."

"And you?"

"I wish I could tell you better," he shook his head. "I touch your hands... you are beautiful to me."

"Am I?" she laughed, happy and easy like a carousel full of children. She resembled a child now, a girl to whom yet nothing bad in life had happened. But the softness of her eyes—a mellow, gentle, durable softness—was the kind that had been gathered early, slowly, bit by bit somehow, like storm-scattered fleece along a thorny path.

"What is it?" she asked watching him.

"I wish I could have stopped whatever was bad that happened to you."

Her eyebrows arched in off-guarded surprise: "Why do you think anything like that happened to me?"

"I just know."

Her crystal eyes hesitated, then turned far away. Her smile broke off. "What's happening to us?" her voice was strained, like the effort of an incoming tide. "It shouldn't be," she added.

He couldn't understand the sudden change: "It shouldn't be?" he repeated slowly, his voice flat and strange to himself.

"No." Her mouth remained closed. The smile gone to another place.

"If you want me to go, I will. Tell me why first." He felt her fingers grow rigid on his hand. He almost let go. His eyes gazed over that abyss, waiting.

Then, her eyes saw his.

"No," she said finally, "not now. There is no need for you to go now." She lifted his gaze slowly, gently: "Your eyes looked like they had gone on the other side of the sun."

"I don't know..." he tried to reply. Her fingers stopped him, resting lightly on his lips. He placed his arm about her waist holding her close. She smiled the same smile, and he felt as if nothing at all had happened between her first smile and the present.

"You know," he said, "somehow you're here, and I'm here...and you're so beautiful to me." He was surprised to be feeling it inside, but he did. He said it: "I'm falling in love with you." He looked at her, "maybe it's not supposed to be possible," he shrugged awkwardly, "but it is."

Her eyes stayed with his: "Feel my hands in yours," she said.

"They've been in mine the whole time."

"How do they feel?"

"Warm, good; why are they shaking?"

"Because I want to put my arms around you."

He touched her cheek, and kissed her. "You know what is happening to us?" she asked quietly, her eyes closed across a distance.

"Should we change it?"

"No," she said simply. "It's just happening." And she was close to him again.

"You're beautiful, you know."

"I'm a bunch of trouble, really," she told him.

"What's your name, trouble?"

"Chris. And yours?"

"Cameron, John Cameron."

"So you haven't told me how long you've been wandering, Cameron."

"A long time. How did you know that?"

"The same way you knew about me."

"It's as if we've met before," he mused, "another life?"

"Do you believe that?"

Cameron shook his head. "I don't know. Perhaps."

"What else do you believe in?"

"Not much."

"Why are you in Greece?"

"I don't know. Just wound up here, that's all."

She tilted her head: "What have you seen here so far?"

"You."

"Thank you. Besides that."

"I don't think I can describe it. I feel at home here: There is a calm, more than I've found before, a life more intense with centuries drifting by; yet still, each day is just a simple day, surrounded by a history so great, not even the living can understand it now... doesn't make sense, does it?"

"You understand it?"

He shrugged; "I don't understand many things. And you, what are you doing here, Chris?"

She gave him a look of mock surprise, "why, sitting here with you, of course, Cameron."

He turned away and smiled.

"I like your smile," she said, "a happy face; sometimes you look like a little boy who'll never stop playing. At others," she paused, "at others you look so serious..."

"Hmm. Are you hungry?"

"I think so."

"Can you read the menu in this *taverna*, Chris?"

"Some of it. What would you like?"

"My arms around you."

She laughed, a clear laughter of bells. "This is a clean, family restaurant, you know."

"So it is. Greek salad then, with feta cheese…"

"And lamb."

"Wine?"

"Red's the best here. Your shirt looks like it's been wrinkled for ages, Cameron."

"It is. Slept in, too, sometimes."

"Your hair is dark and very straight."

"Look who's talking—with all those curls, anything would be straight to you."

"I like yours straight like it is, though. And you cut your salad like a European. Where are you from, Cameron?"

"A little from everywhere. Mostly west coast, I guess. And you?"

"A bit like you - from everywhere."

"Maybe a California girl raised in Europe?"

"Why did you say that, Cameron?"

"A hunch. What kind of wine is this? It's really good."

"Hellas Cellar. I've become somewhat of an expert at my tender age."

"Good. Would you believe I don't even know how to mix drinks?"

"Probably. So what do you do when you aren't wandering, Cameron?"

He watched his shadow etched against the white *taverna* wall. "Nothing. Not anything, really." He glanced at the cat on the wall near his shadow: "Have you noticed how thin the cats are in Athens?"

"Not that one. That one's fat."

"The only one so far. It must be a good restaurant."

"Do you want to hear that song again?"

"Sure. And another glass of wine." He went to the juke box and found the song. He looked back across the tables: Even from a distance she was beautiful, her back taut, slim-curved at the waist, arms folded over the table and her bosom leaning forward almost touching it. Returning to her, he could see the towers of Troy and a fleet of a myriad sails anchored against the horizon—they would remain anchored there forever for her rainbow's smile.

"You look happy again," she said.

"I am. You're here, and I'm here, and you are beautiful to me."

"I suppose all men fall in love with me like you did," she teased without malice.

"Of course. But I was the easiest, I'm sure."

"I'm kidding, Cameron."

"You mean they don't fall in love with you just like that?"

"Not like you."

"I didn't intend to be difficult," he smiled.

She caressed his hand; her eyes narrowed and sparkled.

"Sometimes I can't look at your eyes for too long."

"Why?"

"Like the sun. Too beautiful."

"You look into my eyes," she mimicked his deep voice playfully, "and you see an ocean of blue emeralds..."

"Right. Something like that. How's the lamb?"

"Good. Have some, Cameron, I can't finish it all."

"And dessert?"

"Anything but Turkish coffee here. The Greeks still smolder about that Cyprus thing."

"I wonder if we really did sell them down the river of politics there."

"The Greeks certainly seem to think so. Anyway, who knows? You can't be certain of stuff like that anymore. Governments are nothing but a series of secret meetings and papers."

"So you think about that, Chris?"

"Sometimes. And what do you think about, Cameron?"

"As little as possible."

"I don't believe you succeed in that most of the time."

"For a beautiful girl, you know a lot."

"And you pretend not to, Cameron."

"Shall I pretend I'm not falling in love with you?"

She pressed his hand. "You make me happy just looking at you, Cameron. And I don't even think about why. It's nice to know you're crazy about me same as I am over you. Look," she said, "the waiters are already turning the chairs over and cleaning up."

"We've been here that long?" he glanced around. There was only another couple left. "Shall we walk?"

A high, dim streetlight cast their shadows along the narrow road. She swayed her hand holding his, and looked at him.

"How far away are you staying?" he asked her.

She didn't answer.

"It's not much of a place I have," he said, "but you're welcome there." The sound of pebbles rolled under their feet.

"That's all right," she said quietly.

"Are you scared of something?"

"No," she shook her head. "Not of you, or anything else that matters right now."

"Do you know, it's already the next day," and he kissed her on the lips.

His room was on the second floor along a main street. It was still hot inside. He didn't turn on the lights. There were two chairs, a desk, and a bed in the shadows. She sat on the edge of the bed. He opened the screen doors to the balcony. "It's still quiet, Chris. In a couple of hours the buses and tour cars will start driving below. I hope it doesn't wake you."

Her outline remained still, awkwardly erect on the edge of the bed. She didn't reply.

He sat down and joined her. "It kept me up the entire first night I was here. I told you it wasn't much of a place, Chris."

"I like it, it has you in it," she caressed his hair lightly. "Please come with me to the balcony."

It was cooler outside. She began to shiver. "What's that?" she pointed to a square shadow-topped hill in the distance.

"The Acropolis."

"Persian kings marched thousands of miles to see what we're seeing," she said quietly.

"Not to see it - to conquer it."

"It's odd how restful it looks now," she turned and looked at him.

"You're shivering."

"Yes."

He put his arms around her and they walked to the bed. He unbuttoned his shirt and watched her return to the balcony. He didn't ask why. Her arms rested on the metal railing, her face very still in the moonlight. Then she turned and undressed, the curves of her back uncoiling like a spring. Her skirt and blouse remained where they had fallen; her body retained an outline of light among the shadows, like dew on leaves in a dawn's sun. She left the shutters open, and her arms moved back to arrange her hair as she walked to the bed. She came into bed beside him, under the single blanket and sheet.

Her face came to rest near his. "Why did you say you were falling in love with me?"

He placed his arm under her neck. "Because it's true."

"Why say it so soon?"

"It's been a while since I've believed in tomorrows, Chris. Sometimes tomorrows never come."

"Isn't there ever a future, Cameron?"

"Maybe. I believed in it too much once, I think. I left too many things unsaid, undone. And the tomorrows were too late. Anyway, it doesn't matter now."

"Sounds like it still does, sometimes."

"No, I don't think so, Chris."

"Are you saying it's that easy to leave a past behind, Cameron? Even you don't believe that."

"No. Not easy. Just necessary, and done."

Their faces were close together. "It was strange how you came to me and touched my hand...I didn't know you were listening to that song. I don't think I would have been singing it if I knew."

"I went to that place to listen to it tonight."

"Is that how you choose your places, Cameron?"

"And my girls," he smiled touching her auburn curls.

"Will you tell me now what the song said to you?"

"Someday."

"When you believe it more?"

"Yes."

She tucked her chin below the blanket: "Don't you have any regular girlfriends, Cameron?"

"Not for a while."

"Why?"

He stared at the ceiling. He didn't know what to say. "I guess it's maybe because I don't believe enough, in anything."

"That's a strange answer."

"What about you?"

"You shouldn't believe in me either," she said quietly.

"You should ask me something more possible, Chris."

"Maybe I will." She took his hand, and placed it on her breast: "Is it strange to believe in you, and still ask you not to believe in me?"

He brought her face close and touched it with both hands. "I would do anything to erase whatever unhappiness has touched you—when I first saw you, your eyes looked so beautiful, yet sad. I didn't know such beautiful eyes could look so sad."

"That's because I had seen you. You looked at my eyes," she whispered, "and they had seen yours."

"I don't understand."

She hesitated, then said it quickly: "You were sitting alone like that, your eyes like they had come from a moon-past, Cameron, and I fell in love with you." She added with a small shrug: "You see, I don't believe in tomorrows either, Cam."

He looked at her eyes in the shadows of the room. Outside, the cool air tumbled on the light of the moon. He wanted to say something but only a warm heaviness came to his chest and throat. Still cradling her face in his hands, he kissed her.

Their lips touched slowly, searching the corners, lightly along the edges. Then inside.

"I wish..." he said, "I wish that I could make you happy."

She began to cry.

"It looks like I'm making a mess of it already. I'm sorry, Chris." He caressed her hair along her wet cheeks, then moved away.

Her arms pressed over his shoulders and her breasts against his chest. She tucked her face under his neck: "No," she said, "don't go. I just need to cry." Afterwards, she still shook lightly, her lips pressed tightly together.

"Chris, we don't have to..."

"Shh, Cameron," she touched his lips, "you don't understand. I do want to make love to you."

"But Chris, there's no rush..."

"Please, Cameron, please - don't say anything."

They lay side by side a long time afterwards, their arms touching along their entire length. He pulled the sheet over them. "Are you cold?"

"Soaking wet. You're an electric blanket, Cameron."

"A drawback in the summers of Greece," he smiled. "Maybe you wouldn't complain in winter."

"Who's complaining?"

"I love you, Chris."

"You don't have to say that."

"Not even if it's true? How about singing it?"

"Are you crazy? Get back here, Cameron! Here, that's it."

"I don't know if I can, Chris..."

"We'll soon find out," she smiled.

He lay on his back afterwards, soaking in sweat, his mouth dry. She wrapped the sheet around her and returned with a glass of water. He undid the sheet and caressed her shoulders. Grayness flooded in like mist, framing the open balcony. It was quiet. Not even the birds stirred. It was the coolest part of the morning, when all living things slept. He tucked the blanket tightly around her sides and shoulders, and nudged her cheek with his nose. Her eyes drifted about the pale shadows of the room. "Your eyes were strange then, you know." she whispered.

"When?"

"When I asked you what you did when you weren't wandering."

"I already told you, Chris, I sit and listen to songs in cafes, and think of nothing."

"Only part of that is true."

"All right, then. Sometimes, I think about what an eagle feels like, when it dives into free fall from the sky."

"What does it feel like?"

The trace of an orange hue tinted the gray balcony. "Like having you here beside me."

CHAPTER 16

BUTTERFLY ROAD

A long, late summer. Far away. In the forest, it was still hot in October. He listened, quiet and still. Leaves fell, turning gold from the season of green. The trees knew it was autumn.

Butterflies floated everywhere, hopping on warm currents of air. On the road back, butterflies covered the blacktop, drawn to its shimmering heat. Cars were not something they understood—the roads were carpeted that summer with pieces of butterflies. They left their broken wings on the pavement like small petals waving in the sand.

One lost its yellow and gold wing over his windshield. It was a brilliant fine velvet in the sun.

It was past noon. The noise of cars and diesel buses choking at the stoplights poured over the balcony. Heat pressed into the room. Her face was over his arm with drops of moisture bathing her forehead curls. He watched her sleeping, and didn't move. Far away, in the sun, the Acropolis rose marble-white. The sun's light had been beautiful in other places also, sheets of thin gold. But here it was a transparent being, a crystal gem visiting the earth.

Her hair brushed his arm. She opened her eyes. Her first glance was absent, almost fearful, before her smile returned and her hand touched his chin. "Good morning, Chris. How are you?"

She nodded, stretching over his arm: "And you?"

He kissed her curls where they lay matted on her forehead. "Fine."

"How long have you been awake, Cameron?"

"Just twilight trekking awhile."

"Your arm asleep?"

"No."

"I woke up a few times last night. You were always there. I don't think we moved at all last night from each other."

"Why were you waking up?"

"To feel you close," she nuzzled against him. "What were you twilight- trekking about?"

"Nothing much."

"Tell me anyway."

"A summer back in the States; actually, I guess it was autumn. Only, it still seemed like summer..."

"And what was it like?"

"Different. I guess it was different." Dead end roads, he thought. Lives that ended just like that, without explanations. Worlds that came and were gone in a day, or a night. Mostly at night, he remembered. Accidents. Accidents without cures. Failures. Burned-out beliefs. Things that ended. Beauty lost behind like a butterfly's velvet wing-powder over a windshield. Maybe it was the same with people. Slowly they were changed, molded, hardened, beat down, hurt—until their beauty was lost. Or they died. He remembered something Hemingway had said: "The world breaks everyone and afterwards many are strong at the broken places. But those that will not break it kills. It kills the very good and the very gentle and the very brave impartially." Too bad it was true. But Cameron didn't need to tell her of that. "It was nice," he said, "still hot in the forest, and lots of butterflies."

"What were they like?"

"Like you, Chris, just beautiful."

"They don't die in the winter, do they? They just turn into moths. I'll be a moth, too, someday."

"I'll love you even as a moth," he kissed her hand.

"You shouldn't be so sure," she turned serious, "maybe you won't even be there."

"Chris, I..."

"No, Cameron. Remember what we said about tomorrows? All we have is now. And when we no longer have it," she added quietly, "then we no longer have it." She looked at him: "I don't want you to think anything else. You understand?"

"No."

"Even if you don't understand it now, promise, promise me..."

"What, Chris?"

Her voice changed to a forced normalcy: "Promise me, Cameron, that if either of us has to leave, we will look at the good in the past we had together. Nothing else. Let's not build tomorrows we can't finish," her voice trailed dry as a whisper.

He looked at her in silence.

Her eyes stared back, then suddenly sparkled as she bounced to her knees onto the bed. She knocked him down and pressed her nose against his: "What shall we do today?"

"Whatever you want. It doesn't matter."

"What haven't you seen in Athens?"

He shrugged. "Lycabettus?"

"The 'Hill of Wolves?' Hot, dry, cicadas wailing like sirens—the leaves face the sun with an everlasting dull green, and not even the dust moves in the hot wind—harshly beautiful, clean. Nothing to stop you there, except a sun's light that makes you blind, and also lets you see half of Greece down to the Mediterranean sea. You know, I wish I could have been there with you that first time."

"I like your eyes when you talk of it," she said, "it's like being there again."

"Shall we go there?"

"Maybe. What about a place neither of us has seen before? Then it would be different, the first time for both of us together."

"You won't believe it, Chris, but I haven't been to the Acropolis."

"You haven't! How Come?"

"Don't know. I suppose I wanted to feel the things around it first. I didn't want to go there, just like that, with a taxi or bus, and stare at it. I guess I wanted time to understand the place where it rose, and the people that built it. Guess that's pretty strange, huh?"

"Pretty weird," she laughed. "And how long have you been here?"

"Two weeks. And you know, I am the same way about photographs—I never bring a camera until I feel well about a place. Somehow it doesn't seem like the truth to watch something or picture something so fast, without feeling it first."

"You don't take pictures anymore?"

"No."

"Why not?"

"I'm not traveling to take pictures." But to leave them behind, he thought.

"You know something, Cam?"

"What?"

"I haven't seen the Acropolis either! Strange people, ha?"

"So how long have you been here, Chris?"

"Long enough."

"Why haven't you seen it?"

She shook her head: "It just didn't feel right at the time."

"What's wrong with today?"

"Perfect!" She leaped from the bed. "Firsts to the bathroom!"

They had breakfast downstairs. It was late and the rest of the tables were empty. The hotel doors and windows opened onto the street's bustle and heat. "I'm so excited about going, Cameron; how far is it from here?

"About two miles - you can see the entrance from here. Shall we walk?"

"Sure. But we have to go through the regular entrance, Cameron, I mean the one people back then would have taken. That's the walk I'd like to see, too, the way they walked up there."

"Let's go find it."

The road was cobbled at first, meandering in slow curves uphill. When terracing began along the steeper slopes, the road split. Olive trees stood as silent sentinels covered with summer dust.

"What do you think?" Chris asked.

The entrance rose suddenly before them, as if by a design of its own, etched white against a pale blue sky. Waves of heat compressed against the bulk of the tapering columns flanking the massive tiered steps.

"It looks like the entrance to the Acropolis, citadel of old Athens."

"And feels like it," she pressed closer to him. "Let's go there," she motioned to a narrow path leading directly to the steps. There was another, larger and cobbled, leading off to the side and then to the pillars. "That was probably for scholars," she said, "strolling pensively in white robes."

"And this one?"

"For impatient lovers who ran uphill to see the sights and embrace like mad!" she looked at him: "You know, my hand in yours feels like the first time I loved someone."

He kissed it and gently moved it behind her back, drawing her closer. "And that felt beautiful."

"Did it?" he kissed her on the neck.

"You're breathing fast, Cam..."

"And we haven't even gone up the steps!"

"Let's run!" She laughed, darting away. She suddenly stopped, and returned. "Hold me, Cam. I want to go there with you."

Columns framed the blue sky like a roof. As they climbed the steps, the blue roof expanded into a sky-garden. "Look at that blue, Cameron: The sun's promise to the earth that it will never stop shining."

"Maybe nature keeps her promises better than men."

"That's a strange thing to say," she looked at him.

He shook his head: "I'm not sure why I said it. I'm not even certain it's true." But then he remembered, he remembered the promises of life: The red-cheeked boy of dark straight hair and wide brown eyes, and the death he'd seen behind his eyes; he remembered the square-shouldered youth who walked like a football player and the lumps on his shoulders that grew faster than any medicines could kill them; and the man and the rose... watching it slowly fall from his hands.

John Cameron felt it again. He was holding Chris' hand like before. But it was she who was holding him now.

"Cameron?"

"It's all right. I was just going to say... that maybe since men are part of nature," he said haltingly, "they are also part of its life, laws, and its promises. I guess maybe an accident is just a broken promise..."

She looked at him and held both his hands: "I'm sorry..."

"Why, Chris?"

"You look so sad and far away I can't even hold you now."

"You are holding me."

"Holding you enough?"

"Yes." He touched her face and looked away. "Do you know why those columns look so white, Chris?"

"Why, Cam?"

"There's nothing else white to compare with them - they float above our heads in a cloudless blue sky."

"Is that what you're thinking now, Cam?"

"Yes."

"Kiss me and don't lie."

He kissed her, turning her back gently against the white pillar, her waist between his arms. The marble was hot under the sun, chipped and worn in places, but still warm and beautiful after twenty-five centuries. Suddenly he lifted her to the steps above him, her face resting over his.

"Who are you now?" she laughed.

"A Greek sailor in Themistocle's fleet. And guess what? I'm on shore leave!"

She pretended to pout: "For how long?"

"The Persian fleet has not yet sailed: Artemisium and Salamis are as far into the future as Columbus and America. And anyway, we don't even know about those things yet! I'm on extended shore leave, my lady!"

"Thou shalt not sail a fortnight still, and keep my heart's company "

"Yes, m'lady," he bowed, "an order I'll gladly obey."

"Hmm, only one problem—if you were a sailor, who was I?" she paused, "yes, that's it!"

"What?"

"I'll be one of Solon's daughters."

"Were they pretty?"

"I don't know. I don't even know if he had any daughters. Maybe I'll be a courtesan instead."

"Hmm. I'm not sure I'd like that."

"You, a sailor? You'd love it!"

"Maybe this sailor is different, and doesn't frequent courtesans."

She smiled at him, puckering her lips: "Sailors are all the same, I'm told."

"Not true!" he protested.

"Then why are you holding me like this? In front of this entire public?"

"Because I love you."

She folded her arms and turned her head away: "You sailors always say that!"

"Cross my heart and swear upon the ghosts of Marathon!"

"Marathon hasn't happened yet."

"Oh, I forgot. Well, then…"

She caressed his hair in her hands: "Well, maybe you really are a different kind of sailor…"

He nodded vigorously.

"But then I'm a different kind of Courtesan! Why can't I be a courtesan? If you can be a sailor, I can be a courtesan! Besides, it was just my fortune's lot that it happened that way, see?"

He sighed: "So be it. Actually, you're really built like one."

"Of all the nerve!"

He looked down at the imaginary hat he held: "You're crushing my sailor's cap between your breasts, Chris."

"Hey, sailor, it's me you're after, not my body, remember? You're supposed to be in love."

"Can't I be after your body, too?"

"Us courtesans think that's very *passe*. You'll have to love me on a higher plane."

"Flying planes haven't been invented yet."

"That's the worst joke I've ever heard, Cameron." She kissed him.

"I think it's the worst one I've heard, too. Now, about your body"

She arched her back: "It's nice, ha?"

"Yes," he replied grudgingly. "I'm jealous of all those, those"

"Those what?"

"Whatever those men are that use courtesans."

"Needn't be, sweetie. Courtesans just take it all in stride. Means nothing really. But only Officers, of course—you're my first midshipman, or whatever."

"How can you tell I'm not an Officer?"

"The uniform and insignias, dummy. And you don't have one of those Admirals' saucer-shaped hats."

"That's because you just got through crushing it there," he said.

"I love you even if you're not an officer."

"You do?"

"Yes," she paused, "yes, I do." She looked at him, "now let's go into the Acropolis, sailor."

Marble slabs lay scattered in rubbles about the barren square rock of the ancient city fortress; they slept in silent bulks, alone on a hill carved out of time, hoarding the memories of distant legends.

"Look at it, Cam."

"I see it."

"I feel strange here, Cam. What do you see?"

"Arrowheads, shields with gods of thunder, men in a circle singing, drinking wine from hollowed pumice rock; olive sacks bending mules' dusty backs."

"You too?"

He nodded: "We've been here before, my courtesan, remember? Now let's visit the rest."

"Maybe we really have," she added quietly. She took his hand, and they climbed over the rocks. "Shall we go see the buildings from the center first, or from the outside walls, Cam?"

"How about the walls? Then we can see everything around it first. It was how this place was built—as a monument to this land." He touched the smooth outer walls of the citadel and looked down. There was a precipitous drop. The limestone hill of the fortress rose like a solitary rectangular slab of mountain carved supernaturally out of the plains below. Gnarled olive trees grew at its base, so distant he couldn't make out the branches. He dangled both feet over the edge.

"You seem different now," she observed, "your shirt's all wet and clinging to your back. You look strong."

"And I won't tell you what's clinging where on you—they look good, though. I guess you courtesans never do wear bras."

She blushed a little. "No need to wear one, really."

"Can I touch them?"

"Out here? With all these people?"

"It's all right. I'm a sailor on leave - it's to be expected."

"But I'm a shy courtesan."

"Only a kiss, then, and you can sit here on the inside of the wall."

"You worry me sitting out there, Cam."

"Me too." He sat awhile silent.

"What are you thinking?" she asked.

"I'm afraid of heights."

"Then why are you sitting there?"

"Far off, where the plains open at the foot of the mountains, do you see a trail of dust?"

"I see it."

"The advance column of the Persian host."

"Already?"

"Yes."

She sighed. "We don't have much time left then. You'll have to leave with the fleet."

He shook his head: "I can't leave you behind."

"What are we to do then?"

He glanced over the plains: "I don't know. Look at them, they're spanning out now, covering the entire plain."

"It's amazing," she nodded. "They say Xerxes counted two million men as they crossed the Hellespont. And his fleet is many times ours."

"It's oddly beautiful in a way: All those men marching onto the land… banners, cymbals, colors, flags…that's probably Xerxes there, surrounded by his Immortal Guard."

"Are they really immortal?"

"They say so."

"Aren't you scared?"

"Of course. I wonder why they're coming here, though, to this place."

"Don't you know why?"

"I guess I do. But I don't understand it."

"So we can either stay or go," she said wistfully. "It's very beautiful here."

"We stay, then. Let's visit the rest of this place. We don't have much time, my lady."

Most of the structures had been leveled: Foundations, pieces of columns, slabs dozed in the sun, as if still expecting men's hands to set them aright. To the east, two solitary olive trees cast shadows over a fountain. People drank from its stream.

"Beautiful!" Chris leaped. "Is that a well?"

"Yes. Amazing there's still water in this rock, isn't it?"

"How long will it last, Cam? I mean water during the siege?"

"Not any longer than these walls."

She was quiet for a time. "How many people were inside, Cam?"

"When it happened? About two thousand, men and women. The ones who refused to flee."

"What happened to them?"

They met their accidents of fate, Cameron thought. He looked at her: "About the same that happened to these buildings, Chris."

"And how many days do we have left?"

"Five, I think."

"We better love a lot now, ha?"

They went to the fountain and the water was cool and refreshing. It ran down his shirt as he drank.

"I wonder why they didn't escape," she mused, "when they saw Xerxes' armies covering the plains below."

"Same reason we didn't—look around you." The downing sun left scattered fingers of light, a sun's twilight sacrifice to the earth, over the columns of the Parthenon.

"Yes, it is beautiful, Cam." They sat on a rock; she touched it, feeling it slip under her fingers. "Do you know, Cam, maybe we really might have been here before."

"Yes."

"Sometimes, it really feels like it. Seriously, Cam," she shivered a little, "I can feel those five days we have left."

Cameron looked over the distant plains, the mountains, and the sea. He didn't say anything.

"Isn't it strange, Cam?"

He turned to face her: "It is strange Chris—I love you as if I've loved you before, and always loved you." He held her, feeling her chest press into his.

"I'm so happy, Cam, I want to laugh and sing. They'd think I'm crazy, though. Would you?"

"Sailors and courtesans don't care what others think. They're just happy."

"So you don't mind me being a courtesan anymore?"

"With a body like that, maybe it was preordained. Now I just want to run off this mountain with you and jump into a fur-lined canopy bed."

"You beast!"

"That's what you get for being a courtesan."

"Promise?"

"Furs would be too hot here, though."

"I don't care about the furs, Cam. It's good to just be with you—like playing when we were children, so happy and nothing mattered then."

"That's all well for you, Chris. But my lips are hurting."

"From kissing?"

He nodded. "One more thing you ought to know, Chris."

"What?"

"Your breasts have buds at the ends."

"But they are small...You okay with that?"

"Hmm, yes. The corners of my mouth have had it, though."

"You're absolutely terrible, Cam!" she pushed him away. "I don't understand. Sometimes, you're just crazy and happy, then suddenly so serious, sad. I can see it, Cam; I feel it. I wish I could understand it better."

He shook his head. "Why can't we just stay happy like children?"

"I guess because we finally see the things around us," she said slowly. "Then afterwards we have no choice but to live them. Perhaps, after understanding them better, we can be like children again."

"That would be nice."

"It's funny, though..."

"What?"

"When we first met, it was you who thought I was sad, Cam."

"You were, Chris."

"Most people don't see that. Maybe they're just used to looking at my body first."

"I confess I noticed it too."

"You were too sad to see it then, love. You really were a different kind of sailor, sitting there alone."

"I don't think I was feeling sad, just thinking then. Or rather, not thinking."

"It hasn't been working, has it, Cam?"

"What?" Cameron was startled by the directness of her avenues into his mind. Her eyes rested quietly on his: "So what are you really, Cameron, besides my sailor?"

164

"Just someone in love with you. Nothing else at the moment. And you, Chris?"

"Life's history?"

"Sure. I'm listening."

"The usual childhood, nothing traumatic: I was a tomboy, lots of friends, also liked to be alone a lot. The rest was usual too: Basketball cheerleader, yearbook co-editor, proms, so forth; nice picture in the yearbook as a runner-up princess."

"Only runner-up? They made a mistake."

"I was a rail then, Cam—same height, only twenty pounds less."

"And?"

"That's about it."

"There must be more."

She didn't reply. "What about you, Cam?"

"Oh, traveled a bit, with my parents. First to Australia, climbed a lot of trees there. Mostly eucalyptus, on a land flat as a pancake and bone- dry in the summer. In winter the fields would flood over and the water extended as far as you could see, except for the small mounds and islands of eucalyptus trees."

"Did you like it?"

"Sure. Great place for a kid—all the room in the world to roam, no cars, freeways, or anything for miles around."

"Kangaroos and koala bears?"

"Yep. And iguanas fat as crocodiles. They hung onto the trees like huge scales of darkened bark. Lots of rabbits, snakes, and magpies, too. My dad killed a tiger snake once, right under my bike. But I guess nothing ever seems very dangerous to a kid. And what else about you, Chris?"

"Well, parents got divorced, mother remarried, I was sent off to college at seventeen."

"That's it?"

"Sure."

"College where?"

"Florence." "How was that?"

"Didn't finish, and I wound up here," she smiled.

"And in between?"

"Studied art, classical history, went to parties, caught the sunshine at Capri, and was generally stuffy for a time—you know, doing 'the scene.' Then I did some thinking, but not enough, I guess."

"Why do you say that?"

"The real world, away from books and school, was a shock."

"Did you see your parents much?"

She shrugged. "They had their own world, I developed mine. They sent money. That was it."

"What else, Chris?"

"I liked Florence, the art and history—always did like that stuff. What about you? Where did you pick up on Themistocles and Salamis and Marathon—in Australia climbing trees?"

"Maybe the discipline for it, yes. It takes a lot of discipline to climb eucalyptus trees properly."

"Will you show me some time?"

"Sure."

"Then you left Australia?"

He nodded: "High school, college in the States. Track, debating, cross-country—I was always too slow in cross-country but somehow managed to sprint at the end to keep from losing; then a little rowing on fours and eights, med school"

"Did you finish?"

"What?"

"Medical school."

"Yes."

"And internship and all that?"

"Yep."

"Then what are you doing out here?"

"Drifting, I guess."

"But why?"

Cameron was silent. An evening breeze stirred the coolness trapped under the olive branches. Maybe, he thought vaguely, it had something to do with butterflies on a summer road.

CHAPTER 17

THE GIFT

He walked to the balcony. It was still dark. Cool. Humid. Stars clung to the rooftops of Athena's city.

He watched her curled asleep in the moonlight, her hair like threads of a precious soft metal brought from a distant place of riches and laughter. He touched it, then returned to the balcony.

He felt as if on top of a mountain, wishing he could lift the stars one by one, and store them in his arms. He watched her asleep until they paled, and the city opened its smile of dawn.

She was drying her hair with a towel in front of the mirror. "I think we should leave, Cam," she said suddenly. Her glance came back from the mirror into his eyes.

"I don't see why not. We've been in Athens long enough."

She smiled and continued to dry her hair.

"I thought you wanted to go to Delphi, though," he added.

"Changed my mind. Can't we go to one of the islands?"

"Sure. Which one?"

"Doesn't matter. You pick one out while I go back to my place and pack."

"You want to leave today?"

"No, tomorrow's all right. Any island we can reach tomorrow." She tucked in her blouse in and pressed the snap of her jeans.

"You're crazy, Chris."

She tackled him, landing on top of him on the bed. Her slim waist curved above him with her knees to either side of his chest. He pulled the blouse out of her jeans.

"What are you doing?"

"Undressing you. Breakfast has just been served in bed." Her blouse undone in front, he put his hands underneath. She lowered her neck and kissed him. "You don't mind, do you, Cam?"

"Mind what?"

"I already got the tickets!" She leaped out of reach like a bouncing forest animal, tucking in her blouse. "What's that?" she smiled slyly.

"That's what happens when you're on top of me and suddenly leave."

"Sorry, sailor. Got to go. Lots of things to get done before we leave."

"Why did you get the tickets, Chris?"

"Why not? It was my idea to go, wasn't it? Or are we going to get stuffy about it?"

He pounced on her, pinning her wrists onto the bed. "What are you?" he growled as menacingly as he could, "some spoiled little rich girl?"

"Maybe. Does it bother you?"

"Maybe."

"Are you going to let go of me now?"

"No."

"What are you going to do?"

Hands still on her wrists, he began to undo the buttons of her blouse with his teeth.

Afterwards, she stood up and tossed her hair from side to side to untangle it. It always got curly like that. He zipped up her jeans: "There. So what time are we leaving?"

"Day after tomorrow, nine-thirty in the morning, Olympic Airlines to Corfu. I'll meet you at the airport, Cam."

"I thought it was tomorrow."

"Nope. I have to pack all kinds of stuff. Besides, it'll be more romantic that way—we can pretend we're first meeting on the plane."

"You're crazy, Chris," he shook his head. "I'll walk you home."

"No, you stay here. I'll miss you, Cam. It will be the first time we'll be apart an entire day."

"Two days," he corrected.

"I have to leave. Can you stand it?" she smiled mischievously.

"Not too well."

"I'll even leave my toothbrush here, Cam."

"Thanks, almost as good as a picture. I'll pack it with my things." He jumped from the bed. "But I do want to walk you home."

"No, we agreed, remember? You aren't going to walk me home."

"Why not?"

She shrugged her shoulders. "We agreed, that's all."

"I don't understand it."

"Nothing there to understand. Meet you at the airport, Cam. I love you." She said it, closed the door and left.

People stood shoulder to shoulder, with baggage being lifted over other bags and over people sitting on the floor at the airport. Cameron wondered how romantic it would have been to meet Chris here for the first time. Meeting her anywhere would be romantic, though. He gave his backpack one final push, and slipped into place beside three other people at the Olympic Airlines counter. "Have you seen a girl, curly auburn hair," he motioned to the shoulders, "very light eyes, American"

The girl behind the counter gave him a blank stare, then returned to the rest of her besiegers—some with tickets, some without, all speaking at once and attempting to get their bags at the same time onto the weighing counter. Good God, Cameron thought, whose idea was this? How would he ever find Chris here? He tried to talk to the girl again but was cut off. The girl gesticulated with her hands, pushing away bags; she could barely catch her breath. Suddenly she looked at him briefly, and gave a wide grin. Her hand shot out motioning him over.

"Cameron?" she asked.

He nodded.

"Let me see your passport," she glanced at the name. "Here, Mr. Cameron," she returned it with an accomplice's smile, "and your tickets. Your fiancee is really a beautiful girl. Congratulations."

He stood there holding the tickets. "Thank you..." The girl was already facing the crowd, forehead perspiring, hands waving about in the air.

Cameron walked to the gate for his plane, and waited. He glanced at his watch—ten minutes. Five minutes later, he thought of paging Chris. There really wasn't time left. He stared at the ticket, seat 9D. His pack was already on the plane, along with her toothbrush. He looked at his watch again, then at the plane parked on the runway. He walked out into the hot wind, and stepped onto the boarding ramp.

She sat straight, staring ahead, her hands over her chin. "Chris! I nearly missed you! What's "

"Sit near me, Cam." He noticed her hands shaking. He took them in his. She was crying.

"What is it, Chris?"

"Nothing, Cam. Nothing. I'm happy, that's all. It's just me, and I'm happy," she said holding her hands tightly in his, and kissed him.

"Tell me a story, Cam," she asked later.

"Like at the Acropolis, about a sailor?"

"A happy one, Cam."

"Sure." A happy one, he thought. It struck him he might not know any like that. He looked at her and realized he didn't understand any of this, except that he had to come up with a happy story.

"All right, Chris, put your head here; that's it, on my shoulder. So," he began, "there was a little boy once, who lived in a place so remote that more animals than people lived there. He was too young for school, or maybe there weren't any schools there, so all he had was time to look at things and go wherever he wanted. There were no fences, roads, or machines, and nothing anywhere to make him afraid. In the mornings, after his mother's large breakfast, he would walk across a land flat as the palm of your hand and listen to the music of thousands of cicadas, though he could never see one. Banded colors slithered swiftly through the grass, occasionally raising their heads shyly to watch him, but never close enough so he could pet them; he wondered how they moved so fast without feet, or maybe they had little tiny feet, and he wanted to ask them about it. Heavier things with shiny scales moved huffing and puffing on chubby feet, then panted on rocks or under the shade of trees. 'Iguanas...' he called to them, and they would roll an eye in his direction, their mouths open in the heat. Some things moved very fast and others slowly, some with bright colors, others blending so well he practically touched them before they moved. A caterpillar arched his back, moving like a spring, then raised his head high on a few rear feet, swaying back and forth. It was one of the silent beings, the boy thought; maybe also blind, because of the way the caterpillar had to touch everything before it moved. And there were other beings that spoke or sang, but the boy didn't know their language.

"After the flat lands came green hills, thick as the moss on the trees that covered them. The yellow tail of a cat disappeared without sound into the trees, and deer with small white faces froze into their stillness.

"Then the hills flattened again, and the heat disappeared. The boy would watch a blue rippling color that never ended; it lay under the sun like a blanket of quietly laughing silver. And he would climb down towards it, a cool wind across his face. Each day the boy tried to reach the white-foamed fringe that washed the edges of land, and on days when the wind was very cool and he began early, it seemed as if he would almost get there. Large birds with scooped wings soared lazily above the blue; then they would dive like kites in a silent splash he couldn't hear from the distance. They always rose in a while, to fly low over the water.

"But the boy never could reach that blue place. The sky turned to gold, and he had to turn back before darkness. On days he was really late, white fingers of fog moved slowly between the trees and over the hills; and he liked watching it though he knew it would be very late and cold on the way back.

"It happened that each day he came closer and closer to the sea, until he decided one day he would reach it, even if it became completely dark.

But he felt strangely tired that day, even before starting downhill. Try as he might, at last he realized he wouldn't even get as far as the days before. He turned back to climb over the hills, and it took him longer than any time previously. It was pitch black when he arrived home. He wasn't allowed out for many days afterward.

"When he began his usual journey again, the boy barely reached the top of the hills overlooking the sea. Despite the breeze of the mountains, he felt very warm. He lay on his back, watching the birds fly above. Later he tried to reach the blue shore, but had to turn back in a very short while.

"Days passed like this, and the boy didn't understand why it was harder now just to reach the green hills than it had been to get closer to the sea. He was still glad to reach the hills, though, and watch the silver blue below. He would wipe the sweat from his forehead, and rest in the shade watching the sea laugh in the sun. It was too far now to see the scooped birds dive in the water, but he could still make out their white splashes offshore. Rabbits still hopped on padded feet with their fluff-bouncing ears, and thick iguanas still rolled their eyes at his coming. He understood now why their mouths were always open, because it was so hot.

"On a day when the green covered hills were still ahead, he smelled the eucalyptus scent spread warmly over the chirruping sounds of cicadas. He took off his shirt. He felt good knowing he'd soon reach his perch on the hills. But for now, he stopped to rest, and spread his shirt over the dry grass to lie down.

"A crow's croaking woke him; the boy rubbed his eyes to remove their sleepy darkness. The dark did not go away. The boy sat up. Bellowing of frogs rose and fell. Tiny bright dots winked above. It was cold. The coolness felt good. Curiously, he watched the sparkles above; they were stars. He lay back on his shirt, and followed the sprinkles of light move slowly over the trees. Only when it became very cold did he realize he should be home.

"The next day his parents took him to a place where people were dressed in white, and everything was very quiet. It seemed hard to walk even the length of the corridor to his bed. It was strange, but slowly he began to realize he would never again reach the places of rabbits, banded colors, swooped wings, dark green moss, and the sun's blue laughter. He understood that part of it now, that his legs could no longer take him there. But he still remembered those places, and he didn't mind. Because there was nothing to mind, really, as long as he could remember them. And the rest was just something that was happening, and he watched it slowly happen.

"Slowly, too, he saw that each day he moved less and less. In the same way he understood at some time it would all have to stop. From his bed he now watched the people in white, others in white with needles for his arms, and his parents coming to visit. He knew some day even that would stop. And when all movement stopped, then it would end, and it wouldn't last any longer than that.

"That didn't make him feel sad, only very tired and sometimes very hot and sweating into the sheets. Sometimes, just sometimes, he would wonder why it was happening: He realized he must have done something wrong; something that had made things happen like this. And he wished he could remember what that was, and hoped it was nothing he had done on his walks, because he had never wished to do any harm to the animals and trees."

From far away, Chris pressed his hand: "It's a sad story, Cam."

"We aren't to the end yet, Chris. Just listen." He resumed quietly: "One morning, someone came and told the boy there was a gift for him. His parents wrapped a blanket around him, a muffler about his neck to keep him warm, and carried him to another room. The gift was there, they told him. He opened his eyes wide to see it.

"But it wasn't there. Try as he might, he couldn't see one. Not wanting to disappoint the others, the boy was silent.

"'Don't you like your gift?' they asked.

"He nodded in bewilderment, looking about the room again for a small package. Still he didn't see it. It had to be a small package, he knew, maybe with a ribbon on it. But he didn't see one. He tried again: A small sofa, a table in the room, two chairs, a silver rocking horse with mane swept back and red saddle, a cupboard, a small bookstand... no package. The boy could see he was disappointing the others. Maybe he should go back to bed, he thought.

"Then someone pointed in the direction of the rocking horse: Two feet high, a flowing white mane from arched neck and feet outstretched in full gallop, its large black eyes stared back at him. The boy didn't understand at first. He'd been looking for a small package—that's what a gift would have been for someone who'd done something wrong and couldn't move from his bed.

"Yes... they motioned again, that was his gift! The boy slipped from their hands and walked slowly to the horse. He placed one hand on its white mane. Maybe, he thought, just maybe, it really was for him. And then, if it was, perhaps he couldn't have done anything very wrong after all.

"Inside him, the movement that all this time had slowly been stopping, began to reverse itself. That night, looking into the eyes of a silver horse, the boy understood it was waiting to take him over the green hills to that blue place of the sea."

"Cameron, where is that story from?"

"The place all stories come from, Chris. Now put your head here and go to sleep."

CHAPTER 18

THE COLD

He moved with crutches on the dirt mountain path, throwing one leg in front, bringing the crutches ahead. The pants were folded upon the right leg quite above the knee. A fine dust rose as the man repeated the process on a sunny and dry green hill, on a path above the sea.

Flowers were bright red and gold near the sea. Low tide lapped against the wooden pilings. Bees buzzed around new blossoms, and two pigeons flew overhead with a sound like wind draft. Chris dropped her dusty shoes and dipped her feet into the water. "Wow! Look at this place!"

He sat on a log's edge and looked back into the hills.

"What are you thinking?" She brushed her matted curls away from her eyes.

"Nothing." He touched the iron gate on the old dock. There was no one here now. A dog with dirty white hair long like a sheepdog's passed by with a limp, panting. The sun shone obliquely from the hills far away, embracing the tiny dots of houses like a mother. A warm breeze careened off the water and lifted a gull into the air. A few boats swayed, moored in the clear water, and a rowboat bounced under the pilings of the old wooden pier. Seagulls shouted and cried to one another.

"Tell me, tell me, tell me!" she splashed her feet in the water.

He watched his hand move under the clear water. "That man reminded me of something."

She lifted her feet from the water and came to sit near him. "The one legged one?"

"Yes."

"Cameron," she touched his arm, "look at me."

He didn't blink.

"Cameron, there isn't enough warmth in anyone's heart to let in all the world's cold."

"What do you mean, Chris?"

"Why have you been traveling like this, Cameron?"

"Like what?"

"When I met you, Cam."

"No reason."

"You've been a wanderer for years."

"Maybe."

"What's it all about?"

"That's a good question. I don't know."

"Why did you leave everything like that one day, Cam? What did you leave behind?"

"Car, an apartment, books, my dog…I'll always miss my dog."

"No, I meant, what are you trying to leave behind you?"

"How do you know I haven't already done that?"

"I just know."

"Then I don't need to tell you," he smiled evasively.

"You are going to tell me! You beast!" she squirmed, "get your hand out from there! I want a straight answer."

"I thought that was an answer."

"Playtime's over," she took his hands out and adjusted her blouse firmly.

"Oh, no!"

"Yes, it is. I'm serious. I'm a part of you. You're like a wounded animal still bleeding. I can feel it." Her tone surprised him. She might as well have been describing herself.

"It's nothing that complicated, Chris. I just don't understand how to say it."

"Understand what?"

"I don't know how to tell you, Chris. Maybe on a New Year's, a long time ago, I would have known how to say it."

"Why then?"

"I wanted to talk to someone."

"About what?" she persisted.

He shrugged.

"How was that New Year's, Cam?"

"I should have met you then, Chris. Actually nothing really happened, which was all right, since that girl never did shoot McGuire."

"What?"

"Oh, McGuire was an intern with me. A girl came in quite drunk at New Year's asking for him, and he was off somewhere else. I think she would have shot him; there was a gun in her purse."

"What about you?"

"I got her out of my room as quickly as possible, and went to sleep after the noise and celebration of midnight was over."

"Perhaps I really should have met you then," she smiled.

He returned her smile: "I would have had to work the next day, Chris." "That's all right. You'd have been a bit tired—but you interns can take it, I hear."

"I suppose so."

"How was your internship?"

"Sometimes at night, after finishing rounds, we'd play poker in the lounge, next to the phone, until one of us was called. One guy smoked cigars, another fitted his scuba gear ready to dive the next night with underwater lights, and McGuire usually told jokes, then bedded down with one of the nurses 'til five. At five he'd chuck them back out to the nurses' dorms—and try to get some sleep from five on. You'd have liked him, too, Chris—nice looking, wide sparkling grin, big floppy mustache and green eyes with dark hair."

"I don't like to be chucked out at five o'clock in the morning."

"*You* he probably wouldn't have, Chris."

"How do you know? It wasn't you, was it?"

"Do I look like I fit that description?"

"Only a big more wholesome, but not much," she eyed him suspiciously.

"Well, it wasn't me. I wouldn't throw anyone out at five into the cold. People bump their heads at that time in the morning."

"No, you probably wouldn't. Still, I would like to know how many got as far as morning, Cameron."

He didn't answer, staring now straight ahead over the blue water: "Sometimes when we played poker, and before the night was over, I wondered how the odds ever came that way. Once while counting my winnings, a midnight call came in: I didn't know who it was at first—just a name over the phone. It came back vaguely. Then very clearly. When I got to the exam room he was already sitting on a chair, a teenager with round face, large ears, buck teeth. I had seen him many times before.

"He looked thinner that day, eyes wide as he spoke my name from the right side of his mouth. I didn't know where to begin—I never knew, with him. I asked how he felt. That was really stupid.

"But he just answered and said as best he could that he hadn't passed out today. He had just been dizzy and unable to talk awhile. He was getting better now, he said. His speech was still slurry, especially from the left side of his mouth, and his face on that side was swollen and motionless. His wife, a girl of seventeen herself, touched his face and said another lump had appeared at the bottom of his cheek. It was a firm two inches wide. I finished the exam by looking inside his eyes. The swelling from the tumors in his brain had begun to come out through the discs of his eyes.

"His wife had brought him for his medications, you see. She was still very calm, her hands on his shoulders. But her eyes moved quickly and her breathing was fast. She was seven months pregnant with their first child. They came to the hospital for his medications so he could stay home the rest of his time before the end. But it kept coming, you see, coming to beat him to the birth of his first child. How hard he'd tried to win was written on his face.

"So he'd come back again that night, for his medications as usual. He trembled as his speech choked. He wanted to know which arm I would use—the thin right one full of holes where the medication had already gone to treat the tumors, or the left one, swollen, cold, and white. The fingers still moved, see, he showed me. He moved them somehow.

"I suppose there was still room for another needle somewhere. I looked for one, not wanting to tell them. I did tell them finally, though. I told them he should stay in the hospital for that night. He knew what it meant. He rolled down his sleeve, nodded, and she tried not to cry."

"Cam " Chris began.

"I went back to the poker game afterwards, you know. There was nothing left to do. Except wonder how the odds ever came out that way."

She was silent awhile. "Cameron, it couldn't have always been like that. Good things must have happened too."

"Sure," he paused, "sometimes. Many times. It's strange how you don't remember that as much, though. I liked Pediatrics, you know, that was happy at times, and I never really got tired of seeing kids."

"So what happened?"

"Nothing."

"What do you mean 'nothing'?"

"I quit."

"Why?"

"After internship came Vietnam. I was called for it, went as my duty, returned. The world afterwards no longer was the same place I had believed in. I tried it a while longer, but I guess it didn't make sense anymore."

"How didn't it?"

"I can't explain it," he searched for words, "a bunch of things: One night I was repairing a gash on a man's face; it was two inches long, above his eye. I was in an emergency room, suturing slowly so the scar wouldn't show. The man talked all the time; I let him talk. He got to the part where he'd been in Vietnam, and how many men he had shot. 'How many did you kill?' I asked him as I sutured. 'Many,' he answered, 'so many I don't remember.' 'Are you proud of it?' 'Yes,' he said quite naturally, 'I shot them down like dogs.' And I was suturing him so carefully, you see, so he wouldn't have a scar."

Chris was quiet.

"Afterwards I just began to watch things happen, Chris, without trying to change them anymore. Something inside was gone. That's it, I guess."

"I felt that in you," she finally said. "Cameron… a cold sea of suffering floats out there. You chose a place in the storm, you saw worlds extinguished in a day, in the flash of an eye," she glanced at his eyes. "I can say I understand those things; but you actually felt them. But along the way you forgot, Cam, that there's only so much cold you can let in, that everyone's heart needs some warmth left intact to survive. There is no one without limits for how much cold, suffering, and despair he can let in before that cold stops his own heart from beating."

His gaze returned to hers: "I think… perhaps understand."

She touched his face: "I won't leave you, Cam. I won't leave you until the sunshine again has touched your smile."

He put his arm around her shoulder and watched the boats gently sway in the tide. A seagull landed on a wooden piling, tucking in its white wing tips. "What about you, Chris? It's your turn now—there's a cold that sometime touched you."

She stared past the rusty gate into the sea. "I guess we all fall into the traps of our past. I don't know—sometimes it doesn't even feel like it's past." She shook her head, hesitating: "My story's much more simple, really. I fell in love with someone " she paused, "who died. That's it. That's all," she looked up.

"I'm sorry. Was he a young man?"

"Yes, a young man. Almost a boy."

"Why would a boy die?"

"You know of those things better than I."

"I'm sorry. I shouldn't have asked that."

"It's all right."

"You still love him?"

"I'll always love him, Cam. He died" she stopped. "He died. It was so senseless."

"I'm sorry."

"No," she said, "don't. It is over. It's all right. He was a boy, and I was a girl, and we still didn't know how things could end. You understand, Cameron? Maybe I've learned now," she looked at him, "to love in a better way."

"I don't ask that."

"I couldn't love you less, Cam," she said strangely, "it's the only way I can love you. And we both need the warmth now."

For some reason he still wanted to know how he had died. A morbid medical curiosity, perhaps. He hated himself for it. Cameron didn't ask any more questions. She clasped her hands about his neck: "I love you, Cam."

CHAPTER 19

ANOTHER UNIVERSE

The road crackled softly under the tires. Her head rested asleep on his lap. They were returning from the southern part of the island.

Under the headlights, the cool darkness unwound hills and hedges, dark shapes, silent moon-apparitions shadowing the journey back. The night road curved ahead. Wind blew in through the open window and touched her hair.

A car. A night. A road back: He smiled.

Chris rubbed her eyes: "Where are we?"

"Back home."

"Already?"

"We've been on the road two hours, sleepy head."

"Wow!" she stretched, "I feel good!"

"You should. You put away half the restaurant and an entire bottle of Cambas."

"That much?"

"No less. They even serenaded us before we left."

"I remember—a beautiful little place in the middle of nowhere."

"Remember the flat tire over those rocks on the way back?"

Her eyes enlarged: "No, Cam, I must have really been out!"

He smiled, "There was no flat tire. Let's go to bed." It was hot and they used a single sheet over the twin beds they had pushed together.

"It's so quiet here, Cam."

"Yes."

"Listen to those frogs."

"Yep."

"And the wind from the ocean..."

"And the huge mosquitoes—one of them almost carried you off last night, Chris. By the way, do you have your 'Off' on?"

"Nope. Tastes terrible."

He got up and stumbled in the dark. "You'll taste just fine," he patted it on, "all right, now turn over."

"You're a sex maniac."

"Hey, slack! I'm just putting on some mosquito repellant."

"You know what, Cam?"

"No. What?"

"I'm happy. I mean, really happy."

"Good."

"It's so quiet and beautiful and simple here."

"And you're not really sleepy at all."

"Are you?"

"Grrrowl..."

"You're ferocious, Cam."

"I love you."

She leaned her chin on his shoulder: "How long do you think this will last?"

"Forever."

Her fingers traced the outline of his collarbone in the dark. "Really?"

"Of course."

"I thought you never made plans, Cameron."

"I did once. But I stopped because journeys weren't ending in the places I thought they would, and there were no maps for the places where they ended."

"And now?"

"Now you're here, Chris."

"Listen, Cam"

"Hey?.." He touched her back, slippery under his hand.

"All we have is our time together, Cam. If anything should change, just take the best of it with you, and never look behind. Will you do that, Cam?"

"Chris?"

"But always carry your maps inside, Cam. It's good to know what directions go where." Her warmth pressed closer to him, and he held her in the dark.

"Chris, is everything all right?"

"I'm happy with you, Cam. I'm happy in our time."

He was going to say something, ask her something. He felt her face close, and the droplets on her cheeks. He just kept his arms around and held her close.

"Cameron?" she whispered.

"Yes."

"You know what it is tomorrow?"

"Full moon."

"Are we going to do it, just like we said?"

"Sure, Chris. We'll climb it and meet the full moon. Now go to sleep."

"Are you hot sleeping close like this, Cam?"

"Yes. But I wouldn't have it any other way." Long after she'd fallen sleep, he was still awake. He wondered what she had been trying to tell him. He wondered about many things that wouldn't keep still: Hospitals, images of a past, the way things turned. Perhaps he'd just been around too many wrong turns.

They woke late. Chris peered over the sheet drawn under her chin: "Morning, sweet."

"Morning."

"Who's first in the bathroom?"

"That depends on whether the toilet is plugged or not."

"Sorry about that, Cam."

"That's okay, Chris. I unplugged it last night."

"You did?"

"It wasn't easy."

"I can't help it if I was constipated for five days, Cam!"

"We'll just have to change your diet," he laughed, "or you'll plug all the pipes in this town!"

"Very funny," she shrugged. "Anyway, it's better than getting the trots. Do you think it might have been the wine?"

"It really isn't you, Chris," he said trying to control his laughter, "we just need more water in the flushing reservoir."

"Right."

"But in the meantime, you'll have to go outside..."

She hit him on the shoulder.

"I was kidding, Chris. Anyway, I got it all unplugged, and we can both go in the bathroom and take a shower now."

She jumped out of bed. "What if I plug it again?"

He plugged his nose: "Then it's going to be a lonely shower and you'll have to scrub your own back."

"Since when do you ever scrub my *back*?" she accented the last word and smiled.

"Well, I get around to it eventually, don't I?"

Their clothes dried outside the open window and they took a shower in the small tub with a hand held spigot.

"I'll fix breakfast while you dry your hair."

185

"Such service. Eggs Hollandaise?"

"Over easy and with lots of butter. Will that do?"

She nodded.

"Don't you like my cooking, Chris?"

"It's not that, Cam," she burst out laughing, "I was just thinking how you were able to go in there and unplug it."

"Love conquereth all things. Dry your hair."

"Then I'll pack our picnic basket—are we coming back from the beach before we climb the mountain?"

"Probably; we should pick up some extra clothes. It might get cold up there."

They returned from the beach and repacked the knapsack with food and a wool shirt and sweater. "Where's the wine?"

"Right here. Only it's not wine - champagne!"

"Good God!"

"Why not?"

"Cheese, knife, salami, bread..."

"Right. Fruit in there, too."

"You know how to get there, Cam?"

"Of course not."

She looked at the map: "Two ways, one through Petalia and hiking from there; or driving the longer road by the ocean near Aghios Spiridon, then going up. Either way it's quite a hike to the top. It looks steeper from Aghios."

They took the wrong way: By eight in the evening their rented VW sat over boulders that looked like leftovers from a pyramid. They backed slowly out over a narrow road and returned to the ridge with a small trail ascending the mountain.

"You think that's it, navigator?"

"It's going up, isn't it?"

"Let's leave the car here. We can still make it before midnight."

"Full moon won't be until 12:23."

He patted her behind: "Then we have all kinds of time."

"And all kinds of inclinations."

He looked at her in halter top and cutoffs, leaning against the car: "Why, Chris, the thought didn't even cross my mind," he said innocently.

"Pretty convincing," she nodded looking down, "except for that," she pointed.

"What? Oh, that...well, it's...a Spartan message staff. Let's go up the mountain for a peace parley."

She pulled off her knapsack: "We can go up later..."

"But Chris "

The trail to the mountain was wide and empty; the bone-dry bedrock climbed silently in a sea of coarse bush. In the twilight air, ordinary shrubs opened previously invisible small flowers into the cool folds of night and tumbled out their scents. Gravel slipped under their feet.

"I feel lightheaded, Cam."

"Why?"

"I don't know. I'm not really tired."

"Too hot?"

"No. It's all right now." A pink hue remained to the west. "Is it going to be dark when we get there?"

"I think so." A bell rolled over the silence, echoing. A bearded goat hovered comically with its four feet cramped over a small rock. Under its neck shook a copper chime. The rest of the flock scattered along the path, followed by a shepherd with staff and face invisible under his hat. It was quiet again.

"Aren't you cold in those shorts, Cam?"

"My legs never get cold. Look at that valley, Chris. Strange in the light of the moon "

"I'm scared, Cam."

"Why?"

"Because there's nothing out here, yet anything could really be here."

"Anything?"

"It feels like quite anything could be here."

Cameron laughed, "Then we should be prepared for anything. Dragons with fiery breath, stalking tigers, ghoulish ghosts"

"Don't make that voice, Cam. It scares me."

"All right. Come here. Give me your hand."

"What would you do with a ghost, Cam?"

"That's simple - I have my entire anti-ghost outfit with me."

"Really?"

"Yep. See that bottle of champagne? 1971, a good year."

"So?"

"In the time the ghost takes to drink it, we split."

"But *I* want the champagne, Cam."

"Whoo, whooo, whoooh" he intoned, "we're here!" The wind swirled in desolate gusts, blowing over darkly sculpted forms; rocks balanced upon barren rocks, as if they had just rained from the sky. They were on top of Mt. Pontekrator.

He removed his knapsack. "Put your sweater on, Chris."

"It's already on." She was shivering. He took his wool shirt and settled it over her shoulders. "Let's find a place away from the wind."

"Is it full moon yet?"

"Twenty minutes to go."

Black shapes of other islands squatted over the water far away. An unbroken chain of mainland hulked behind them like an antediluvian apparition through the night's lunar haze. Around them circled the space of an ocean—dark, flat, unknown. An occasional sliver of silver moon streaked the legend around them.

The moon became full. The valley floor dove in a V cleft, a lighted wound into the folds of the mountain, eerie with moon shadows.

"It's amazing," she said. "Like a day; another planet's dim day, and the wind from another universe."

"And we're the only ones here."

CHAPTER 20

THE SONG GOES ON FOREVER

Olive trees. Mountain slopes under a noon heat like fire. Not even the air stirred. Rock-terraced walls put up by hand over centuries circled the folds of the mountain. The mountain floor found shade under a forest of olive trees. Sunshine fell like drops distilled through their branches.

"Stop it!" she wiggled, "that tickles!"

"It's supposed to...Hey, wait!" he contorted under the sheets, "that's not fair, I'm more ticklish!"

"Only here," she said, "it's totally fair."

"God, I don't want to get out of bed."

"Neither do I."

"What time is it?"

She looked at his watch: "Eleven. Hey, Cam, we've been all over the rocky part of the island. Let's go to the sand."

"Where's it sandy?"

"The western beaches of the island."

"Is it sunny?"

She parted the curtains. "Of course."

"Is it going to be sunny there?"

She rolled him over: "Get out of bed you lazy sailor, out of your bunk! Reveille!"

"They never pulled on *that* for reveille before."

"I hope not. Out, out! You've got distant shores to conquer, towns to plunder..."

He promptly dove under the covers again: "Sorry, I'm a lover, not a fighter."

"All right, then. The first two ships have already done all that. You're on the third ship."

He peeked from under the sheets: "What do I get to do then?"

"Well..." she sat coyly on the bed, "let me see—pillage, plunder... what's

left?"

"Conquer!" he leaped from under the covers like a true Viking. His hands fell on thin air: She'd bounced deftly out of his way, smiling behind the doorway.

"Got you up, didn't I?" she said.

"Us Norsemen don't take too kindly to losing our morsels," he furrowed his eyebrows fiercely.

"But you're not a true Norseman. If you were, you'd already have caught me."

He pounced once more: Just as he was about to reach her wrist, he slipped on the rug.

"Uh! Did you hurt yourself?"

He closed his eyes and stopped breathing. As soon as she was close, he turned her quickly over the rug. Her laughter quivered under him, her breasts touching his chest. "If it were for Norsemen like you, Cam," she laughed, "the Irish would never have red hair!"

"I'm really quite ferocious in action, you know, Chris. Well, almost ferocious."

She attempted a swift escape.

"No way," he tightened his grip. "Be still, Chris. I'm pondering something."

"What?"

"Punishment befitting attempts to escape from a Norseman sailor."

"I thought you were a Greek sailor."

"Then it would be easy."

"Oh no, you don't!"

"Hmm. Maybe not."

She hugged him. "I love you, come here"

"Right now?"

"Sure."

"I'll try not to slip on the rug this time…"

She placed her arms across his neck: "I don't think you will"

They were back in bed. "What time is it now?"

"Two thirty."

"Geez!" Her legs stretched under the covers.

"Now look who's not getting up."

She put up her hands: "I'm just a prisoner, sailor, remember? From a sacked village."

He looked at her: "Sacked is right. Aren't you ever going to get up?"

"That's what I kept asking you," she smiled.

"I thought I was up."

"Oh, no, you don't! Not again!" She jumped out of bed quickly. "That's it. To the showers!"

"All right," he moved closer.

"Keep away from me!"

"I promise…a shower, Chris"

"You promise?"

"Absolutely. Actually, you've really done me in."

"Doesn't look like it."

"Come on, I'll wash your back."

They dozed under the sun. He turned his head and watched her lying on the flat rock beside the clear water. Pebbles glittered all the way from the bottom. Her skin was shiny from lotion. She was turning brown. "I thought we were going to the sandy part of the island, Chris."

She turned over and settled again. "Not enough time. Tomorrow."

"You're getting burned there; they're turning red."

"You won't be able to bite them anymore."

"Nothing there to bite."

She looked at herself wistfully: "That's true. Not exactly a feast, ha?"

"Actually, Chris, any more and never mind, bad joke."

"What? Tell me."

"Well, it actually happened, see; someone came into Emergency and"

"And?"

"He had lockjaw, you know. On one side only, but he had it, all right, and we had to use all kinds of muscle relaxants to reposition his jaw."

Chris looked at herself: "Well, you've got nothing like that to fear here, Cam."

He opened the bottle of wine. "Where's the bread?"

"Here. How many apples left?"

"One."

"That means neither of us will have it, Cam, because it's the last one, and each will want to give it to the other."

A crunching sound came: "Have a bite."

"Cam, you're turning practical again!" she said excitedly.

"Sure. Haven't I always been?"

"Yep. Hopping on moon pebbles and watching the clouds from above."

At night they walked to the end of the beach: A river's mouth flowed past the rocks and away into the distance. Stars from the dark sky reflected onto the calm ocean; the river's end fell into the sea, rippling their reflection. They stood outside a restaurant over a cliff by the trees. The ocean could barely be heard. Beach tents and campfires hovered like fireflies below. He balanced on a timber in the sea mist, and lifted her up. He held her in his arms.

"What are you thinking, Cam?"

"That I've been waiting for you, Chris, from so, so long ago..." A piece of heaven couldn't have been held any more carefully in his arms. She smiled, a signal sort of smile between them, and he knew then that no pain could ever kill that happiness.

They went inside the restaurant, talked slowly, and touched each other's fingers. "What are you going to do now, Cam? I mean later?"

"I don't know."

"Why don't you start again?"

"I suppose I could."

She placed her hands on his: "But remember to keep warm this time, Cameron. At the center of yourself you need to stay warm, and never let the cold in again."

"How do you do that?"

"You do it because you've touched the cold, you've been at its center where it freezes souls, and you've returned. Now you can bring others back from the same place."

"Is that what you've done with me?"

She looked at his eyes: "I would give all the warmth I've ever had, to do that."

"You already have. You're the best that's ever happened to my life."

"Really?"

"Yes."

She looked at him seriously, perhaps sadly: "Will it be enough, Cam?"

"Yes," he replied.

"Remember that, Cam."

He caressed her hand: "You know, once on a ship's bridge, I watched the lightning of bombs burn through a night like it was day. When they stopped the sky became dark again, and our ship sailed a night pebbled full of stars. I felt so small and powerless then: How does one small being begin to make a difference?"

"You're ready to find out now, aren't you, Cameron."

"I suppose so. Losing can't be half as bad as not trying. And this time," he winked, "I promise to bring along my warm long johns."

She gave him a hug across the table.

He woke early. He wasn't certain why, but he was completely awake. Light had begun to seep through the slots of the wooden blinds. He walked quietly and opened the window. Below the balcony, across a small dusty street, the azure Mediterranean lapped calm under the sunrise. In a doorway, a dog rummaged over a bone. A cat rubbed sinuously against a tire. Sea smell drifted cool in the dawn's air. A wagon hitched to a mule with large ears creaked to work below. He glanced around him: In a small room with peeling whitewash she slept curled inside the sheets, her hair sparkling at the edge of dawn's sunrise. It was strange that after all his drifting, at a point where nothing more seemed left, when the future seemed as lost as the past he'd left behind, he'd finally found all there was. He looked over the sea: Small fishing boats set out with their nets, the sun placed its arms over the earth, and Chris was still asleep. He understood now, that after losing everything he had, he really had everything.

She stirred awake and sat at the edge of the bed: "Cameron, what are you doing up?" He smiled, and she saw his face and his eyes in the sunshine.

"I thought you wanted to go west today, Chris. So we'll go west. As far west as you want."

"Cameron," she said quietly, "sit by me." She raised her hands to his face and touched it carefully, slowly, watching him. There was a softness he'd never felt before.

"What are you thinking?" he asked her.

"Are you happy, Cam?"

"Yes, Chris."

She looked at him: "Like that song when we first met," her voice was surprisingly gentle, fragile, "it will go on forever and ever."

He took her hand and kissed it. "Yes."

She saw the sun on his face, and touched his smile with her fingers: "I love you, Cam. Don't ever doubt that."

He took her in his arms and held her for a long time as they watched the eastern sunrise.

They went to the other side of the island. Digging his toes into the sand, he held her over the rolling breakers and kissed the salt from her lips: "Shall we leave for town soon?"

"If you want, Cam."

"You're getting burned. It's hotter on this side of the island." They toweled off and ran uphill to the main road. He watched her skip barefoot and the arch of her back. He caught up and placed his hand inside her jeans pocket. "You have a beautiful back, Chris."

She smiled and preened: "You mean I have a good ass?"

"That's a better description."

"Property of all good courtesans," she shrugged, "we can't help it."

"I've got an idea," he nuzzled her.

"What?"

"What if"

"What if what?"

"If I take a ring from the sea and make you this sailor's lady."

She looked away. "Sorry, sailor. Nothing but officers, you know. Maybe in a few years, after you've distinguished yourself"

"Then I will, my lady," he touched her hand to his lips. "What ten perilous tasks are assigned to me?"

"You don't understand," she looked at him.

"What?"

"I mean, courtesans can't wait that long. By then," she patted where his hand was, "we'll no longer be as nice." She laughed and darted away.

He caught her by the waist. "You're right, I don't understand."

She looked at him, but he didn't recognize the look in her eye.

"Shall we go into town for lunch?"

"How about by that old castle near the canal?"

"Sure."

She hummed. "What day is today, Cam?"

"I don't know. The 23rd, I think."

She was silent and looked wistfully at the canal with bouncing small boats moored at the opening to the sea.

"You're not very hungry, Chris; haven't even done away with your quota of wine."

"Pass it on, sailor!"

"We could go on into town and pick up some things. After all, if we're going west, we'll need"

"Are you really going to do it then, Cam?"

"Sure. Might as well start again sometime. You want to, Chris?"

"Oh, Cam!"

"Are you happy?"

She was crying. "Yes, Cam, yes."

He placed his hand on her shoulder and dried her cheeks: "There you go again, just like at the plane. Please, Chris, you worry me when you cry. Even if you're happy."

"I won't cry," she stifled a sob, "I promise I won't."

"Good. Shall we go then?"

"Let's go home, Cam. I want to be with you."

In the evening they had dinner on a restaurant's terrace by the sea. The town's lights winked far away; vines climbed along the side shielding the sea wind. They sat by an open fireplace and music played from somewhere.

"It's nice here, Chris. I'm glad you picked it."

She pressed his hand.

"A toast," he lifted his glass, "to the navigator that brought me here."

She drank from her glass and looked at the fire. It blazed brightly in a smoke-colored brick hearth. He followed the gaze of her eyes: "What do you see, Chris?"

"A cave...white ice all around. A fire, crackling warm, pushing back the ice fields"

"What else?"

"Men and women huddled...a child in a corner, shadows Their faces are coarse, worn of cold; their hands ragged from wood and stone tools. Their eyes are empty days, nights of hunger. But they're not cold," she said as if surprised at what she saw, "the wrinkles on their faces aren't frowns. Someone takes the child into her lap the child extends his hands, smiling, cradled safe in someone's dusty arms" She paused. The music carried a Spanish tune, *Vaya con Dios, amigo* she turned away. The tune faded, *Vaya con Dios,* my love...

"What about you, Cam?" she asked. "What do you see?"

He hummed the tune. "Wait a minute," he said slowly, "Yes. You are right, their eyes are not cold. They are strange, patient; they watch the small child's hands extended to the fire's warmth They've waited for ages, for the emptiness of ice to melt And before that another ice, before even a fire was there And above the ice in a hall of gods, mead flows in the sun's reflection, while god-feet walk on mountain clouds with wings of gold. They quaff and laugh as a transparent lyre plays to the vaults of heaven. But there...in a corner of the heavens, a dusty brown hand reaches up...Scalding and burning, silently it removes a piece of fire from the rocks of heaven. He descends slowly, carefully, face and mouth tight and still, cradling the fire over sharp rocks and cold distant crevices - never spilling a twig - nor uttering a sound's breath that might disturb the sacred fire.

"By all rights, he deserved the thanks of men and gods alike: From the ones, for having thought of it; from the others, for having done it. Instead, a vulture gnaws forever on Prometheus' insides...While his opposite, Epimetheus, having loosened the plagues of hell, lies in a soft bed of silks " Cameron patted her hand and laughed: "I'm sorry, Chris, I got carried away. Legends, tales of a past: Tales of games of an ancient time, told by ancient men who played by different rules. Isn't it strange they'd make up legends like that?"

A lady with an armful of flowers stooped over their table. He picked a white rose, lifted Chris' chin, and tucked it in her hair. There was a glistening below Chris' eyes. "Hey, are you crying again?"

"It's the story, Cam. You know I cry at stories."

He touched her cheeks. "But it hasn't ended yet, Chris," he took her hands in his. "You see, legends and stories have their own rules, and life and dreams have others. I spent a long time in those different places;

and sometimes I believed, and at others I stopped believing. But there is something that goes on, something you taught me, something that's no longer a dream, Chris. And that's how the story ends."

"How's that, Cam?"

"It's a very simple thing. But you'll have to stop crying first; you promised not to cry."

"Yes," she looked at him, "I did promise." She added quietly, in a barely heard whisper: "...But I didn't think anything like this would happen."

"Are you sleepy, Chris?"

"Yes, Cam. Let's go to bed."

He held her close that night, their faces touching, like they had been from their first night in Athens. He had a long dream, of legends, halls, castles, and an Acropolis burning down: In the flames, smoke, and walls crumbling around them, he needed to reach her to tell her of the end of a story, of a song that went on forever. At last, she was near him, her signal smile returning his: "Are you happy, Cam?" "Yes," he replied. "I love you, Cam," she said calmly. He saw her smile again like that, and he awoke.

She was gone.

CHAPTER 21

THE THIN CATS OF ATHENS

The moon was a deep orange, rising; the sea quiet, glass. Gulls flew and boats returned. Fishermen docked by the pier and laid out their nets to dry. Clouds passed in shrouds playing the sunset and new moon for their colors of evening.

It was as if nothing had changed at all. Everything went on as it was.

Cameron felt sleepy, his head heavy. Was it still a dream? He shook his head: Doors and windows were closed. He got up and threw them open… Daylight: What did you expect? he asked himself. He held his head under the cold water tap and reached for the towel. Maybe she'd gone to the store—stores were already open at this hour. He checked his watch. Yes, they were. So she'd just gone to the store. What was the matter with him, anyway? She'd be back soon.

He took a stroll along the shore. He returned past noon and the room was still as he had left it: Towels untouched, curtains unmoved. Her things were still in the drawer, her toothbrush on the cupboard. He felt strange now. He put on his hiking shoes to walk to the airport. It was positively stupid, though, he thought: She was probably exploring some unknown part of the island, scampering over rocks like a goat. He took off his shoes and tried to take a nap. Even so, she had always told him. Something could have happened to her—unlikely, but it could have. He sat up and tied his shoes again, wondering where to start. The western part of the island? The mountains? Even by car it would take all day. He needed to get to the airport and rent one. Better yet, he would call.

"Yes, sir."

"Avis, please."

"This is Avis."

"I would like to rent a car."

"What kind of car?"

"Any kind."

"Yes, sir. We have"

"Are you at the airport counter?"

"Yes, sir."

"Did any planes leave today?"

"One, sir. To Athens, nine o'clock," said the voice.

"Hmm. You wouldn't happen to know if any Americans were on board?"

"A few, sir, I think."

Cameron tried to describe her: "Twenty-four, slim, jeans"

"A young girl, without baggage?" asked the voice.

Cameron felt cold inside his chest. Skipped several beats. Numbness. A strange sensation. His throat tight, he tried to describe her again.

"Yes, yes, I think so," the voice said. "Now, will you be needing a car?"

"When is the next plane to Athens?"

"Tomorrow, sir."

"Nine o'clock?"

"Yes."

"Please book me on it." He gave the voice his name, then hung up and sat down. Steady, Cameron. Sit and think. He paced instead. Then began packing. Within ten minutes he'd thrown his things together and her toothbrush. He sat and thought again: What if she'd gone to Athens as a surprise? It was a surprise, all right. She might even be back tomorrow—some reason, some crazy reason women have... And what if it wasn't Chris at the airport, and she was sleeping under the sun on some beach of the island?

What if it *was* her?

The chill slowly moved inward, shook, slid like a glacier spreading across his left chest.

Why?

He tried to think. He couldn't think.

Why?

Process, he thought—damn it, Cameron, use a logical process of thought! First things first: He needed to find if it really was Chris on the plane; if it wasn't, she could be in trouble somewhere on the island, and he'd have to search systematically, inform the police. If it *was* her... Cameron stopped. If it was her, he'd need to think again.

In either case, he had to be logical. Case in point: He had to give an accurate description, have some way to start the search. So how does one describe a beautiful girl: "Excuse me, I'm wondering if you've seen this beautiful girl " he said out loud. Great, just fine; that would really do fine. He whistled suddenly—he remembered that a boy at the town square had taken their picture, kissing. She'd laughed, and the boy had scrambled away. An instamatic, an old box camera - who cared? He needed to find it, find the boy. Piece of cake in a town of ten thousand.

The next day Cameron found him. The picture verified that Chris had left for Athens. She'd used another name on the passenger list.

"Yes, that's the girl."

"Did she have a return flight?" he persisted.

"No, sir. One way."

Cameron slung his backpack over his shoulders and climbed aboard the metal-winged enclosure bound for Athens. He left behind, in the room they had been, an address of a hospital in the States.

On the streets of Athens, searching for faces, looking at waists, hair of that certain color, a certain walk, waiting for a face to turn, it finally sunk in: She was gone. He sat on a park bench and realized Chris was gone.

Night came but not sleep. He was in his old room in the city. Their room. He got up after a few minutes each time he went to bed. His mind had no thoughts that came clearly—only that she was gone. Cameron went outside and began walking under the lights of the streets. When the lights turned to morning he still walked, making mental notes - of what - he couldn't remember. He passed the swollen body of a dead dog twice; morning restaurants opened, streetsweepers combed the streets, bells chimed on produce carts. It was a gray, lukewarm morning. He opened his coat to the wind and rubbed his hands. He wasn't tired— there were still places to go, streets to feel underneath, time to pass...

With newly found energy he bounced across the street and recommenced the journey. He didn't stop to examine where: He retraced his paths haphazardly, back to the main square, spanning again the rest of the city randomly. Like a shadow he paced, covering walks of dirt and stone. Time and hunger didn't exist. Until sometime at night again, legs stiffened and hands shaking, he finally stopped and sat on a sidewalk curb.

Why? he asked himself again. He turned and looked at his shoes. Slowly he stood up and began walking back to wherever he'd come from.

The same room: Shadows played in the balcony, forms; laughter and her back and waist in the moonlight, her eyes on his...He couldn't stay. Without direction, he tumbled out once again into the night.

It passed by as if motion didn't exist—a night and a day and a city like a series of long hallways. Fleetingly he recognized the alleyways, bridges, and colors of signs. Keeping his hands in his pockets kept them from shaking, and the legs no longer felt pain. At some corner he stopped and gazed at colors: Neon flashes, blue, orange lights, brighter orange, yellows, greens, red. They were all there. He picked out a sign with colors and bottles on the entrance, and moved in that direction.

On a beach at Piraeus waves with white sounds at night washed ashore. He lay on the sand. In the darkness, there was a rolling inside him like a river searching in many directions for the sea. It was too bad, he remembered, that it had happened on that night when he'd felt the happiest in his life. And this time, he'd lost his love by trying to keep her. He pulled the bottle from his pocket and looked at it in the moonlight. He raised it in a toast: "To you, my lady, and a song that goes on forever."

Silence. Pebbles answered over the shore. Slowly the bottle did its work, and he dug a place into the sand, away from the wind, to sleep.

In the early morning he awoke to a rain that parted almost as soon as it had begun. He shook his clothes and took off his coat. The city rooftops shimmered moist under a morning sun. Clean wet cobblestones slid under his feet on the way back. It was still summer, and the sun would soon be driving city dwellers towards the beaches.

Sitting on a wooden bench at a bus stop, his clothes made whorls of drying vapor. He took his hands out of his pockets and looked at them. They still shook. He tried to control the shaking. They steadied somewhat.

All right, that's more like it. Now you know she has left.

Yes.

Why?

That's for another time to find out.

But for now, you have to decide.

Yes. That decision has already been made, a long time ago.

All right, I know that. What's next?

Eat, clean up, then find her. Turn the world upside down. But find her. This time with a method, a process, with reasons and places to start. Just like Diagnosis 101.

That familiar thought sent a chill inside him: What if...she was in a hospital somewhere? It had crossed his mind before, when she'd talked of maps, journeys, and their time together. Was that what she'd been trying to tell him? Surely he would have noticed something, a symptom, a pain, some detail...Through his racing brain paraded the list of gruesome enemies: Lupus, lymphoma, leukemia, Hodgkin's... There would have been a sign, though; she had appeared well, lost no energy...Still, it was a possibility.

He began a systematic check of the hospitals in the city. This time he didn't want to find her: Not that a wheelchair or her skin pale and drawn would have made a difference to him. He just wanted to see her. A smile grew on his face as he walked past the last hospital's stone portals: Nothing yet. So wherever she was, she was healthy, not in a hospital. The thought kept him happy for the rest of the day. He kept the thought to himself, quietly inside, as if even the wind overhearing it could change that luck.

He watched ships being unloaded by the city's port. Sailors moved about, leaving their ships for the city. Cameron smiled. Perhaps he really should join the Greek fleet. He could sail or go someplace else—it wouldn't make any difference now, he had little chance of finding her here. He had already checked the passenger lists daily, they knew him at the airlines by now, and he didn't even need to show the photograph anymore.

So what else was left?

He wired the island.

Nothing.

Anything else?

Cameron returned to his room. There had to be some clues: He dipped into circuitry of the past, words, gestures, her smiles, crying at times, the way she looked...The first time she had looked like that, when she'd asked him to promise, to promise no tomorrows...Why?

He jumped up: Cameron, you've been blind! He paced agitatedly about the room. She'd been trying to tell him all along, and he'd never caught on! "Cameron, carry maps, always carry maps..." And the shadows on that first day they met, and on the plane..."When we no longer have it, then we no longer have it..." He repeated the words over and over to himself: She had been attempting to tell him, in her own way, that she would remain to rebuild his past, while he rebuilt her present. Then she would leave.

But why?

Electrons clicked, jumped over voids in his brain; possibilities raced through his mind: He rummaged through every conceivable plot, every misfortune, fortune, or soap opera, and even simple solutions. He laid them out before his mind and examined them.

Now to test them.

At last, he was thinking again, stepping from place to place, with directions, moving from possibility to probability. The first place to cover was her method of disappearance: He had checked buses, trains, planes, and ships. She could have also left by car. But he had been to the rental agencies also. Or by private car?... There was still another simple solution: He went to a private airstrip. He took the picture from his wallet and placed it on the counter.

The man took it between his fingers: "Yes, sir?"

"Did this girl leave a few days ago?"

"Very pretty girl," the man said, "hard to forget someone like that, eh?" He looked at Cameron, then the wallet.

The customary monetary lubrication of hands and memory ensued. "Was she here?"

"Yes."

"Where did she go?"

Requirements for further lubrication.

"To Istanbul."

Cameron thought and paused: "With someone else?"

"Yes. Two men."

"Can you describe them?"

The man behind the counter looked at him curiously, as if in a cat and mouse game. His whiskers were sleek as he smiled: "One older, one younger—you know, strong, big—a valet or bodyguard."

"Bodyguard to whom?" Cameron asked.

"Why to both of them," the man smiled. "The young lady is married."

Cameron controlled himself well. The man glanced in his direction: "Don't you know who he is?"

"Should I?"

"Sandeman, Mr. Sandeman. I thought you and the young lady... well, in the picture..." he glanced at it again.

Cameron removed the picture from the man's fingers and returned it to his wallet.

It was Cameron's last night in Athens. He had not been able to sleep in their old room. His bag was already packed and he opened the balcony doors onto the street. He lay on his back in the bed.

She came to him, her arms around his neck, and kissed him slowly. There was softness in her movements as she touched him, and the same softness in her lips and voice: "I love you, Cam."

Waking up he felt sadder than at any time since. It had been more real and slow than anything he could have ever imagined in life.

Looking back over the balcony, rooftops, and streets in the morning light's leaving, the same thought struck him as at first: The cats were very thin in Athens, and the pigeons extended their wings on the sidewalk to cool them from the heat.

CHAPTER 22

A TRAIL

Floodlights fell on Piazza San Marco's Cathedral. Rows of gilded pillars drifted evenly into the night. Under the new moon, domed ducal palaces yawned empty, its ancient inhabitants, traders, pirates of caravels, alive only in the stone eyes of a long tailed lion with wings, alone on a pedestal for centuries - the lion of Venice.

A band in white tuxedos played violins in the square. A camera crew made a movie, rolling silently with microphones and lights following their characters. Two couples, oblivious to the cafe crowds and movie crew, danced on the square's tide-moistened cobblestones.

He sipped the dark Venetian coffee and tried to fit together pieces strewn over cold, warmth, and time. Watching the movie takes, he realized how strangely fact and fantasy weaved with each other.

Tonight Cameron waited. It was the closest he had ever gotten. Always he'd been days, weeks behind: At Istanbul the private plane had landed and left again before he'd even arrived. In Venice he'd finally caught up. There were four of them now—Chris, Sandeman, and two others. He'd seen her tonight. The sight of her had taken his breath away. After his momentary hesitation her light blue dress disappeared within the polished teak cabin as the motorboat pulled away. She probably hadn't even seen him. Perhaps the others had, though: People had stared at him as he ran to the edge of the dock while the boat bounced away on the irregular chops of Venice's canals. When it was out of sight, he turned away from the ocean darkly lapping the improbable stone-rimmed city, and returned to his hotel.

He was getting closer now with each day. Perhaps finally close enough to test some theories. Cameron purposely didn't arrive at his hotel until late. He checked the mailbox—nothing. Checked the doors and windows—no one had been in his room. In a way, he was disappointed. Nothing had happened.

What if something had? What would he have done? He had no plans for that. Only an improbable theory, and nothing yet that he could do about it. Cameron brushed his teeth, fluffed up the pillow, and lay down.

"I'll always love him, Cam," she had said of the boy, the boy that had died. "He was a boy and I was a girl, and we still didn't know how things could end...He died...It was so senseless." Or had he died? There was also Sandeman: Seldom seen; between planes, limousines, yachts, almost invisible; talked of in international consortiums of wool, liquor, petrochemicals, Sandeman's hand extended wherever power and money could reach. Perhaps it had also extended over Chris and the boy she had loved. In that case, he hadn't succumbed to some strange disease, or met some untimely accident. In its own way, perhaps it had been an accident: Planned by Sandeman.

Well, it was an improbable theory. Ridiculous, actually. He himself knew little of Sandeman directly: Power, yes; money, yes; bizarre methods to keep accumulating both, yes. Answers for the rest would have to wait.

By sunup Cameron was already checking the boat docks; if he hoped to catch up with Sandeman it had to be soon. Sandeman had unlimited funds and time to keep traveling, Cameron was running out of both. By evening the Venice hotels had yielded nothing, and the boat garages and docks had failed to turn up the polished teak boat.

Cameron took the ferry from St. Mark's for Via Roma - it was the sort of happy place that Chris might visit. In the ferry's wake the city appeared strangely compact, solid by the edge of the sea, yet somehow fragile—like a lily pad that could be reclaimed at any time by the sea. In a churchyard by the water several boys played soccer; boats bounced in open garage vaults at the entrance of homes.

Cameron turned and saw it: To the far right of the red fire station boats, inside a freshly painted yellow "garage", was moored the teak boat. Cameron got off at the next stop and retraced his steps. A young man tended the boat. Aquiline nose, light green eyes under dark shocks of hair, tautly pale skin—everything about him looked Venetian, from the way his nostrils tested the sea air to his casual sea-supple stride on the boat. He'd been Venetian bred for generations, and as such, wasn't likely to be one of Sandman's men.

"Hello," he motioned to the young man on the boat, "do you rent this?"

He was startled to find Cameron on the narrow gangplank, then just shrugged, "No."

"It is not for rent? I believe I saw some tourists aboard yesterday."

The young man paused a moment from his chores. The boat was spit-polished above the waterline. Cameron jumped on, extending his hand: "Hi, I'm John Cameron."

The sailor couldn't conceal his annoyance, but reflexly extended his hand. Venice was a formal, very polite city. "You must not be on this boat, sir. It belongs to someone."

"Oh, then it is not for rent. I'm quite sorry. Do you mind if I look about a bit? I'm thinking of buying one like this, or perhaps building one." Without awaiting a reply, Cameron swung around the railing and below deck. He glanced around rapidly: A pair of movie tickets in an ashtray, a pot of coffee, a portfolio...The young man was indignantly behind him.

"Mister..."

"Cameron, John Cameron, dear chap." He gave his name again on purpose. There was no point in hiding it. Perhaps it would facilitate Sandeman's hand. That would bring him closer, which is exactly where he wanted him to be. "Yes, a beautiful boat indeed. How much would this run?"

"You must leave immediately, Mr. Cameron."

"Well, of course, I shall go. Do you wish my card for Mr. Sandeman? It is urgent that I see him. You see, I wish this boat as a prototype—I'm sure we can arrange something. Where is he staying?"

"You must go," repeated the seaman, "Mr. Sandeman allows no one on his boat."

"Then where could I see him? I must talk to him immediately."

"I know not where he stays."

Cameron complied with the tug on his shoulder and followed the seaman on deck. It was a polished and slippery deck. The sailor's splash ruined the carefully polished sides. Cameron dashed back into the cabin towards the portfolio. While the young man angrily sputtered sea water and groped for the ladder, Cameron rifled its contents. There was the record of a telephone call on hotel stationary: The hotel's name, Saturnia International. Cameron stuffed some papers in his pocket and tossed the rest onto the boat. "Thank you! I wouldn't let Mr. Sandeman know someone's been around his boat while you were on guard!" He winked and waved goodbye.

The Saturnia International Hotel had the same quality as the teak boat—sparklingly in wood tones polished from top to bottom. Except for the marbled entrance which was vacuumed every time more than five people walked across, the walls and beams were made of ship's timber and appeared like the interior of a ship's cabin. Sandeman apparently liked the sea. Cameron strode in rapidly and deliberately: "I wish to speak to Mr. Sandeman."

The clerk was dumbfounded: "I...We don't give out our guest list."

Cameron continued without pausing: "Is Mr. Sandeman still here? There is a girl with him. I represent the girl's family," Cameron opened his wallet, "detective; the family wants to find her whereabouts. What is the suite number?"

"They're gone, sir," the clerk blurted out, "they all left this morning."

Cameron could have smashed his knuckles on the desk. "Do you know where they went?" he asked calmly.

A shrug returned from behind the desk. "We are not in the habit of inquiring about our guests. Mr. Sandeman is a welcome guest here."

"I shall let you know if I require your further assistance. Thank you." Cameron gave a short bow and left.

Damnation! He'd lost her again. Cameron walked into the first cafe he could find, and with pencil and paper began checking over the rest of the portfolio papers he had in his pocket. He would follow Sandeman as far as necessary: He didn't know how, he didn't know where, but he would.

He returned to his hotel to pack. There was an envelope in his mailbox.

It was from Chris.

CHAPTER 23

DESERT MADNESS

A fine dust blew, settling within the makeshift tent. Through the opening he could see the camels' elongated necks, detached eerie shadows in the desert haze. Behind them was a void - a transparent mirage. The shadows pulsated in the afternoon heat that fell like sheets of glass shattering on sand.

How long had it been? A month? Three months? A year? He didn't remember. Days, months had telescoped in and out, beyond the realm of calendars. There was no time in the desert. Time was something at the end of a compass needle, pointing in one direction, N.E. 17. All he knew was that he needed to get there.

Why?

Silence. He didn't remember that either. There were no answers in the desert. It was why he had stopped: To reorient himself. Reorient himself? A strange smile crept over his lips. Yes, he had to be careful: One could travel alone in the desert for only so long, without being careful. He hadn't realized that at first. He had covered a distance he didn't know, over a time he couldn't guess, on his way to a place he'd never seen. His mind had been sucked dry like the desert sand around him.

He had stopped now, to repeat his coordinates again - N.E. 17 - and to repeat the other coordinates of his life. The wind settled. Only small whorls remained playing on the desert floor. He felt the grit on his palms and glanced from the tent at the dark shapes of two camels. He didn't know much about camels—how much longer would they keep going? His own water wouldn't last for over a week now. And in that time he needed to get somewhere.

Where?

Silence again. He shook his head. Maybe that place didn't even exist.

What had happened? What had placed him here, on a final journey that bore no footprints, left no traces other than his own, eclipsed in a few hours by the wind? What was he following? What would he do when he reached it? He needed to recall what there was left for him to do. He looked at his hands: He needed to recall who he was.

It was strange: Without memories now, he felt curiously free; like a wolf surveying a vast domain of desert that was his, yet never really his, nor anyone else's. That was part of the freedom, and part of the trap. Wolf-eyes continued to watch the even cloud-drifts of sand; distant sunrises placed him to sleep, sunsets and moon shadows parted his eyes, brought him awake, to keep moving to a place only wolves dreamt of.

He nodded, tired from the night's journey. In sleep's twilight, thoughts began, then evaporated again... Something about a fortress, a castle, a hooded cobra slithering down its walls... He bolted upright in the small tent, perspiration over his eyebrows: He saw again the twisted coils, wrapped around the bucket swinging from the water well, sliding with measured deliberation like a clock's pendulum through space. He had fired two shots, point-blank range, and the coils loosened like smooth tendons of jelly onto the ground.

He touched the side of his holster automatically now, peering at the edges of his tent meeting golden sand. Its colors would also be gold, he knew—one had to look for the eyes and dark ribbing of its hood. Carefully, in slow motion, he unholstered the 9 mm parabellum.

Nothing. Not a ripple over the sand. Only a slow wailing of wind past the tent. He re-holstered and wiped his brow with dusty hands, grating like wet sandpaper. Get a hold of yourself. You need sleep.

Yes, I do, he nodded to himself.

But sleep at times like this came only with strange images, jolted out of a past...There was something he still had to do...about the end of a story... miles of desert and a Cobra dangling...He placed his head in his hands. His hands shook. Had any of it really happened? How had it come to this?

I don't know, he answered himself.

Maybe you should find out.

How? Here, in this desert?

Silence. He was getting used to the silence. He was used to images and phrases drifting before his mind. There had been silence even before his guide had died: They seldom talked; it was amazing they had even reached an understanding about their destination. He had met the guide at a trail's dead end, at the edge of a desert town where the name of Sandeman evoked only blank stares. "Sandeman," he had tried once more in a small stone hut, and this man nodded. Nothing else was said. He'd drawn a map and placed a compass on it—an unspecified number of miles into the desert, in the direction of N.E. 17.

They began their silent, steady coverage of miles that same night. The guide never asked why he was going there; and he, for his part,

214

never asked the guide why he was willing to take him. Maybe he'd had his own reasons for going. Not anymore: The guide was dead.

He had buried him. Dug him into the sand of a desert's night after waiting through the day with his corpse. He was used to seeing the dead; but not waiting with them. He would feel their pulse, touch their chest, look at their eyes and close them. But unlike the rest, this one had been *his* guide, whereas of the others, he'd been *their* guide of sorts. In any case, endings before their time, accidents; accidents he'd stared at plenty of times, unable to explain: Just staring, and wondering by what luck, by what act of fate...

Perhaps the guide's death hadn't been an accident after all. They had been traveling all night and into the day, to find a well. Judging by the even tracks they left behind, the guide navigated the desert like a sailor. They found the well at the end of their straight line. The guide dismounted as usual, his normal slate expression broken by a trace of curiosity as he scanned the sand and approached the well. Suddenly, his head and neck lurched back. It was already too late. It was around his arm. He saw the guide grasp its hooded neck, shaking to free himself, while the rest of it uncoiled from the well. The bucket dangled back and forth like a clock in the air.

He didn't know how much more time passed before he'd splattered its hood at close range. He dropped the pistol on the sand and knelt beside his guide. A cross with a knife; a tourniquet above the biceps. He watched the guide's eyes, his breathing. There was nothing more to do. No more tricks of life left to pull out of nowhere. It caught up with him here, again—at the end of the line.

He applied suction; set the tourniquet again allowing the arterial pulse through, but occluding the lymphatic and venous circulation to retard the venom's flow. Still the pulse became fainter. He adjusted the tourniquet. Fainter still. Then fast, in a sudden rush as if racing for the time...It stopped. He looked at the guide. It was easier to look at him now, the understanding gone from his eyes. The breathing, sporadic for the last few minutes, was gone.

Automatically, as if from an indexed stack of computer cards, possibilities sorted themselves before his mind. The process was mechanical, self-circuited, built-in for involuntary retrieval:

Process: Diagnosis, Multiple Systems Envenomation
1. Ventilatory failure
   a) Muscular paralysis, neurotoxic origin.
2. Circulatory collapse
   a) Cardiac arrhythmia and standstill, cardiotoxic, hemorrhagic, and hemolytic in origin.
   b) Vasodilation, neurologic and/or humoral origin.
3. Probably other factors he didn't know about.
4. Probably other factors no one else knew about yet either.

Process: Treatment alternatives
1. Primary treatment - antivenom - not available.
2. Cardiopulmonary resuscitation - end result, envenomation continues longer than life can be sustained by C.P.R.
3. Amputation of entire limb. Repeat: Initial amputation of limb. End result - bleeding, infection.

Process: Neat, logical, clean.
Chances: Nil.

It didn't matter; it didn't matter that he knew the certainty of the outcome. He began CPR. Continued for hours. Sweat poured through his shirt, over the arms, neck, onto the guide and the bright golden sand. The guide's face slowly turned blue. Purple in spots. Where he massaged the chest, ribs had begun to crack. Half open eyes. Where the broken ribs met the breastbone, purple blotches began to seep from the anticoagulant properties of venom. The guide was dead.

It had all been a precise, efficient process: On a certain road, to a certain end, as before. A summation of the past. Instead of the automatic process, he could have held his hand, and asked his name. Funny, he hadn't even known the guide's name: He'd thought there would be plenty enough time for that in the desert.

He waited through the rest of the day's heat, then buried him at night. He took the 9 mm from the sand and replaced it in its holster. Had the guide's death been an accident? Perhaps. He shuddered at the remains by the well's bucket: On either side of the shattered neck hung its hooded ribs, mottled a yellow gold—*Naja Nivea*, South African Cape cobra. Out here? Absurd. Over a thousand miles away. Of course, he couldn't be sure. Nothing was ever certain. Perhaps it was just a coincidence—like the string of coincidences he had finally followed to here. Did Sandeman really live in this desert, by some man-made oasis? Did he know he was being followed? Did Sandeman exist at all?

He sat beside the sandy mound he had dug. What was happening here? Some sort of bizarre game to be played out in the desert? Was he hunter, hunted, or neither one? Everything merged in the desert: There were no differences other than life and lack of life. He'd been lucky so far. It would take more than luck to get him out alive.

Perhaps he was already dead...A short spasmodic laughter turned the camel's heads. He stared at their obsidian eyes. Perhaps this was some sort of game for his soul...No, he realized: He had seen the eyes of the guide, his eyes as death had guided him away. So he himself was still alive; alive and drifting in a desert sea, where memory failed, events, traces, even his own footprints vanished. In a drifting course towards a forgotten dream...

And if he reached it, what then? He had no plans. The desert would probably take care of that, though. It didn't matter. He would go as far as he could. Wolf-eyes lived each day, crossed unknown distant spaces unfolding by night; wolf-eyes watched, moved, and guessed. Wolf-eyes, now tired, slept.

He awoke on his back, his boots out of the tent. He glanced up: A line of reddish hue disappeared into a net of darkness; small, brilliant dots glowed like droplets over a web. Sunset.

It was time to move. He converted the tent into his robe and packed the camels with gear and the remaining water. At the beginning of each night's journey he never thought. Thoughts did not matter then. Realities did not matter. Memories were washed clean. There remained only movement, drifting to compass point, N.E. 17.

But each night before leaving, before starting for a new place that would look just the same as the one he had left, he reached into his breast pocket, and unfolded a note. It was too dark to see now. No matter. He folded it back carefully, and replaced it in his pocket before leaving.

CHAPTER 24

MAGIC

Early morning. No one on the slopes. The wind numbs his face. Along the drop - empty, quiet, shadows. To one edge of the trees, the sun breaks through. He skis there to warm himself. Then into the powder of the forest. Sunlight cuts through the trees. The skis break up drifts of snow. Over one drifted edge he jumps. He turns to a stop:

A rabbit leaps on padded feet.

A butterfly glides up, down, spirals. A white and yellow butterfly, with golden dots and wing tips, at eight thousand feet in a winter's snow.

Why did it come back now?

Why did anything come back now?

So odd in a place like this.

Perhaps it was the fire, he thought. As odd and strange as anything that had happened to him: Fire blue, dark blue in the night, dark, darkest near its heart; edges ice blue, crystal day; its center twilight blue. Strange fire. Alive alone under a desert night.

Where did it come from?

It didn't matter. He'd never seen a fire like that before. He shook his head and turned away; his eyes adjusted to the night. An even dark nothingness—or everythingness. He was the nothing here. He shrugged and watched the stars. A strange fire like the stars above... It was nothing, he thought: One began to see things after weeks alone in the desert; one created something, to fill the void. He touched his arm to the fire. A blister rose. The fire was real.

Of course it was real. One of the camels had stumbled upon the wood tonight, in the middle of an untracked desert. He'd dismounted to light it and make coffee. Only he didn't make coffee after all. One couldn't use or change a blue fire like that. Crap, he thought, just put a pot of coffee on that fire...

Not on that fire.

Then get going. The desert night is for traveling, not wondering about fires. You need to keep moving.

Why?

Silence. He dreaded that question. He dug his palms into the cool, night desert sand. His hands circled and clenched, until it scalded like an ice water river. He let go, watching the silvery specks fall. Tiny silvery specks of sand, catching the light of the moon. Or was it of stars?

It didn't matter.

Nothing much mattered.

What did matter, then?

How the hell am I supposed to know?

Silence. He hadn't really said it. Nothing but thoughts in an empty desert; he was alone with a strange blue fire casting shadows into the night. How much time did he have left? As much as there was water remaining. He hadn't even checked how much that was. Not really any point in knowing. It would last until it ran out, then it would be over. Unless he hit a well. With the death of his guide, it would only be by luck if any waterholes happened along his course. The guide had taken that knowledge with him.

That also didn't matter. Done, as all the rest. Drifting now, to where he didn't know, along a course N.E. 17.

He stared at the fire again: There with its blue cave-heart, as if silently storing within its being another twist of the road ahead, but without surprises—there were no real surprises left. Roads had led deep and deeper into a darkness he had long ago forgone to second guess: Roads had branched, and he had chosen one of the branches; small roads, dirt roads, fantastic paths with green grasses sprouting absently without the knowledge of human foot. Why had he taken them? It could all be explained, he thought, if one had a place to call end.

He shrugged and tried to laugh. One couldn't laugh out here. The end? What end?

He had a compass, he answered himself. A compass set N.E. 17.

He did laugh now, a strange, mocking laughter, lying there with his arms stretched bare over the sand. He was slowly becoming used to the idea of never getting out of this maze: Perhaps there had been an end once; perhaps he had even chosen roads to reach it. He didn't remember now. It was pointless thinking of it. No roads here, no paths or mountains or forests. Any of that would have been easier. Of all places, he knew this the least—unmarked, untracked, open—desert.

Hear that, fire? I'm lost. Or maybe I'm crazy. Maybe both. He stared into its blue flame, lapping at the edges of night.

Are you crazy?

No, fire blue.

Are you certain of that?

Of what?

That you aren't crazy.

I don't know what certainty is. I haven't found it, fire blue.

Yes, you have. You thought you found it, many times.

You're right. Not many times, though. Only a few. But then, it always escaped.

Has all of it escaped?

Yes.

Every last bit?

I think so.

Think again.

Slowly, he looked at his hands before answering. Yes, fire blue. Yes, it has.

Then why are you here?

I don't know. That, too, is uncertain. That's the most uncertain of all.

You're confusing it all.

Of course. That's because it *is* confusing. It has to be, since it's all uncertain. I don't want to talk of it anymore.

You have nothing left to lose.

That's true. I don't, fire blue. I suppose that's why I'm here.

Isn't that a kind of certainty?

Certainty? I just move. I don't know what will happen at the end. I don't have any idea. You call that certainty? Besides, I no longer want any certainty. It has always escaped. I don't see the point of it. It no longer matters. And I believe that's where all this began—nothing mattering, right?

At least it matters a little, to know why you're here. Otherwise wouldn't it be a kind of waste?

Yes, I suppose so. One doesn't like to think in terms of waste near one's death.

Do you think you'll die, then?

What I think of it and what I feel are two different things, fire blue.

So, be an odds-man: What are your chances?

Chances no longer matter to me.

I guess we won't find any certainty there. Let's try another track.

Damn! You're going to drive me up a wall with this certainty crap!

I'll shut up then.

He paused. No: I can't sleep, fire blue. Besides, I must be moving soon. There isn't much time.

All right, then: I guess you still want to know whether you're sane, why you're out here, where this all might end. Perhaps we should start at the beginning. Your name?

Yes, the beginning...

What is your name?

"John Cameron," he actually whispered it into the darkness. Perhaps even in a whisper it still carried some sort of identity. Perhaps.

Isn't that a certainty?

We're at it again, I see.

Yes. I thought you wanted to know if it's been a waste or not.

All right. John Cameron, that's my name. But that's just an accident, fire blue. A name attached when I was born. It's even an accident I was born at all. Births are as accidental as deaths. You won't find any certainties there, fire blue.

But was it an accident?

That I was born? Of course.

Really? How can you tell?

I guess I don't know. But then, it doesn't really matter.

Look, you have nothing to lose, Cameron. We've already determined that: Nothing to lose, so you can think of whatever you wish to think. Now think.

Well, then: I I know the date I was born, because it's been written in a birth certificate. Also a baptismal record, with middle and first names reversed as I recall. Now none of these are certainties—they're accidents, pieces of paper.

As you wish, Cameron. But what you're recounting are just facts told to you. What do *you* remember?

Remember? Ah! Sort it out now? Everything?

Something, whatever comes to you.

Whatever comes? Why not? A photograph, an old black and white photograph; a baby, a few months old, in white knits, bare pudgy arms and feet, arching backwards, reaching up with his arms...There was a smile on the baby's face.

Go on.

There is a man in the photograph, smiling, cradling the baby in his right arm. A lady in a dress with flowers laughs and holds a string of white pearls above the baby's hands.

Well, then.

Well what?

It was you. Your father and your mother.

Yes, I think so.

You *think* so?

Silence. A second image arrived - another photograph. Two people in a sidewalk cafe, together somewhere on an island...The image remained as the desert night enveloped him, timeless, as it had enveloped other beings, dreams, spirits of ages before and to come, keeping it all within its vast quiet. Above, the stars shook their live silvery spiderwebs, connected by the imagination, fantasy. Like a string of clear white pearls and so very quiet; they were so bright, yet without sound. It was impossible, he thought; there had to be sounds about the stars. He lay still and listened. He could hear them now: Laughter, a good merry laughter from far away, of lives untold, fantasies real, dreams yet unspoken, kept in guard for the future, for other dreamers of distant times and distant places. And each dream was different, yet all were the same in a way—of what should be and could be, but isn't. And anyone past and future, that had dreamt or would dream, plucked them from a place no one knew, but everyone suspected. And the stars guarded their dreams, kept them lit, and laughed happily, because they knew: They knew they weren't dreams at all.

A falling star skipped across the sky. Gone like a match-flame in a storm. John Cameron shook his head. Had he really seen it? Had any of this really happened? Along many roads dreams had been extinguished. Now another dream, once real, faded over a desert's void. And if this dream was nothing, then that was all there was.

Nothing.

Nothing that matters.

Fantasy, stars, silence, desert.

At least, that was no worse than the realities of many others.

Well? The question returned.

Yes, fire blue. He collected himself: Photographs, smiles, pearls, laughter, a kiss in a cafe...Cameron stood up. It was all so long ago. He really needed to keep moving. There was little use in attempting to squeeze certainties out of a past which had brought him into this present.

He paused in front of the fire before leaving. He didn't put it out. After a while, looking back through the night's distance, he saw the blue flame had disappeared.

Had it been there?

Had he seen a falling star?

Desert madness? Night dreams? Insanity? Just fantasy? Or maybe magic?

It doesn't matter, he thought. There is a dream still left.

And if you found that dream? If you found that it was real - would it answer all the rest?

"Ah! I don't know," he whispered into the night, "but that would be magic!"

CHAPTER 25

THE SHADOW

It danced its blue dance. Silent. Unexplainable. Behind it something vague, colorless, shapeless moved - the fire's shadow. Both fire and shadow had come from the same place: Unknown. They were unexpected companions in an unlikely journey of forgotten beginnings, and an end drawing near.

Days and nights had gone by. How many? It didn't matter. Time didn't matter. He needed to keep going. He stopped because the pile of wood was there again—stacked in the same way in his path—lined up like a trail along his course, without tracks leading to or away from it.

He dismounted, unloaded the camels, and unfolded the tent's refuge from the sun. At least it was simple now: As simple as it had been once on a hill, a long time ago, win or lose... He shook his head: Things had become complicated since then; he didn't remember exactly how. But finally, here, it was simple again: One stopped in the heat. Slept. Lit a fire. Moved in the dark. For now, he needed to sleep. Tonight he'd light the fire again before commencing his journey anew.

Star shadows, webs, nets of night. He awoke cold. Releasing the corners of his tent, it swirled over his shoulders and became his robe. He walked to the camels to bring a pot of coffee. The camels were gone.

He rubbed his eyes; searched the place where the camels had been. Only small depressions left in the sand, tracks wandering lazily away under the pale moon. He sat next to the pile of wood. It didn't really matter. Nothing had changed. It was still just that simple: He kept going, he kept going until he stopped. There was no need to stop yet.

Cameron leaned over the wood. His hands shook as he lit it. The flame was blue, blue as the first time. He touched it once to be certain. It was there.

Where was the fire coming from? What was its purpose? Perhaps there was none. It was there, and that was all that mattered. There had been many things before that he hadn't been able to explain. It was fitting now this last journey would be the same. Perhaps eventually, before the end, he'd make some sense of it all.

Blue fire with your blue glance, talk to me again.

Why? About what?

I'm alone here. I need to talk. Can you understand that?

I'm a fire. I don't understand the things of men.

Nor I of fires. Or the things of men. So whether I talk with you or with myself, it makes no difference. Which is it to be?

Silence. He *was* alone here. He and a strange fire in the middle of nowhere. Glancing at his few odd remaining possessions - a canteen, rope, a pistol, a riding stick without camels - he wondered how many miles he had left. An ice-wind swept across his left chest. He wondered what that feeling was.

He moved closer to the fire for warmth. Behind its blue flame, strangely flickering, contorted a dark wizard, a keeper of secrets, a sorcerer - the fire's shadow. He probed its black recesses, attempting to read its unearthly visage.

Who are you, fire blue?

You still do not know, Cameron?

Should I? Have we met before?

Perhaps, Cameron. Perhaps.

Of course, a few nights ago; now our paths cross again. Still I do not know who you are, or why you are here.

Nor do I know you, Cameron, or why you're here. You haven't told me.

Yes, that's true. I don't know myself. Is it what we talked of before, remember?

Yes, I do remember.

Cameron examined the shadow. He hadn't paid much attention to the fire's shadow before: It moved with it, but was apart from the fire, vague, cold, indistinct. He stared at it. There was something familiar about it.

He stared, and the same chill returned into his chest: He suddenly remembered, and understood. It was so pat, so obvious now. Like the times before. Only then, he hadn't really known what it was. Now it finally dawned: The shadow was his death. He had seen it before many times, seen it coming for others. He'd even seen it near himself, before he had known what it was. But tonight, he not only saw - he felt it - he felt himself dead. Not the how, or exactly the when, but an ice-wind continued to spread within his left chest. Gradually, he became used to the cold.

So we have been close before, shadow, haven't we? Many times.

Perhaps, Cameron.

Do you know, dying doesn't matter to me now.

I know. That's why I'm here.

Then you really are my death?

What do you think death is, Cameron?

I don't know.

Yet you say you've seen it, many times.

I have. Still, I do not know what death is.

Nor can I tell you then, Cameron.

It's all right, it doesn't matter, he answered. It was strange to be holding this conversation with the shadow of his death - strange, yet somehow singularly appropriate - here, at the time of the moon's peak, at the absence of the sun's warmth from earth.

But it is different now, Cameron, isn't it?

Yes, I suppose it is.

And you wish to know certain things before you die.

Cameron nodded. The blue flame moved ahead of its shadow. Yes, fire blue, let's talk.

Why are you here, Cameron?

To discover whether dreams are real.

What does that mean?

I'm not sure, fire blue.

Perhaps we should start again at the beginning then.

Yes, he replied. Silence. He realized he didn't know where to start.

You still seem to have trouble beginning, Cameron.

Yes.

Well?

I don't know, fire blue.

Why don't you just begin anywhere?

It's the same no matter where I start: The past is a ruin of whatever certainties you wish to name; the future is spun of dreams; and for the present, look around you.

I see desert, Cameron.

Yes, fire blue. And you can't believe anything in the desert.

Haven't you ever believed, Cameron? In anything?

Maybe.

What was that like?

I guess I believed once that some things mattered.

Like what?

I don't know, fire blue. I guess I don't remember.

You must have thought that what you did, studied, worked for mattered—what was that?

I suppose so: Science, humanities, medicine, the scientific process, people and what happened to them; I thought that made a difference.

Did it?

He shook his head. No, fire blue.

But initially you believed it did?

Yes, I suppose so. I believed that sickness could be healed, misfortunes could be smoothed, that wrongs, at least in some small part of the universe, could be set right again. I believed that the powers of reason, laws, the scientific process, medicine, persistence, were certainties that could achieve those ends. I believed that clues existed, rules could be followed, to prevent the bad from happening, or change it into good.

And what happened?

Nothing. The beliefs lost.

How's that?

Certainties ended, fire blue. Beliefs were destroyed. Accidents, diseases, death took their place. Accidents caused by acts of man, or by whatever controls his destiny when man does not, visiting the earth at random, shot like a bolt from the blue: Visiting beds of white on quiet hospital nights; visiting small dusty villages whose only fault is that they lie along a road one side needs to transport soldiers, and another side needs to stop them; visiting children with beautiful eyes and a bleeding death already inside them; visiting fathers of children yet unborn. Visiting, visiting...maiming, destroying - without reason, without anyone or anything able to stop it - like butterflies broken along a sun-drenched road by machines they don't understand. Yes, fire blue, beliefs lost. A blind deck of cards reigns instead, an accidental machinery of fate that grinds up people and beauty alike through each day's sun with an unpredictable toll. Life is a game without rules, certainties, or promise.

I'm not sure I understand all of it, Cameron.

Nor am I, fire blue. It has something to do with a card game of long ago, something about a large-eyed boy without tears, a man and a rose....

Do you want to talk of that?

No. I don't think it will help to explain anything.

What shall we talk of, then?

Perhaps we have talked too much. I should be moving soon. There isn't much time left.

Where will you be going?

He shrugged and glanced at the fire: I'm not sure that place even exists.

Still, you are going.

Yes.

Why?

It's the only place left, whether it exists or not.

The fire turned slowly to embers. He needed to go now. He had rested enough. Cameron stood up, touched the canteen to his lips; his eyes swept the dark vast expanse. They tried to adjust to the empty darkness, then returned to the place where he stood. He realized now he had reached the edge of his life. And he was finally too tired to go on. He sat down next to the embers.

There was a bit of flame left.

Wait, Cameron, wait: You have forgotten something.

What? He dug his palms into the sand. Forgotten what?

Almost instinctively his hand reached slowly to his breast pocket. It touched a worn and faded note. A photograph fell onto the sand. With coarsened dry hands he lifted it to his gaze by the fire. Then he unfolded the note carefully, and by the fire's last remaining light, read:

Cam

I'm writing you because I could never tell you this in person, and ever leave you again. It was difficult enough to do once.

Do you remember that time when we left for the island on the plane? I tried to leave you then, as I had tried many times. But I succeeded only once - when you were the happiest. I hope you understand why it had to be then. It gave me some of your strength.

I'm ashamed to say I almost made a run for it with you. God knows I wanted it so. But some runs cannot be made without losing one's soul. As it is, part of me will always be with you. I don't expect you to understand all of this now, nor can I explain it. Only to say that had I left with you, I would just as surely have left a part of you outside me.

You must know part of the story by now, or at least guessed, since you have followed so far. You probably know I am married to Sandeman, just as you must know I still love you. To keep that love for you, I must remain where I am. It is something you taught me.

Perhaps it was foolish of me to have ever been with you. Selfish, foolish, and I hope you forgive me. I had guarded against it ever happening, but I really hadn't guessed there would be anyone like you left. I will always remember you as you were on that dawn with the smile in your eyes, and our first and last evenings together. And yes, it was all worth it.

For now, God be with you, my love. You will not see me again, nor receive another letter. It's just too hard for me to do more than once. But in another time, another place, when a song of any language plays in some distant corner of the universe; or a sun, worlds hence, shines upon another Acropolis; or a fishing-boat docks by some remote village; or a broken-down cart you might be driving winds its way slowly over a rubbly street I might be sweeping, our eyes will recognize each other. And yes, even as courtesan and a sailor - we shall know each other, always.

'Til that time, Cam, remember to stay warm inside your heart. And should yours or mine ever forget and become cold again, God grant our love's return.

My Love, Chris

Cameron folded the note exactly as it had been. He stood up. Behind him, a fire slowly dimmed. It was only after a long time, and his stride had already become automatic, that his hand replaced the note inside his pocket.

CHAPTER 26

THE MAN AND THE ROSE

He spent his time in the white bed. He was dying; he was dying all the time, and probably knew it. But no one on the staff was certain that he knew, because no one had really told him.

From time to time he would pick up the dark red rose from his bedside table, bringing it close to his face. When the intern saw him that day, the man's hands were weak. The rose fell. The man's eyes followed the fall. "Ah..." was all he said.

Cameron stretched out on the sand, like the night before. He was tired. Somewhere along the way, he'd become tired. He didn't remember where. He stared at the empty canteen and placed his head on the sand.

There was no blue fire tonight. He simply invented it just the same, with its remote blue glance. It didn't matter now whether the fire was real or not: He was used to its conversations; they were companions in a journey's same direction, if not destination.

Cameron shrugged. So it was one step further now, staring into the night at a fire that wasn't there. But why not? There was no reason he shouldn't think of anything he wanted with the time left.

Like where it had all begun...

It could have begun anywhere.

But was ending here, in the unlikelihood of this desert.

Hear that, fire blue? We need to talk.

Go on, Cameron.

I'm drifting. I don't know where this all started, or where it will end.

No one does, Cameron. I won't find out any sooner than you will.

It isn't that. I'm not complaining. Of the things I've seen, the worst ones didn't happen to me. They drifted past me. Or maybe I drifted past them. That's something I've never understood.

Perhaps it would help to find where the drifting began, Cameron.

He tried to remember: Images of a New Year's past, of a redhead holding a basketball in his hands, a man watching a rose fall...I don't know, fire blue, he said finally. I guess it just all added up slowly.

How?

I saw things happen. I saw them happen, and I couldn't change them. Worlds were born, faded and died each day; entire lives were extinguished without fairness or reason in less than the blink of an eye...

When was the first time you felt it, Cameron?

Felt what?

That uncertainty, Cameron, that end of the line: An end that surpassed all your skill, knowledge, scientific process; the uncertainty that drained like a trailing wound; an end arriving despite all you had given, without any more to give.

Perhaps that's what it was, fire blue. Perhaps that's where the drifting began. It even sounds good. But it is too late for answers now.

Why do you say that, Cameron?

It feels very late.

So you're letting it all go again. As you've done before: Because you couldn't make sense of the things going on around you, because they didn't add up, because you couldn't bundle them up between the laws of fairness and reason—you stopped believing. You didn't find answers to questions, so you drifted. You didn't see love, so you went on alone.

You consider that a form of failure, is that it, fire blue?

Perhaps I am.

I don't doubt that it's a great weakness myself. What else is new? I'm weak—that I can live with.

It's no longer a question of living, Cameron.

That's true.

So let's not talk of time, or how late it is, or all that bullshit, Cameron.

Let's talk about you, about weaknesses, about lost beliefs.

You're right, fire blue. Maybe the beliefs weren't destroyed after all. Maybe I wasn't strong enough to follow them.

And what are you doing now, Cameron?

Now? Staring at an imaginary fire under a desert night.

You didn't always do that, Cameron. There was a time when you braced your back, placed your brain, your being against that machinery of fate. And sometimes that machinery slowed, sometimes it even ground to a halt. You were thrown ten yards back at times, but at others, you moved ahead. Good things did happen, Cameron, changes did come—you also saw that.

He tilted his head: Yes, fire blue, they did. But they couldn't keep ahead of the rest, you see, like the man with the rose... why did that have to happen? Why him?

Tell me about it.

I was an intern then.

Go on, Cameron.

He had a wife, three children, a home, thirty-six years of life on this earth. And a tumor inside his brain. It was diagnosed and operated; removed as well as brain tumor could be removed. By the time he had regained the use of the right side of his body after the operation, the tumor was growing again. Life for him became that of a specialized ward full of brain tumor patients—a year of it. Antimetabolite drugs slowed the tumor's growth, but never really stopped it. He still could feed himself at first, his hands shaking in the journey from plate to mouth, sending the fork into precarious spirals.

"Hel...lo," the man would say at the intern's arrival.

"Hi. You're eating well today," the intern replied.

"Hand moves...moves...moves..."

"Take your time. Keep eating."

"Hand moves...well!" he would say in a suddenly successful lurch for words.

"Sure. How's the food?"

"Food...food...the food..." The man put his fork down in obvious perplexity, trying to think.

"That's all right. Take your time. It will come." The intern placed the dessert tray closer to the man.

"Food..." the man repeated, his forehead pensively frowning, lips forming and reforming.

"No," said the intern, "just eat."

"Food very good!" beamed the man unexpectedly, and his left hand resumed the fork's spiral path.

"Good," the intern nodded, and pretended to watch the TV above the bed, until his patient's meal was finished.

"Children were here today," said the man with apparent ease.

"They came all the way from Sacramento?"

He nodded contentedly. He was a thick-chested man, of curly chestnut hair, moon face, and bristles of a growing beard under his heavy mustache. The mustache gave him a leonine look—a tired lion lying quietly in bed, with a smile always present except when he had to search for words.

"It was pretty good that they came, ha?" said the intern.

"Sure. Good." Large square hands rested on the covers. They were not hands one would associate with tremors or weakness. Suddenly the man's mouth opened again, puckering, sputtering without words. He tried again: "Wren...ched right-o, left them...I...I...I...They shouldn't see....I...I..." It was his worst effort of the day. It would come on suddenly like that, without any warning.

"You were talking about the children," the intern patted the large hand, "you know what you want to say?"

The man nodded, then closed his eyes.

"But you can't always say it. I understand that. Don't try too hard."

He opened his eyes and shook his head: "No. Times some see me mad...No..." He looked down, "no." The right hand rested uselessly on his lap. The left one shook.

"Do you want to write it down?" the intern asked. Sometimes that worked.

"Yes," the man said easily this time. The pen in his left hand traced a few lines resembling letters, then crashed, slashing down the page towards the bottom. The man turned his eyes to the intern. His hand released the pen. "What the hell," the man said with a cracked smile. He lay back and closed his eyes.

The intern thought he should leave.

"Stay," the man said hoarsely, his eyes opening, "Stay."

The intern sat down. At two o-clock the man's wife would return. She was meticulous about that. Then she would stay the rest of the day. She'd gotten an apartment next to the hospital.

The intern glanced at the man: It was strange, normally the brain tumor would have killed him by now. But he had gone through most of the year, many times on the verge of dying, and then on astronomical doses of steroids he improved again. He would improve enough to go home, and in a few days or a week something else would happen: Either slow bleeding as a side effect of the medicines, an infection, or something totally whimsical and unrelated, like a fall or a blood clot, and the man would be back in the hospital for months. This time it had been a blood clot. Strange that his blood had clotted in a lower calf vein—everywhere else it wasn't clotting at all, leaving purple spots the size of match heads spreading like a rash, enlarging spontaneously like wine stains inside the skin.

The wife arrived at 2 o'clock. "Hi," she said.

"Hello."

"How is he today?"

The intern didn't answer.

"Is he asleep?"

"Almost. I'm not sure he ever really sleeps."

"How is he, really?"

The intern shook his head and looked at her. "You know he's been this bad before. Maybe, maybe...I don't know." The intern turned around and left.

The next day, during morning rounds, the man was sitting up in bed.

"Good morning. How are you?"

"Ah, not bad," the man grinned.

It was like that. The intern knew the man would die. Yet somehow along the way, he'd seen this man throw the odds book out and get better. The intern himself had begun to believe now, the same as his wife had always believed, that perhaps it would all end well somehow.

"You're talking well. It's the best you've done," he told him.

"I can walk, too."

"All in one day? Show me. Let's go to the lounge."

Weak and swollen from the medications, with a cane, the man walked. His face was rounded like a child's from the medicine, and his stomach and back protruded.

"It's nice outside."

"How are the flowers in the park?" he asked the intern.

"Good colors. Maybe we'll take a wheelchair and see them."

"I got mad at my kids the other day," said the man.

"Why?"

"I don't know. It just happens. I don't want it. Don't know it even."

The intern had seen the man's daughter crying. "It's all right," he touched his shoulder, "they understand you're still not feeling well."

"Wo...wo...woo...end. Tch...can't...like that..."

"Say it slower. Try again."

"To...to...torrow. It's nothing I can..."

"Easy. Let it go a while."

The man studied his plump and purple stained hands, then lowered his swollen chin onto his chest. "Oh, what the hell," he said quickly, "I always fuck it up." His mouth remained open after the sentence as if surprised he had said it. His teeth, shining white and clean, were as strong as ever; his wife brushed them every day. But she couldn't keep him from seeing his brain disintegrate slowly, while the rest of his body still lived.

"She did a good job on your hair," the intern said. "It looks good that way."

The man smiled. With unchanging eyes he looked at the intern: "I'm going to die."

The intern sat without moving. He'd been able to guess this would happen sometime. He had even prepared a speech or two in the past. But by now he too, had begun to believe: A belief that a different end was needed, deserved, and would therefore somehow happen. That left no more room for any speeches.

The man smiled again, just like before. It was one of the reasons the intern had begun to believe. "You know," said the intern searching for words, "your boy looks just like you. You have a good wife, two daughters, you're leaving much of yourself behind"...The intern was experiencing some speech difficulty himself. "They're your life, your example " His voice seemed to be returning an echo.

When the echo was gone, for the first time, he saw the man cry. Cameron put a hand on his shoulder: "You can cry all you want. You're still the bravest man I've ever met."

A few days later, Cameron walked the man's wife home. "I guess you'll be going back tomorrow," he said.

"Yes, I think so."

He pushed the elevator button. "It would be better for you if you kept busy."

She nodded. "They saved my spot at work," she said quietly. "It's been a long time"

"Yes, it has." He glanced at her eyes. He didn't know what to say. "I'm sorry. I just I was beginning to think he would make it, you know. I warned you so many times that he wouldn't; but then each time he did, so I also began to think I'm sorry. I should have prepared you better, I didn't do the job."

Her back was to him. "I was prepared, you see. But I always believed he might still make it."

The elevator came. "Goodbye," the intern said.

"Thank you."

On his way back that evening, Cameron recalled the three of them sitting together on those last days. The man, as well as he could talk, had been telling his wife a story: He ended it, clearly and suddenly as he sometimes could, by saying, "Kiss me and I'll turn into a prince."

It was evening again. In a desert now, an imaginary fire flickered to a halt.

That's the story, fire.

All of it?

No, Cameron remembered: I guess there is one more thing.

What else, Cameron?

Several days after he died, his wife walking somewhere found a small canvas painting. Above a dark red rose were the man's same exact words: "Kiss me, and I'll turn into a prince."

Cameron turned his eyes into the night. When they returned, the fire had disappeared. He realized it didn't matter now: From this point on, whenever he needed, it would come back. It would be traveling with him—it was one of the gifts. One didn't have to believe in gifts for them to be there: They came quite simply, without anyone's knowledge or expectation, stumbled upon sometimes, like a butterfly on a high snowy peak, or a rocking horse, or the improbable words of a dying man returning to life.

CHAPTER 27

A VERY SIMPLE THING

She sat quietly on the edge of an Emergency Room exam table, puffy fingers pressed together, eyes gazing on the floor. He lifted her chin slowly, but was not prepared for it. He had worked Emergency a long time, he knew those things did happen. Still, he was not prepared for it. Sometimes it was better if one had time to prepare oneself beforehand.

Her right eye was swollen shut, purple. Her cheeks were red. A mangled cut ran from above her eye and across the cheek. He kept his eyes fixed on another spot and tried not to blink. Doctors didn't. Doctors just worked. Doctors worked no matter what. He would too, in a little while. For now, he tried not to blink, or think of how it had happened.

It was an accident, he pretended. Someone hadn't really beat her and cut her. But he knew someone had. Someone really had.

Slowly her eyes moved a little. The hands of a five-year old touched the stethoscope around his neck, and she opened a broken smile.

God, he thought.

Where are you?

And where are we?

It was odd what one remembered now. Strange what came back to fill a void soon to close. It had to be soon now - he was counting his steps - each step in the sand was slow enough to be counted, silently or out loud. He could stop at any time, of course. It would make little difference. But there were some thoughts still left, and with them the steps also continued. A journey's end didn't arrive until everything stopped altogether.

He tilted his neck upwards: A crescent moon rose over the desert. No wind. An even gold mantle spread silent to where sight lost itself. Orange glowed above, slowly paling into an ice blue darkness. Under the coolness of the moon, it seemed easier to remember. He remembered how it had first begun, he remembered the time he thought it had ended. And now he also remembered why he was here: Finally it was really so simple; in a way the steps of his present journey had already ended; and another had just begun.

Suddenly, his eyes narrowed at the edges of light. He blinked, attempting to get used to it. It had come as if from nowhere, the desert night's horizon broken by shapes of lights, domes, shadows of walls. He couldn't believe it. Another desert mirage: In a while, in an image's afterglow, the domes and shadows would dissolve again into the night.

They didn't. He pressed his eyes and opened them again. The walls were white under the moon, smooth and high, cradling domed roofs within. Signs stood before a softly lit, iron-grated entrance. He moved past them without looking. His heart pounded, a heat racing within. He moved without knowing what he would do next. He had lived just to get here, and now that he was here, he didn't want to think... "Good day. I'm John Cameron. I've come to take Chris back..." He tried it out into the night.

Right, he thought to himself, that would do just fine. Sure it would. Actually, there wasn't much more he could do. It wasn't so bad, really. No matter what happened next, he knew now that he'd been doing all along exactly what he should have been doing. There was nothing else he would rather have done. His eyes narrowed against the light as he went into its range, and his steps continued towards the gate.

He was surprised that nothing happened. He'd expected something: A sound, a noise, something; perhaps not even a pain, but an impact, a heat inside or searing cold, the sand rushing up to greet him. He was prepared for that. It wouldn't stop him; he would keep going. But nothing happened. His steps had taken him to the gates. The gates slowly opened.

In contrast to the lights outside, it was dark. A few dim lights at foot height scattered about what seemed to be a garden. Landscaped forms rose around him like a fresh forest night, resembling childhood dreams, journeys at the edges of steaming black forests. A fragrance of flowers and fruit floated in the air. Cameron stopped moving and waited.

A form moved out near the gate. Cameron touched his belt.

"Are you expected here, sir?" The abrupt yet calm manner of the question was as surprising as the question itself. The man was clad darkly, appeared almost featureless where he stood.

"No, I don't believe so." Somehow, at this time and place, there didn't seem to be any point in deviating from the truth.

"Are you lost?"

"No, I don't think so. Is this Mr. Sandeman's?"

"Do you know him personally?"

"No, indirectly. We have some things to discuss."

The man betrayed no curiosity or hostility. Perhaps it was too dark. "Which one, Junior or Senior?" His very calmness resembled more a dream than reality.

Cameron stood still, staring at him. "I'm not sure, really." He wished he had better words for the occasion, better plans. But it was too late to come up with any plans he didn't have. He was here, and to continue what he was here for, he had to proceed in the same way he believed.

A bright yellow L-shaped light broke open as a doorway parted. A metallic clang rasped, followed by the softness of something rolling over a path. Cameron thought he recognized the sound, something familiar...

"What is it, Francisco?" Something unsteady was carried in the youthful voice, almost a wheezing.

"Someone lost, sir. States he wishes to speak to one of you."

"He does?" Darkness gave way to a young man of late twenties, sandy brown hair, swollen eyelids, breathing rapidly from the exertion of rolling his wheelchair with one hand. The shoulders were broad above the dangling thin legs, his nose and jaw were sharp-lined; from his pale face peered eyes that perhaps had glimmered in different, happier days. Their light was now gone. The young man came to a stop, his eyes moving slowly under their puffy lids. Insomnia? Alcohol? Depression? Cameron's mind slowly engaged into its process.

"How are you?" asked the young man wheezily.

Cameron had been about to ask him the same thing. "Tired, I guess," he answered, "thirsty."

"Ah, good. Come with me." He waved Francisco away.

"He's armed," cautioned the figure by the gate.

The eyes tried to open under their swollen lids: "Oh, well," the young man looked at Cameron ingenuously, "I suppose everyone should have that out here. I'm sure the gentleman wouldn't mind leaving it until he needs it. I don't believe you have any plans for needing it here, do you?"

Cameron stared at the walls, the gate, the wheelchair: "No, I hadn't intended it."

The wheelchair rolled closer. "How did you get here?"

"Most recently, on foot."

"Care for a drink?"

This is insane, thought Cameron: He had just emerged from nowhere, a strange half-dead figure caked with sand, now an equally barely alive apparition was inquiring whether he wanted a *drink!* Cameron took the parabellum slowly from his shirt, removed the clip, and tossed it to Francisco. "Which way?" he asked the young man, positioning himself behind the wheelchair.

Whether from weariness, alcohol, or wheezing, the seated ghost acquiesced to someone pushing his wheelchair.

"Will you be all right, sir?"

"Quite, Francisco." He waved and motioned Cameron forward.

"I would still like to check him, sir."

"No need to," the young man coughed drily. Then, "asthma," he explained to Cameron, "wasn't like this before..."

Cameron wasn't sure if the statement was directed for the cough or wheelchair. He wheeled the young man over a smooth walkway, past a cold marbled entrance, into a cavernous carpeted living room lined with hanging tapestries; a fire burned in a large square hearth lined with stone. A bottle of scotch stood above the ledge—no glasses, just the bottle.

"Welcome," the young man swept expansively with his shaking hands. The shirt sleeves dangled loosely over his bony wrists.

"Thank you." Cameron replied.

"How do you like it?"

Cameron nodded. "First class."

"I hate it."

Cameron looked at him.

"Sit down, sit down," the young man patted a place by the hearth. He reached for the bottle: "A drink? Forgive me... no glasses."

Cameron accepted the bottle. The amber liquid was the first to touch his throat in days. He coughed violently: "Perhaps I could have some water now," he said when his speech returned.

"Of course. I'm sorry. There's water behind the bar. Maybe some glasses in the cupboard. I never use either of them, you know. She hides them," he winked. He studied Cameron again: "You've been walking out there?"

"Yes." Cameron gulped a glass of water, then one more. The heat in his throat gave way to a strange feeling. His gaze wandered over the figure in the wheelchair: *You've been walking out there?* The irony of it settled like a spirit's shadow over both of them, laughing at them from the dark recesses of the room: Cameron had arrived aching and shaking from a journey that had almost killed him, to find someone whose insides begged to be only given that same chance.

"How far?" the young man asked.

"I really don't know." Cameron extended a glass towards him.

"I don't get much of a chance to talk to anyone here."

"Neither did I," Cameron replied.

"You're exhausted, no?"

Cameron nodded.

"There are many types of exhaustion," the young man vacillated between drunkenness and lucidity, "would you mind if we still talked some?"

Cameron sat down. None of this connected: He had expected a place of danger, guarded by gorillas, impregnable walls, perhaps even a moat with murky waters below. Instead, he found a warm fireplace and someone in a wheelchair. Cameron was numbed by the strangeness that this night had brought.

"You're different," said the man in the wheelchair suddenly. "I don't meet many new people here, but you're different."

"Why do you say that?"

"Because you came here." The young man coughed and squelched it with a prolonged tug at the bottle. "Asthma," he explained again, "in other places it's even worse. The desert's not so bad, you know. The garden makes it worse," he shrugged: "She wants it, though. I never tell her about it. I don't ever tell her. Shh..." he placed a finger over his lips, "it's bad enough for her out here."

Cameron turned cold inside. If this was... then Chris was... His mind began to spin. Out, outside of him, outside this room, into a space of colorless cliffs, suspended in nothing... He grasped the sides of his chair. When it had steadied, he glanced at the bottle. He understood now the need to reach for it, the need to reach inside its momentary calm, that lasted for however long it was full. "Usually, asthma gets better in a moist climate," he heard himself say for something to say. "Either that, or sometimes a very dry climate."

The young man shrugged. "There are molds in the moist climate. I'm allergic to them. Anyway "

Cameron gazed at the walls for something to focus upon. He stared without seeing. Inside he was still spinning. Slowly images blurred at first, then black and white and some in color reached him from the wooden frames where they lived on the walls. Images of days gone by, pictures, photographs of another time now far away. They might as well have been of another world: A perfectly tanned youth in shorts and

T-shirt grinned with white teeth as his muscular arms and legs carved an oar smoothly through water in a shell-of-eight. Cameron followed the curve of tendons and muscle, mouth firmly set in disdain of pain wrenched from them during rowing, not just for victory but for sheer feeling of speed under hull, in an effort to drive body and soul to a place they both had been, almost the edge of the universe. Cameron closed his eyes... It hadn't been that long ago. The photograph of the young man, now in the wheelchair, was also of himself. They were the same.

A sound came across the room, words...the young man had said something. Cameron opened his eyes.

"You used to row?"

Cameron nodded. "Yes."

"Probably at about the same time I did, eh?"

Cameron saw the half-hidden eyes, the pallid, wax-glistening skin under the fire's light. Once they had been the same; they had touched the same paths, before something different had happened to each.

The young man was silent now, focusing his gaze blankly behind the walls. Away in another corner of the same room, his eyes gleamed forward from a photograph's face, victorious hands holding a rowing jersey aloft.

"I see you won a few," Cameron spoke into the silence.

"Yes. I won a few."

It was dawning on Cameron: The slow, seeping knowledge of the secrets between these walls, the secret of the three of them, the reason everything was ending here.

"And you?" the man cocked his head.

"Oh, I used to row. Not very good at it, though. Not tall enough, you see."

"Not even for the light crew?"

"It's not the same thing," Cameron answered.

"No. I suppose it isn't."

"They kept me because I could row either port or starboard. That was the main reason. If someone was having an off-day, I could step into just about any position."

"Funny, so did I," the young man glanced at him: "I rowed port or starboard also. Isn't that something?"

Something, Cameron thought. Yeah, something. Something the way fate perversely weaved strange bonds between them.

"I don't sleep well anymore," the man said, "without the workouts. It's not like before, you know. And my wife's asleep... So, I drink. Do you still row?"

"Not much now."

"You should, you know, while you still can."

While you still can... Love while you still can, cry while you still can, soar, dive, disappear into oblivion, Cameron... Leave while you still can... Leave. It's all the same thing, Cameron, it all meets up at the end of the universe...

The young man coughed in a spasmodic bout, then lifted the bottle: "Alcohol," he intoned clearing his throat, "do you know they even use this stuff in inhalation treatments for asthma?"

"Not internally, I don't believe."

"Absolutely," affirmed the young man, "it's good for you. Have another?"

It burned all the way down. To the two of them caught in this strange night's web, it felt good.

The young man extended his hand: "Robert John Sandeman, Jr."

His fingers were bony and long. Still a rower's hand.

"John Cameron," the sensation of holding a strong, compressed spring in his hand came fleetingly, then was gone. Vanished like a moment out of the past, like an unused callus, like victory on a paper photograph.

"Where did you row?" Cameron asked.

"Doesn't matter now. Seems like a long time ago." Robert Sandeman watched the ice clink desolately within the glass.

"I'm sorry."

"No need to be, Cameron. Most of the time I'm sorry enough for myself."

"I guess all of us feel that way one time or another."

"I haven't gotten used to it, Cameron. Don't know if I ever will. One wouldn't think it would be that difficult, you know?"

"I don't think I'd be able to know that."

"There you are: Tired to the bone, listening to my drunken crap. If you'd rather go to sleep, just say so."

"No. I can use some company myself."

"You know, perhaps you won't believe this, but aside from my wife, you're one of the few people I've talked to...since it happened." He raised his glass apologetically: "That's because I'm presently quite drunk. Helps the asthma," he winked, "and helps to talk and to sleep." He shook his head: "You see, I live here because I haven't gotten used to the idea of living anywhere else, of facing the world...as a cripple. My father built this, a retreat for me. To present myself elsewhere, in such weakness, being wheeled around by my wife..."

"There are weaknesses in all of us. In many forms. I haven't shown my face to the outside world either, come to think of it."

"Why you?"

"Mainly, I guess because I didn't believe enough," Cameron replied.

"Ah! What's there to believe in?" Robert Sandeman Jr. shrugged.

"Myself? The accident that put me here? Look at me: Drunk in solitary splendor...You know all about me now, Cameron. I wonder even that my wife returns, that she always comes back. I send her on vacations—send her away hoping she won't return to see me like this again. She always comes back..." The glass Sandeman held in his hand seemed ready to explode.

Cameron felt something falling inside him, falling...

"I'm sorry. That's enough of me, Cameron. What about you? What happened to you that brings you here across whatever is out there?"

"Me? Same as you—there was nowhere else to go."

"How's that?"

Cameron wondered if he knew how much he knew. "I got lost," he replied.

"Easy to do, out there alone."

"My guide had an accident."

"Where is he? We can send out a party"

248

"He's dead."

Spontaneously, quietly, the young man said: "Often I wish I were." The bottle was empty. He had another wheezy coughing bout.

"You should take something for that," said Cameron.

"Ah," Sandeman Jr. held up the empty bottle, "can you get me another one?"

"No, I meant something else; something for asthma."

"I forget...do you see? I forget...the medicines. I never had asthma... before this. It came afterwards, with it Maybe it's because I want to die. Don't you think so?" He looked up with bloodshot eyes, gazing through a mist, wondering how much further he needed to go to destroy himself. "You understand, Cameron? "

"Maybe I do."

"Will you help me?"

Cameron stared without blinking. Robert Sandeman Jr. met his stare directly as he could, with a dignity that made everything else about him disappear: "I want to die, Cameron. Do you understand?"

Cameron stood up quietly. His hands were limp by his sides. His legs began to give way slowly. "No," he shook his head. "You can't."

"Why?"

Cameron remained silent.

Robert Sandeman Jr. nodded at the parabellum's bulge within Cameron's shirt: "You kept another clip, didn't you?"

Cameron didn't answer.

"Well?"

"No," Cameron lied.

The figure slumped into his wheelchair, wheezing heavily.

"Where's your asthma medicine?"

"Somewhere...in the drawer"

Cameron brought two pills. "Take both. Usually it's better with food, it makes you less nauseated that way."

"You know something about this stuff?"

"Yeah. A little."

"A doc of sorts, eh?"

"Something like that."

"So you won't help me?"

"Guess not," Cameron smiled.

Sandeman swallowed the two pills with water. "How did you wind up here, Cameron? Why would anyone be out here?"

Learning, Cameron thought—still learning the things he didn't know. Sandeman wheeled himself with one arm. From somewhere he found another bottle. "A few anthropologist docs came out here, hunting for something or other in the desert. They found some fires there once, or a type of wood they say: Appears and disappears in the desert, gives off a strange blue flame. No one knows how it got there or what it's for. Is that why you've come, Cameron?"

What is it to be, Cameron? What will you do now? Cameron put his hands inside his pockets. They shook as he spoke. "Yes," he said. "Yes, that's why I'm here."

Sandeman Jr. gazed at him through the bottle's liquid amber, "And did you find what you came for?"

"I believe so."

"Was it worth it?"

"You know," Cameron now smiled, "It's always worth it."

Robert Sandeman Jr. squinted. "What was it?"

Cameron shook; it turned outside him, within him: He saw it now in her eyes by a fire's story; he saw it now on a clear day's dawn by an open window over the sea; he saw it now in her eyes crying... He finally saw; and believed it now.

Cameron took the bottle from Sandeman's hand, and extracted a long drink. "It's an old Arab legend," he began, "some call it myth, some call it magic. I suppose no one will ever know. This wood strangely appears and disappears, covered and uncovered by winds and sand. Like misfortunes and accidents, the sands and fate-winds from the sky swoop down to quench it, scatter it, cover the fire. The Arabs call this the fire-spirit: They say it is not made of the parts of man, nor his limbs, nor the things man builds, nor of any of the things outside him. It needs none of those things, and burns whenever it is lit. It can never completely be covered, nor will it ever really die."

Robert Sandeman gazed at his bottle. "Have you really seen it?"

"Yes."

"Find out how it got there?"

"No. I'm not sure anyone ever will."

He looked at Cameron: "And you, Cameron, what do you think of this legend?"

"I don't think it's magic at all. I believe it's true."

"If it isn't magic, what is it?"

"Something very simple, you know. Very simple, and all that anyone ever really has: What one has inside that's given, more than received, and can never be taken away by anything that happens."

Robert Sandeman shuddered once, his hands trembling: "You think I still have that left?"

"Don't you?"

"I love her...I still love her inside..."

"Then take care of her. We're all the same way, and need care."

Robert Sandeman was silent. He glanced up after a while: "We're both tired. I'll show you to your room. In the morning, my wife and my dad can show you around this place. I don't think I'll be in any shape to join you," he smiled, "maybe later, when my hangover wears off."

"Maybe later then," Cameron agreed, "I can't stay."

"Why not?"

"I'm a night traveler, as you see. You might call it part of my profession. In a way, we're both night travelers, searching for something lost. I've already spent more time away than I should have. It's time for me to return. And for you also."

"How will you go?"

"I'm not sure. Where's the next town?"

"We usually fly in. But there's a jeep road heading east, half a day's ride. We always have a jeep ready to go. You can leave it in town if you like, with my name."

"Thanks."

"I'd like to talk with you again, Cameron."

"Maybe we will."

"Yes," Sandeman smiled, "with another movement of the wind over the sand. Anything else, Cameron?"

"Yes," he took the bottle from his hand and raised it: "To you."
"And you, Cameron. Take care."

Enveloped in the drone of the jeep's motor, Cameron no longer felt tired. He had come to tell her, tell her the story's end of their last evening by the fire: He had wanted to tell her that in a game without rules, without promises or certainties, there was still something left, something that went on forever and ever. And it came very simply, with every touch of someone, with every meeting of their eyes, every warmth after the cold; it was the Christmas in the snow, the gifts of a rocking horse or a rose, a butterfly over a mountain, or a blue fire in the night. And no, it wasn't magic, and it didn't die, and it wouldn't burn out even with the last cinder of the universe.

Though he could no longer tell her now, he realized he didn't need to. She had known it all along, and had taught it to him: She had shown him kindness and love, simplest and strongest of all.

The roadbed was hard under the wheels, and easier to follow now. He turned off the jeep's lights as the eastern sun dawned.

THE END

CPSIA information can be obtained
at www.ICGtesting.com
Printed in the USA
JSHW021919251022
32145JS00001B/16